MALINDA JO MUZI
INVISIBLE
Loyalties

PINK
ROSES
PUBLISHING

Merion Station, PA

INVSIBLE LOYALITIES
Malinda Jo Muzi

Published by:
Pink Roses Publishing
PO Box 307
Merion Station, PA 19066-1019
Orders@PinkRosesPublishing.com

http://www.PinkRosesPublishing.com
All rights reserved
Copyright © 2008 by Malinda Jo Muzi

Publisher's Cataloging-in-Publication Data
Muzi, Malinda Jo 1942–
    INVSIBLE LOYALITIES
    by Malinda Jo Muzi

ISBN: 978-0-615-17801-1

1. Crime 2. Loyalty 3. Jewish 4. Murder 5. Ethnicity

Library of Congress Control Number: 2008926238

Jacket Design: ATG Productions, LLC, Christy Moeller-Masel, Phoenix, Arizona
Book Design & Typesetting: ATG Productions, LLC, Cory Olson, Surprise, Arizona
Printing: Freisens, Altona, Manitoba, Canada

Printed and bound in Canada

For Elliott

Also by Malinda Jo Muzi

Psychology: A Biographical Approach
The Child Through Time and Transition
The Experience of Parenting
Your Kids, Their Lives: A Parent's Guide to Raising Happy,
Competent, Caring Children

ACKNOWLEDEGMENTS

No author can survive without a relentless editor, and I have been exceptionally fortunate in my professional and personal relationship with Harriet Goldner. It was Harriet's 'one more go-around,' over and over, that made *Invisible Loyalties* finally visible.

ATG Productions, headed by Kelly Scott-Olson, once again created a beautiful book for me. I want to thank Christy Moeller-Masel for her special cover, and Cory Olson for her interior design.

I am grateful to live in a township protected by the men and women of the Lower Merion police department. My apologies for the literary license I took when writing about their organizational structure. I do know that the county comes in on murder investigations but I prefer to keep my smartest and best-looking police characters close by.

You can't put things right again. That's impossible. But things have to count for something. People have to reap what they sow. There isn't justice, but you can't stop wanting it.

Peter Collier
Downriver

CHAPTER ONE

Saks Fifth Avenue should have been moved years ago. The venerable department store sits alone among a series of medical and financial-service offices strung along the suburban side of US 1, known as City Line Avenue, the broad highway separating Philadelphia from its western outskirts. Everything else decent has retreated from the city limits and, except for the Saks store, the once golden mile of City Line is littered with discount shops and low-end restaurants that invite Philadelphians to cross the once forbidden dividing line between the city and the rest of the world. A gateway to the legendary Main Line, the surrounds of City Line are now distinguished by the number of car thefts and purse snatchings reported each Thursday in the local suburban paper.

Miriam Lavin was among the most undaunted and steadfast of Saks' customers, a relic from the days when affluent Jewish women relied on the store for Bar Mitzvah gowns and cruise wear, before Philadelphia's western suburbs became integrated and white families fled over the line to what they hoped was safer territory.

Miriam refused to betray her favorite store even after marriage to her second husband, Morrie, forced her further out than most of her cohorts, into a Valley Forge country condo, a thirty-minute drive from Saks on a good day. Miriam made the journey to Saks twice a week: on Wednesday nights to get her hair done, and on Friday nights to browse the sportswear and fine china departments. The Saks visits did not alleviate her sense of loneliness and isolation, but they at least got her out of the house. "I've got no one to cook brisket with prunes for anymore now that Morrie is gone," she often complained to the manicurist in the beauty salon, a single mother of three children. "Two lifetimes I've lived: two houses, two children, two husbands, two funerals."

Two inheritances, the manicurist thought, in anticipation of the meager tip Miriam always gave her.

A careful woman by nature, Miriam Lavin didn't worry about the area's crime statistics. She had been approached menacingly only once, on a night when she had parked her car in an exposed area just beyond the first floor entrance to the store. The ruffian had been a homeless drunk rather than a mugger, and the store's security people had simply returned him to the city side of the avenue, where he belonged. Miriam now parked in one of the underground, protected spaces beneath Saks. She regularly pulled her steel-gray Cadillac, purchased by Morrie six months before his death, into a handicapped spot just outside the store's lower-level entrance. The car was identified by a license plate bearing the initials MAL and a wheelchair symbol that should have been relinquished two years earlier, when MAL stopped breathing and, therefore, ceased to be disabled.

This Friday night was to have been a quick trip. "I'm giving my granddaughter an engagement party tomorrow," Miriam told the saleswoman in china and crystal, "and I must have three place settings of Rosenthal right away." She took a Saks post-Christmas sale brochure out of a large fabric Gucci handbag, opened it, and pointed to the black-and gold-rimmed pieces she wanted. "I'm in a hurry," she declared, tossing Morrie's American Express Gold Card and the brochure onto the counter. "Gift wrap them as fast as you can. I only have a few minutes. I've got to pack tonight. I'm leaving for Boca Sunday, for the winter." Miriam had a habit of telling everyone her business in hopes of provoking envy, a trait she projected from herself onto everyone she met. "My grandson's law firm paid for the place after I sent a big malpractice case their way," she concluded, speaking as if her grandson owned the law firm when, in fact, he was a new associate doing the grunt work in an old, Waspish Philadelphia organization.

Basically an unattractive woman, Miriam, at 78, did what was described by her girlfriends at the condo as "the best with what she's got." She relied on her Saks beautician to "do something" with her straight, bleached, pale blond hair. The beautician, partly out of revenge for Miriam's extravagant boasts and frugal habit, pulled Miriam's hair back into a chignon, a style that, unfortunately, called attention to her slightly pockmarked, sagging face and drooping eyelids. A tall, slim woman, Miriam countered her facial imperfections by dressing stylishly, in mostly Ann Klein and Bill Blass, purchased wholesale in New York through a niece's clothing store. Her jewelry—mostly heavy gold and diamonds—came from 8th Street in Philadelphia, where she imagined she got a good deal on bracelets and pins because the owner of the store she frequented had been represented by her "grandson's law firm" when the jeweler had run into trouble for buying stolen property, some of it from Miriam herself.

While the saleswoman packed and wrapped the Rosenthal pieces, Miriam made two quick trips: one to the lingerie department on the second floor—where she bought the bride-to-be a sheer, white nightie—and the other to the first floor perfume department—where she picked up a bottle of Obsession for the maid-of-honor, an older granddaughter not yet betrothed and the object of benign kidding within the family. "My Molly will find herself a man one day soon," Miriam assured the woman behind the Calvin Klein counter. Miriam used the word "my" in a proprietary way when speaking of her children and grandchildren, as if they were lamps. "If my Sandy, not half as pretty, can find someone, it's just a matter of time for my Molly."

"From your lips to God's ears," the perfume lady answered. She was used to old Jewish ladies and their family problems.

Miriam had Florida on her mind when she returned to the third floor to pick up the china. Without bothering to thank the saleswoman, she gathered her credit card and packages and hustled off to a bank of elevators. She hit the down arrow and glanced at her watch: 9:10. Just enough time to press ahead of the other shoppers before they rushed to leave the cavernous parking lot at closing time.

Miriam exited the elevator at ground level. Ignoring the security guard stationed in the lobby leading to the parking lot, she walked directly to the gray Cadillac. She scanned the area around the car before hitting the alarm switch on her key chain. It was quiet for a Friday night with only a smattering of shoppers heading for their cars. An unseasonably warm January left little reason to shop for sweaters and boots, even at half off.

The alarm deactivated, Miriam opened the trunk of the Cadillac and dumped her packages into the storage space. She closed the lid slowly, allowing the electrical system to secure it. Ever cautious, she looked around again before unlocking the driver's side door. Miriam got into the car and placed her Gucci handbag on the passenger's seat beside her. She reached for her seat belt but before she could buckle up a burgundy Malibu sedan pulled behind the Cadillac, blocking its retreat. The driver, a woman in a black coat, her hair covered by a black scarf pulled low on her forehead, wearing sunglasses, pointed to the rear of the car. "Your trunk is open," she called out.

Annoyed at the delay, Miriam got out of the Cadillac and walked toward the back of the car. "Thank you," she said testily, barely looking at the sedan or its driver.

"No problem," the Good Samaritan responded. "Happens to me all the time," she concluded, without driving away.

Miriam pulled up on the lid of the trunk. It was closed tightly. Puzzled, she turned, and started to say something to the woman in the burgundy car. "There's...."

It took only a split second for Miriam Lavin to realize that her position tonight was far from enviable. She saw a hand come out of the driver's side window, got a fleeting look at a gun, and probably didn't hear the shot much before a bullet hit her above her right eye and tore through her brain. Her key chain flew from her hand as she fell back against the Cadillac trunk and slid down the car, her blood splattering the wheelchair symbol on the license plate as she hit the concrete floor of the parking lot. She came to rest on her right side, her bloodied face looking toward the rear wheel of the sedan. The Good Samaritan got purposely out of the Malibu. She picked up Miriam's key chain from where it had landed a few feet from the car, walked past the dead woman, reached into the Cadillac, and grabbed Miriam's handbag from the front seat. Her last task before getting back into the sedan and driving off was to stop for a second and kick the body of the consummate shopper.

CHAPTER TWO

etectives Rhonda Robinson and Colin McKendrick, newly appointed to the investigations unit of the Lower Merion police force, sped into the Saks parking lot 40 minutes after the call came into police dispatch from the mall security office. They were both experienced officers, Rhonda in juvenile affairs and Colin in traffic safety. Neither had ever been part of a murder investigation before, and they came upon the parking lot scene gingerly. "Car parts, body parts, all the same to me," Colin remarked nervously as Rhonda pulled her unmarked police car behind the flashing lights of an emergency service ambulance. Rhonda had just gotten into bed when summoned to Saks, and she had quickly dressed, sped to police headquarters in her spiffy red Saturn, changed cars and picked up Colin, who was still at his desk investigating a township carjacking.

A dozen officers were on the scene and the garage was swarming with what seemed like half the upper brass of the police department. The investigations unit was at work sealing off the garage, blocking all entrances and exits, and checking every car parked in the Saks lot. Its commander, Sergeant William Sutor, spotted Rhonda and Colin and called them over to where he was examining the body. "Rhonda, what took you so long? Colin, those people over there, interview them. Find out who saw what; let's get to it," he instructed, pointing to a cluster of Saks employees and customers who had gathered to peek at the body.

Sutor was the man in charge. He had been on the force 20 years and had worked on a dozen murder investigations, one of them the case of another officer, his best friend, who had been killed trying to apprehend a burglar half his age without calling for backup. Sutor, at 42, would have made the same decision as his buddy, and he would have been comparably dead. Sutor was acutely reminded of his age every time he carried his 6'4", 230-pound body up a flight of steps. Today, bent down and looking at the wound in the dead woman's head, what he thought of first was how much his knees throbbed with pain.

Sutor yelled out orders as he sifted through Miriam Lavin's hair looking for a spent shell. He turned to Rhonda, "Is the medical examiner here yet? Make sure the DA was notified. Get some men to check the lot for shell casings. One might have flown a good distance. Could have been run over by a car. Look carefully. If they find something that even resembles a shell, bring it over here."

The pain in his knees forced him to stand up. He'd played football in high school in hopes of getting a scholarship to college. Instead he got joints that predict the weather. "Rhonda, radio in and get more lighting. Where's the photographer? We need photos from every angle." Sutor had joined the Lower Merion police force after he returned from a Marine Corp stint that took him to no more dangerous a place than Japan. He took this easy duty as a sign that it wasn't in the stars that he die violently. Lower Merion had its share of crime, particularly in areas near the city; a half a dozen cars a week disappeared from township driveways, a handful of burglaries were carried out, and a handbag here and there was snatched; but murder was a rarity, and when it did occur invariably the killer was the master of the house or a co-worker of the victim, some poor soul who never saw it coming.

Rhonda Robinson had worked with Bill Sutor before she came into the investigations unit, and she knew what he expected of her. He had hired her as a result of a township affirmative action initiative, and her initial duties at the juvenile division had put her under his command. At a later date, when she was less intimidated by him, Rhonda thanked Sutor for hiring her over the many well- qualified black men who had applied for a job in the conservative but generally safe community. Sutor told her he would have hired her as the first black female on the force even without the program. Although she knew better, she accepted his words as a compliment and let it go at that, particularly after he promoted her to the investigations unit. The animosity her promotion caused among white men in the department led her to work obsessively to prove herself worthy of her position, and her efforts led Sutor to rely on her more than he did any of his other officers, white, black, male, or female. Rhonda aspired to be the first black superintendent of police in a mostly white suburb. She figured it would take her twenty more years, right up to age 50. Sutor told her that with his help she'd be there on her 40th birthday.

"Don't touch anything! Don't walk on anything!" Rhonda was proficient in what not to do at a murder scene because Bill Sutor had drilled into her head that crimes are solved by evidence only. "Most of the time the evidence is at the tip of your toes—until you step on it," Sutor repeatedly cautioned. "No O. J. Simpson screw ups," he lectured her more than once. With this, her first crack at murder, Rhonda didn't want anyone squashing her initiation ceremony. When an ambulance paramedic tried to move toward Miriam's body, Rhonda put her hands up to block him.

Colin McKendrick searched for a witness to the killing. He interviewed three Saks security guards and the handful of shoppers who had gathered near the body. None of them had seen anything. The lobby guard stated he had heard the shot but thought it might be a car backfire, although it did sound too strong for that. The closest thing to a witness was the middle-aged Saks saleswoman who first noticed the body and ran to get help. She identified the dead Miriam as "one of my best customers."

"What's your name?" Colin asked.

"I work here at Saks," the saleswoman replied.

"I got that," Colin responded. "What's your name?"

"I'm in lingerie. Panties, bras, and nightgowns. We have lovely things, you know." The woman was overweight, over coiffed, overdressed and over jeweled, the perfect look for a Saks saleslady.

"Madam, your name?" Colin repeated. "Your name and address, please." He opened a spiral notebook, labeled one of its five sections "Witnesses," and began taking notes. He had learned how to outline in 12 years of Catholic school, and he organized his pages now just the way he had in third grade. Other people used Day Runners and note pads, but Colin figured his way had worked for Sister Mildred and it would work for Bill Sutor, who wasn't half as tough as his elementary school nun.

The saleswoman was indignant. "Why do you need to know it? I haven't done anything wrong. I came out of the store, was walking to my car and what do I find? A dead body. So what do I do? Like any responsible person, I call the police. And what do I get for my trouble? This interrogation."

Colin appealed to her vanity. "If you don't give me your name right now, I'm going to let you sit in a police car until you do. How would that look on the front page of the *Main Line Times*?"

The saleslady muttered her name was Fromma, "with two m's, don't forget," and she was a part of the Freedman family, the "one that has an interest in the music fair." She insisted she hadn't seen or heard a thing as she approached her Mercedes, which was parked in a handicapped space next to the Cadillac. "Back problems," she emphasized to Colin, certain he was about to put aside his murder investigation and give her a ticket for illegal parking. "I've been seeing a chiropractor."

"What's her name?" Colin asked pointing to the body. He tried to put some authority in his voice, although a part of him knew he had left the power piece of his personality back with Sister Mildred.

"Dr. Henrietta Walsh. Her office is in the 191 building. She'll tell you about my back."

"The victim?" Colin insisted, exasperated. He felt sure he would blow his first murder assignment, and his voice quivered slightly in apprehension. He hadn't wanted to be a cop, never really liked the work since taking the job, but at 35, with a wife and four kids to support, he knew there was nowhere else to go. When he had been in the traffic division, life hadn't been so bad. He had been around his true love—cars—but he needed the money that a promotion to investigations offered and, as the son of a wife abuser and drunk, he needed a William Sutor to guide him into the ways of being a grownup man. "Do you know the victim?" He reworded his question, "Did you know the deceased?"

"She usually buys Chantelle, that's how I know her. It's not the best, but some of it is quite nice. She buys for her granddaughters. I call her when we have a sale. Twice a year. Half off." She shook her head sadly, knowing that the woman on the ground with blood splattered on her head and face would never again come to a Saks discount day. "One of them is getting married soon. The older one can't find herself a husband to beat the band."

Colin became more frustrated. "Mrs. Freedman, what is your customer's name?"

"I don't want to be involved in this," Mrs. Freedman insisted. "I'm just minding my business, going home from work, with my aching back, and what happens? I stumble across a murder. And now I'm a suspect. You're talking to me like I did it. What do I know? I'm minding my own business. I don't want to get involved in this. I come from an important family. We don't need the publicity. We get lots of publicity. I have an uncle...."

Colin grabbed Mrs. Freedman by the arm and pulled her toward a patrol car. He instructed the driver, "Take this woman to the station and keep her there until I get there, which may be three in the morning. She's withholding information. Don't let her make any calls."

"Her name's Lavin!" Mrs. Freedman blurted out. "Used to be Herzelman!" Her face became flushed and she started to sway. "A good customer. I knew her when she was married the first time. Such a tragedy when he died. A car accident, I think. No, maybe he's the one who fell down the steps. Anyway, nice fellow. Used to come shopping with her and sit in the car and wait. The second husband didn't come."

"Her first name?" Colin asked.

"Miriam," replied Mrs. Freedman, still worried. "I shouldn't have parked next to her."

"I doubt that's what killed her," Colin observed, jotting down the name she gave him.

"Miriam Lavin, that's her name," verified Mrs. Freedman.

"Let me ask you this," Colin inquired carefully. "What time did you notice the body?"

Mrs. Freedman thought for a few seconds. "Nine thirty," she asserted, shaking her head affirmatively. "Nine thirty."

"How do you know it was nine thirty?"

Fromma put her hand on her hip defiantly. "How do I know? What do you mean how do I know? I'm supposed to work till nine thirty, I work till nine thirty."

"Did you see anyone at all in the parking lot?"

"Like who?"

"Like anyone, anyone at all."

"I saw Miriam Lavin."

Colin wanted to strangle Fromma Freedman. His mother had worked her whole life as a domestic in the homes of vaporous women like Fromma Freedman, and the thought of it angered him every time he met a

Main Line lady who looked as though she had never cleaned a countertop in her life. "Did you see anyone who was alive?"

"Alive?" Mrs. Freedman seemed puzzled.

"As in breathing," Colin said.

Mrs. Freedman looked toward Miriam Lavin's body. "No. I only saw..." She paused in revulsion. "I only saw you know who."

"Did you see Miriam Lavin tonight?" Colin asked.

"Of course," Fromma stated.

"Where? What time?"

"I just told you. I saw her lying next to her car. At 9:30, when I left work."

Colin bit his bottom lip to keep himself from telling Fromma Freedman she was the dumbest human being he had ever met. Dumb like a fox, he thought.

"Did you see her earlier tonight? In the store."

Mrs. Freedman nodded. "She bought some lingerie."

"Are you sure?" Colin pressed.

"Sure I'm sure. She was my last sale. She bought a white lace nightgown for her granddaughter. Her granddaughter is getting married, you know."

"What time was that?"

Mrs. Freedman shrugged. "I don't know, for sure. Right before the store closed, I guess."

"So you saw her in the store shortly before she was killed. Is that correct?"

"I guess so," Mrs. Freedman answered hesitantly.

"Mrs. Freedman, let me ask you this? Did you notice anyone driving through the parking lot when you were walking to your car?"

"No."

"Did you hear anything?"

"No."

"Did anything strike you as unusual? Did the victim talk to you?"

"No."

"Did you notice anyone else walking to their car?"

"No."

"Can you think of anything that would be helpful?

"No." said Mrs. Freedman. "Can I go now?"

"No," Colin declared, with great satisfaction.

Colin walked over to Bill Sutor who was huddling with the people from the coroner's office. Sutor's hand was held open to them; he was showing off a spent shell. "Looks like a 9mm. It was in her hair." Sutor pointed to Miriam Lavin's body then turned to address McKendrick, "What took you guys so long?"

"Her name is Miriam Lavin," Colin offered. "She's a Saks customer." Sutor, his boss for only a few months, was his imaginary self, if only because Sutor was a bachelor who spent his paycheck on $700 custom-made suits, whereas Colin had a dozen people to consider before making a decision as trivial as whether or not to get his ear pierced, which he hadn't done because the dozen people, most of them in his wife's family, had disapproved. This was his chance to impress his idol. "Miriam Lavin," he repeated.

Sutor handed Colin a registration card he had taken from the Cadillac's glove compartment. "Morrie Lavin. Valley Forge Towers. Know the place? You live out that way, don't you?" he asked, brushing a bit of dirt off his navy pinstriped suit. It bewildered Sutor how men his age were able to put on jeans and jogging suits and leave the house for anything other than camping in the woods or running around a health club track. The thought of going out in public in play clothes insulted his antiquated sense of social propriety. At 9:40, when the night patrol supervisor called him about the murder, he had been home watching television, and his tie had still been knotted. "Your neighborhood, isn't it?" he asked Colin.

Colin nodded. He lived out that way all right, but his section of town and Miriam Lavin's were as similar to each other as Monte Carlo and Calcutta. "Classy building. It's actually three high-rise buildings. Tenements for the elderly rich." He resented the Valley Forge people in their expensive houses and condominiums while he lived only a few miles away in a shabby Bridgeport row house. "Who told you to get tied down just out of elementary school and have a bunch of kinder, Sutor once asked him after listening to one of Colin's gripe sessions about having no life, no freedom, and no money.

"What did I know?" Colin answered, which remained the truth.

"This is the only ID we have so far. Her handbag is missing. So are her car keys."

Sutor called out to Rhonda, who was talking to the Saks security people. "Get the Saks people to give you an accounting of every transaction Miriam Lavin ever made. Bring the manager down here, if he isn't already. Trace every step this woman took tonight in the store. Where did she go? What did she buy? Who did she meet up with? Anything and everything she did."

Reviewing findings from his interrogation of Mrs. Freedman, Colin flipped through the pages of his spiral notebook. "She bought a lot of underwear." He went on to speculate, in an effort to impress his boss, "Looks to me like an attempted carjacking. A robbery and a carjacking."

"Look again," Sutor insisted. "She's wearing expensive jewelry," he noted, pointing out a delicate gold chain with a Star of David on the end of it rimming Miriam's neck, a diamond heart pinned to her jacket collar, a thick gold bracelet on her right wrist, and a gold and diamond watch on her left. "She was shot here," he observed, leading Colin to the back of the Cadillac, "and yet the driver's side door was open. Did she get in the car, forget something, and then get out again? Was her purse taken while she was in the car or when she was walking toward it? Did the killer leave the car door open?"

"The robbers pulled her from the car and walked her around the back," Colin suggested. "Then they took her handbag."

"Then why didn't they take the car if that's what they came for?" Sutor asked. "Why not the jewelry?"

"The thieves were in a hurry," Colin concluded. "Maybe someone was coming. That Freedman woman. From the pajama department."

Sutor surveyed the scene again. "Expensive pieces," he muttered, mostly to himself. "It's not a carjacking," he asserted to Colin.

"Then what is it?" Colin asked.

Sutor shrugged. "A purse snatching, maybe, but its not hard to take a purse off an old lady without killing her. A broken hip when she falls, that I can see. I can't remember a purse snatching around here that ended in this kind of violence."

"That's why I say it's a car jacking. Ten to one, it's a carjacking gone bad," Colin insisted. "I've worked on three of them over the past year. It was inevitable that one end in murder." He looked at Sutor, who was distracted. "Maybe she refused to give up the car. Maybe she put up a fight."

When Sutor didn't answer, Colin changed the subject. "Who's going to do the honors with the family?" he asked, silently praying that he not be chosen. "Who's going to tell them?"

"I will, " Sutor replied, "along with Rhonda. She's good at family contacts."

"The saleslady said the victim was a widow. She may not have a family."

"Old ladies who do their shopping at Saks have more family then they know what to do with."

Colin chuckled, "Maybe one of them bumped her off."

"It wouldn't be the first time," Sutor noted, seriously.

For the next two hours Miriam Lavin got the attention she always imagined herself worthy of. She had been enamored of people in the medical profession, and one of their finest, a county pathologist, was there to pronounce her dead. Her head hairs were examined and her clothing was scrutinized; it was like a Wednesday night out at Saks for her. Miriam loved lawyers, and a few of them showed up from the district attorney's office to watch her get zippered into a body bag, put on a litter, and loaded into the EMS ambulance for a trip to nearby Lankenau Hospital, where she would rest until a family member identified her body, and a staff pathologist cut her apart during an autopsy.

Morrie Lavin's gray Cadillac, along with its handicapped tag, was hitched to a police tow truck to be dragged to a township garage. Patrol cars pulled away from the crime scene; bystanders, including Fromma Freedman, were permitted to go home. By shortly after midnight, the parking garage was empty. It was as though Miriam Lavin had never existed, which was the point of her murder.

At midnight Rhonda and Colin left the Saks garage and headed back to police headquarters where they met up with Sutor, who was waiting for Rhonda in the parking lot. Colin was happy at the thought of soon being in a warm bed while his comrades spread the bad news. "Who would kill a little old Jewish lady in the parking lot of Saks?" he asked. "Why didn't they just rob her and let her be?"

"This wasn't a robbery," Sutor said, "It was an execution." He opened the passenger side door of his patrol car for Rhonda and held it until she was comfortably seated.

"No way." Colin said. "Maybe a carjacking gone bad."

Sutor slammed the door. "You have cars on the brain, Colin. It was premeditated murder. An execution. You'll see."

Colin, who knew better than to argue with his boss, waved to Rhonda and headed across the lot, to his own car, and home.

CHAPTER THREE

Goldsteins' Funeral Home on North Broad Street in Philadelphia was forced to open its partition in order to accommodate the many relatives and friends of Miriam Lavin. The blue steel coffin holding the body was closed, and there was speculation among the mourners that the personnel at Goldsteins' had lacked the skills needed to cover the bullet hole adequately. Some postulated that the autopsy had further shattered the dead woman's face. Neither theory was correct; Miriam had long ago dictated that her body was not to be viewed upon her death.

Seated in the front pew, to the right of the coffin, were members of Miriam's immediate family: two daughters and their husbands, plus the lawyer grandson and his wife. Behind them sat four granddaughters and their assorted fiancés and mates, as well as another grandson. The daughters seemed distraught, the lawyer looked bored, the granddaughters were fidgeting, and the other grandson, a preadolescent, was playing with his Game Boy.

There was a spray of white roses on the coffin; and, every so often, a mourner made his or her way up the aisle to touch one of the flowers before turning to offer condolences to the grieving family.

It had been five days since the murder. This meant that the Jewish funeral service, traditionally accomplished within 24 hours, was past due. For a Wednesday there was quite an assembly at the funeral home, and the rabbi, a clean-shaven young man a month out of rabbinical school, made note of the crowd in his eulogy.

"It is a testament to Miriam Lavin that so many people took time out from their busy schedules to be here today," began Reuben Cohen, who had been secured by the funeral home two days earlier because, for all her talk of religion and her insistence that all her children and grandchildren marry Jews, Miriam Lavin had not belonged to a synagogue, nor had she attended services at one, not even on the High Holidays; and, therefore, she had no personal spiritual advisor to lead the mourning for her.

The rabbi, who had interviewed Miriam's family the day before, now presented their evaluations of the dead woman. "It has been said that friendship is man's greatest gift. If this is so, Miriam Lavin was the most beneficent of women." The truth was that most of the people in the room had never met Miriam Lavin in their lives. The friends Rabbi Cohen alluded to were, in actuality, the neighbors, colleagues and comrades of Miriam's children and grandchildren. As one mourner put it after listening to the eulogy, "How many friends can a woman of 78 still have?"

Rabbi Cohen went on, turning into a social comentator. It was his first funeral, and he wanted it to be memorable. "Violence and mayhem have become the order of the day. There seems to be no escaping it, even on a pleasant Friday evening in the suburbs. Most of us here thought we could flee the terror by leaving the cities where we were raised. But as Miriam Lavin's tragic death demonstrates, there is no escape. As the Talmud tells us, 'For one who dies of natural causes, 99 die of an evil eye.'"

The rabbi went on to talk about how societal conditions are breeding the lawlessness that brought Miriam to her sorry end. He mentioned overcrowded environments, parentless homes, and joblessness. No one in the audience gave a damn. Their houses had unused rooms in them; these people were available to their kids, too much so; and if clothes and haircuts were any indication, everyone in the room was fully employed or at least being supported by someone who was.

"I'd like us to join hands with each other," suggested the rabbi, whose earliest career was as a camp counselor, "in a gesture of oneness; as proof that we, as human beings, can live together in peace." It had turned into an encounter-group funeral. Miriam Lavin would have hated it.

As the mourners reluctantly reached out their hands to each other, a woman rose from her place on the back row of the chapel, walked down the aisle, and stood for a moment in front of the coffin. She was wearing a purple velvet, floor-length skirt with a matching cashmere sweater; amethyst chandelier earrings dangled to almost her shoulders; and her red curly hair was held up by a comb of roses. She appeared to be in her mid-40s, and there were clear remnants of the beauty she undoubtedly had been in her youth.

The woman tore a white rose from the coffin bouquet, gave a hint of a smile, turned toward Miriam's daughters, threw the rose at them, and quickly exited down the aisle of the chapel and out through the back door of the sanctuary.

A buzz swept the room and 300 heads turned to see the hasty retreat.

Miriam's daughters were at first stunned, but their paralysis swiftly turned to anger. "What the hell is she doing here?" "Who let her in?" "Why didn't someone stop her?" They talked as though tickets were needed for attendance at a funeral. The grandson who was not playing with the Game Boy leaped to his feet and pursued the purple figure down the aisle.

Rabbi Cohen attempted to calm the crowd by refocusing on Miriam Lavin's attributes. "The Bible says, 'A virtuous woman is a crown to her husband.' Miriam was the devoted wife to two men. The first, Leonard, with whom she had two daughters, Bernice and Susan, and the second, Morrie, who she married in her later years and took care of through his long and devastating illness."

The rabbi paused to look at his notes and take a sip of water. "This was not a woman who complained about her fate in life despite years of raising her girls alone while Leonard worked two jobs so that the family might prosper. The love that Bernice and Susan have for their mother was Miriam's reward for all the sacrifices she made along the years, and it is to Bernice and Susan that our hearts go out today." The rabbi gestured to the front pew, where Miriam's daughters sat. Their lips were pinched together and one of them, Bernice, was flush with rage.

The grandson returned, shaking his head to indicate that the intruder had escaped. The rabbi continued to praise Miriam's devotion to her family. He went on to name each grandchild and nearly everything Miriam had done for them, including helping pay their college tuition, planning their weddings, and even picking out furniture for them when they moved into their own places. "She was a hands-on grandmother," the rabbi observed. "She was always there, whether they needed a helping hand or a shoulder to cry on. Very few grandchildren have been as fortunate."

The spell had been broken. Miriam's daughters were too agitated to concentrate on the rest of the eulogy, and the crowd was too interested in finding out from each other what had happened. At a signal from a funeral home employee, Rabbi Cohen wrapped up his talk. "It is pleasant to find rest among one's ancestors," he concluded, then requested the attendees join him in reciting the 23rd Psalm.

All six grandchildren and two sons-in-law had been chosen as pallbearers. Following the rabbi's final blessing on Miriam Lavin, the appointees rose and accompanied the coffin to a side door leading to a hearse. The rest of the mourners were instructed to leave the chapel a row at a time, beginning in the back. Those going to the cemetery were to wait in their cars for further instructions. Relatives and friends were invited back to the deceased's Valley Forge condo following burial at Mt. Sharon Cemetery.

All but two men and one woman filed out of the chapel. Lagging behind were Bill Sutor, Rhonda Robinson, and Colin McKendrick, the Lower Merion police department representatives. The three came together at the center aisle from different areas of the chapel, where each had been unobtrusively observing the assembly, while fellow officers stood outside the entrances photographing everyone who had entered.

Rhonda spoke first. She was tall, with a runner's muscular body. Aware that her light skin had eased her way up the career ladder, she straightened her hair, had her nails professionally done, and wore contact lenses. Her suit was Evan Picone and her handbag Coach. Like the woman in the coffin now being placed in a hearse, Rhonda felt right at home in upscale stores like Saks. "Not a murderer among them," she judged.

"Shame to get murdered at that age," remarked Colin. He was wearing a Phillies baseball cap over his curly, light hair, which was too long for his boss's taste. "Damn shame." A deeply religious Catholic, devoted to his mother, Colin had been moved by the rabbi's eulogy and social concerns. "I feel sorry for the family." McKendrick had three sisters and four brothers, so he knew a lot about families and their pain. He was the youngest of his clan and the fifth family member, beginning with his grandfather, to go into police work. At 5'6" he had always felt insecure about his physical abilities. He considered his three years as a street cop to have been the worst in his life, and he felt eternally grateful to Bill Sutor for bringing him inside, first in the car-theft division and, now, in investigations.

"Shame to get murdered at any age," Rhonda commented. Born and raised in Philadelphia's inner city, she wasn't half as sentimental as Colin when it came to mothers and dying.

"She was a fine lady," Colin commented, as if Miriam had been a close friend or relative.

"Somebody didn't think Miriam was so fine," Rhonda suggested. She was reviewing the signatures in the leather condolence book provided by the funeral home and confiscated by Sutor after the service.

"You mean the redhead in the purple dress?" observed Sutor, amazing Rhonda, who had never known her boss to notice what a woman was wearing. "Who is she? What's her connection to the dead woman? What was she doing here?"

Rhonda handed Sutor the condolence book, "Here's an interesting autograph." On the last page, following a long list of mourners, were the carefully printed words: *It couldn't have happened to a nicer person.*

Chapter Four

*I*n traditional Judaism, the period of mourning called shivah lasts for seven days. Miriam Lavin's family shortened their mourning period to three. Relatives and friends poured into Miriam's luxury condo overlooking Valley Forge Park, the site of George Washington's Revolutionary War encampment.

Bernice Eisenberg, Miriam's oldest daughter, made the decision to prematurely dispense with grieving. She organized the mourning affair, choosing Miriam's apartment as the place to receive guests rather than her own home, where she would have been forced to feign hospitality to her relatives and family friends. She ordered trays of corned beef, roast beef, pastrami, turkey, coleslaw, potato salad, rye bread, rolls, and the condiments that went with cold cuts. She sent her son out to pick up cases of soda, and ordered her sister's husband to count the bridge chairs and set them up. Her daughter was instructed to tidy the bathrooms in the apartment, and two of her nieces were told to keep their feet off the coffee table. Bernice reminded her husband to sit quietly in the corner and keep his hands off the booze.

The apartment was set on a 13th floor corner, in the first of the three towers built in the '70s. It had an expansive view of the front courtyard and its cascading fountain. The rooms of the apartment had been interior decorated in navy, white, and peach by Morrie Lavin's late, first wife Arlene. The living room was so massive it had been divided in half by a white silk sectional. A wall of mirrors reflected the elegant crystal and china left behind by Arlene when she had died suddenly of a heart attack 13 years earlier. Arlene's collection of artwork and ceramic figurines was displayed in the entrance foyer. There were photographs everywhere—on Arlene's Steinway, the glass coffee table, and the sleek credenza: a baby in a carriage, a couple in wedding attire, dozens of framed school shots, teenagers on the beach, an elderly woman in front of a Chinese temple. There were no photos of anyone who might have passed for Miriam's first or second husbands.

Bill Sutor gave Miriam's family time to settle down from the funeral before going to the apartment. He arrived just as the last of the shivah guests were leaving. He'd worked on the Main Line long enough not to be impressed by the trappings of money. "Nobody gets out alive" was his motto whenever he drove past the huge mansions of Gladwyne and Villanova whose inhabitants foolishly believed their money insulated them from the sorrows of the world; and he thought of this as he surveyed the near-perfect place and remembered the body on the parking lot floor.

The door to the apartment was open when Sutor arrived, and he walked into the living room. A teenage boy was sitting alone on the couch sorting baseball cards. The coffee table held the remnants of his corned beef special lunch. Sutor recognized him as one of Miriam's grandsons, her younger daughter's kid. "Is your mother here?"

The boy pointed toward a hallway. "In the bedroom" he mumbled sullenly, without looking up from his Phillies pack.

"Thanks," Sutor responded, heading down the hall. He passed the kitchen unnoticed by the group of women wrapping food and chatting amiably. The bedroom door was open but no one was in the room. "Mrs. Ganardo?" Sutor called out.

Susan Ganardo did not hear her name spoken. Following her older sister's instructions, she was busy going through Miriam's closets, gathering up the clothes she wanted for herself and her girls. A bleached blond, like her mother, skilled enough with makeup to camouflage a beak nose and weak chin, Susan's clothes came not from New York designer shops like her mother's but from off-price stores in discount malls. The navy suit she now wore was too tight and too short.

The condo's two walk-in closets were packed. One closet was shelved, and at each level there were sweaters—woven, embroidered, knitted, sequined, and appliquéd—arranged according to shades of colors, from black at the top of the closet to white at the bottom; each piece was carefully covered in plastic. The second walk-in held dresses, pants, jackets, and shirts, all meticulously arranged by color. A series of glass-fronted drawers held carefully wrapped belts, scarves folded in quarters and separated from each other by tissue paper, and still-packaged stockings.

Susan had surveyed her mother's earthly belongings and wondered how she would cart the items she wanted

home and where she would put them. Her house, in a
New Jersey suburb, had no space for this overflow of
goods. It was a modest, two-story, vinyl-sided tract home,
cramped enough since two of her three daughters, well
into their 20s, still lived at home, one after dropping out of
college and the other after a divorce. With a 13-year-old
boy in one of the bedrooms, there was simply not enough
room for their grandmother's wardrobe.

Susan and her husband, Lenny, were both
schoolteachers. The card collector was the only product of
this second marriage, and Susan and Lenny were looking
forward to the day the kids from Susan's previous life were
on their own. It crossed Susan's mind that with the
inheritance she would receive from her mother's estate,
this would be possible sooner than she and Lenny had
expected. The thought eased Susan's anxiety as she
continued to rummage through her dead mother's closets,
stacking dresses and sweaters on her mother's bed.

"Mrs. Ganardo?" Sutor called out again.

Susan interrupted her perusal of a scarf drawer. She
poked her head out of the closet.

"I'd like to speak with you," Sutor said. He held the
condolence book in his hand. They had talked briefly the
night of Miriam Lavin's murder so an expression of sorrow
was unnecessary.

Susan came out of the closet, a stack of pants over her
arm. She was embarrassed to be seen in the closet on the
day of her mother's funeral. "For my daughters," she
stuttered, in defense of the raid on Miriam's wardrobe.
"Bernice thought I should take them."

Sutor closed the bedroom door so they could speak
privately. "I'm sorry to intrude on you at a time like this,

but it's important to stay on top of things as they happen. I'd like you to take a look at this." Sutor opened the condolence book and handed it to Susan. "Do you know anyone who might have disliked your mother enough to write this?" he asked, pointing to the offensive remark.

Susan stared at the message. "This is disgusting! I can't imagine anyone writing this!"

"Your mother had no enemies?"

"None," Susan insisted. "This is sick!"

"Somebody didn't like her."

Susan was silent.

"Mrs. Ganardo, tell me about the woman in the purple dress. You seemed very upset that she was at the funeral. Is it possible she wrote this?" He held out the book again, but Susan wouldn't look at it.

"I don't know," Susan answered, as she sat down on the bed. "This isn't the time to talk about this. We're sitting shivah."

Sutor looked at the clothes stacked on the bed. "There's no better time to talk about this. The more we know and the earlier, the more likely we are to catch your mother's murderer." Sutor glanced around the bedroom. It had been professionally decorated: teal green and peach chintz, balloon shades and matching spread, coordinated dust ruffle and pillows, matching furniture pieces, and figurine lamps in pairs. The one extraordinary piece in the room was an aqua-colored Oriental carpet. The furniture and carpet had belonged to the first wife.

"My mother was killed by a robber, someone who wanted her handbag," Susan observed. "Wasn't she?"

"I don't know," Sutor admitted. "It's too soon to tell."

Sutor walked over to the bureau where an elaborate collection of perfume bottles was arranged. He looked at Susan through the mirror over the bureau and asked his question again. "Who was the woman who tossed the flower at you?"

The bedroom door slammed open against the door jam, and Bernice abruptly entered the room. She strode over to Sutor and angrily demanded to know, "What are you doing here? We're in mourning." Bernice was well into her 50s but she looked older because, unlike her sister, she didn't touch up her graying, closely cropped hair. Her skin was scarred from teenage acne, and she disdained the use of makeup to cover her blemishes. She was masculine in her appearance and tone, square-faced and broad-shouldered—a big-boned woman with a strident voice. It crossed Sutor's mind that the Jewish gene pool had failed this family miserably when it came to looks.

Sutor gazed at the open closets and the clothes on the bed. "I'm sure this is a difficult time for you," he commented, making no effort to keep the sarcasm out of his voice, "but there are things we have to know."

"Come back later," Bernice commanded.

"I'm not here on a social call, Mrs. Eisenberg. This is a murder investigation."

"Investigate some other time." Bernice was used to intimidating the people around her, and she thought Sutor would be no different than a family member.

"I'm investigating now," Sutor insisted firmly.

"My son's a lawyer," Bernice informed him.

"I'll keep that in mind if I ever get a parking ticket," Sutor answered. Although he wondered why she was threatening him, he persisted: "Who was the woman in purple?"

"What difference does that make?" Bernice argued.

"I'll determine that after I find out who she is." He felt an immediate dislike for the daughter of the murder victim, and it occurred to him that if the mother was anything like the daughter, she had gotten what she deserved.

"She's a family problem," Bernice responded, going through the stack of sweaters on the bed and picking one out.

"Problem enough to kill your mother?"

Bernice pulled the sweater from the pile. "This will look good on my Wanda," she declared. She had inherited the proprietary trait if nothing else.

Bernice started to leave the room. "That's all I'm saying."

Sutor blocked her way. "How much of a problem is she?"

"Problem enough to have made my mother's life miserable," Bernice replied testily. "If you'll excuse me, I have things to do."

"A name," insisted Sutor, taking a pad of paper and pen from his pocket.

"Melanie Marconi."

"What is she to you?" Sutor asked.

"She's my mother's second husband's daughter," Susan blurted out.

Sutor tried to clarify the relationship. "Miriam's stepdaughter? Your stepsister?"

The connection sounded too intimate to Bernice. "Let's just keep it as my mother's second husband's daughter."

"What was the problem?" Sutor asked.

"Go ask her," Bernice suggested, defiantly.

"I plan to," Sutor responded, "but first, I'd like hear your side of it."

Bernice tried to wave him away. "She was jealous of her father's love for our mother. She didn't want her father to get married again after his first wife died."

Sutor looked at Susan. "Is that your view too?"

Susan remained silent and began folding the confiscated sweaters.

"Did your stepsister resent your mother, Mrs. Ganardo?" Sutor asked.

Susan answered with a simple, "Yes."

"Did she have a reason to?"

"No," Susan answered emphatically. "My mother was a perfect lady."

"How long was your mother married to her second husband?"

"Six years," Susan replied.

"Was the marriage happy?"

"How could it be with all the trouble she had from Morrie's daughter?"

"You mean Melanie Marconi?"

"She hated our mother."

"Why?" Sutor asked.

"She was jealous of her father's affection for our mother?"

"She's crazy," Bernice offered. "Melanie Marconi is a lunatic."

"What was your relationship with your stepfather like?" Sutor asked Susan.

"It was good," Susan asserted. "My mother was devoted to him, and he to her. He was sick for many years, with cancer, and my mother took care of him. She was a wonderful wife."

"The only problem in the marriage was that daughter of his," Bernice insisted.

"What was your stepfather's relationship with his daughter?" Sutor inquired. "Was he on the outs with her?"

Susan shook her head in disgust, "He thought she could do no wrong."

"He was a fool," Bernice offered. "Morrie was a complete and total fool."

"You're saying Morrie didn't have problems with his daughter but your mother did?"

Neither woman answered.

"How long ago did Morrie die?" Sutor asked.

Susan answered, "Two years."

"Have you had contact with Melanie Marconi since?"

"Thank God, no," Bernice declared.

"Did your mother have contact with her?"

"Not really." Bernice replied. "Who in their right mind would want to have contact with her?

"What do you mean 'not really'?"

"She ran into her once in awhile," Susan suggested.

"Where?" Sutor wanted to know.

Bernice and Susan looked at each other. They both realized that they were giving away more than they intended to. "We don't want to answer any more questions," Bernice stated.

"Where did they run into each other?" Sutor repeated. He looked at Susan, who he had already chosen as the weak link in the family. "Mrs. Ganardo, where did your mother and her stepdaughter meet?"

Susan avoided Bernice's eyes. "In court," she said. "For the past two years they were battling to the death in court."

Odd choice of words, Sutor thought. "What were they fighting over?"

"Things," Susan muttered.

"What things?"

"The stuff in the apartment," Susan replied. "The stuff that belonged to Melanie's mother. Some silverware and china, a few ceramic figures."

"Let me get this straight. Your mother kept silverware and china that belonged to Mr. Lavin's first wife and his daughter took her to court to get them back?"

"Yes."

"And that's it? That's what the fighting was about? That's why Morrie's daughter interrupted the funeral? Because of some silverware and china?"

"Yes," Bernice insisted. "That's all it's about." She brushed past Sutor. "I'm not saying another word. If you want to question me again, you can do so through my son." She gave Susan a look of warning. "Not another word, Susan. Do you understand me?"

Susan nodded.

Sutor closed his notebook and put it back in his pocket. Two years in court over dinnerware. There was not a doubt in his mind that the daughters of Miriam were lying through their newfound sweaters and scarves, although he was sure people had killed for a lot less than a soup bowl and bread plate.

Chapter Five

*Rh*onda kept elaborate notes, a habit since her days at Temple University, where she had majored in psychology, earned a place in an honors program, and had been in line for a graduate assistantship until her college boyfriend proposed marriage, impregnated her, and got himself killed doing a drug deal a month before their daughter, Carly, was born. Rhonda's goal of becoming a family therapist was dashed when her mother reluctantly agreed to baby sit only until Rhonda finished college and not a day after. Instead of applying to graduate school, Rhonda mailed applications to five area police departments. She was still determined to get an advanced psych degree and, with Bill Sutor's help, she arranged a schedule that enabled her to fit night school classes into the few spaces left in her day after fulfilling her job obligations.

Rhonda, who outlined her notes at work as carefully as when she was in class, read to Sutor from a yellow, lined legal pad: "Miriam Lavin's stepdaughter is a college professor, PhD, English lit, 45 years old. She's a widow and has a teenage son."

Rhonda had been at her desk since 8 A.M., arriving after she had spent an hour at a women's health club doing sit-ups and aerobic exercises. She had access to the police athletic facilities but, since her dashed college dream, she avoided men whenever possible. The dossier on Melanie Marconi reminded Rhonda of her lost ambition, making her feel like a failure and a fool in comparison. While growing up, she had been mortified by her mother's unmarried parental status, and now she was in the same predicament. Had she completed her education in family dynamics, she would have learned that this was almost inevitable.

Rhonda cloaked her feelings of inadequacy and sense of life's betrayal in sophisticated manners, fine dress, and strict personal boundaries. She did not keep a photo of her daughter on her desk and never mentioned the child while at work. She pretended the father of her child had never existed.

Sutor suggested they question Melanie Marconi together. "You look like a college professor," he remarked, nodding approvingly at Rhonda's tailored, calf-length, hunter-green wool suit and pink silk shirt. "Maybe you two will have something in common."

"Actually we do," Rhonda said, as she closed her notepad. "She teaches at Temple, the center city campus. I went there." She reached under her desk and pulled up a sleek, black leather briefcase. "I know the place well, but I don't remember Dr. Marconi." She put her notepad in the briefcase and drew out a set of keys. "I'll drive," she offered. "I don't want to pull up to the college in a police car. It might spook the kids."

Rhonda and Sutor drove into Philadelphia in Rhonda's Saturn. Sutor's large frame was crushed into the passenger's seat, and his bad knees were jammed against the air-bag compartment.

The college is in the Fairmount section of the Philadelphia, just a few blocks north of the city's center. They found a parking space amid the sprawling complex of gray stone structures tied together by tree-lined gardens and courtyards. Sandwich wrappers and plastic cups polluted the campus grounds, just as when Rhonda had been a student, and dilapidated food trucks lined the curbs outside the classroom buildings. Despite a January chill, students milled around singly or in cliques determined by ethnicity. Black students huddled together in groups of four or more; the white kids were either alone or in the company of one other person; sounds of Vietnamese rose from a circle of Asian students chatting amiably among themselves at a distance from the others. There was little overt tension between the groups and not a hint of contact, verbally or physically.

Ever efficient, Rhonda had called ahead to find out that Dr. Marconi held an office hour at 11 AM. They arrived at 10:59, and Sutor was pleased, as Rhonda knew he would be. He hated to waste time and prided himself on never being late—or early—for an appointment. Rhonda had achieved her status by understanding Sutor's devotion to order, and by making his life easier in the office. She had come to Lower Merion after a three-year stint with the Philadelphia police, during which time she had earned four commendations. Once employed in Lower Merion, she organized a neighborhood town watch group in Ardmore, the primarily black section of the township, and the crime rate there dropped 20 percent. Because of her community connections, Sutor increasingly relied on her when crimes occurred in Ardmore. He speculated that black mothers imagined Rhonda as the girl they had hoped their daughters would grow up to be, and this would make them more cooperative when the face of one of those daughters appeared in a police lineup.

Dr. Marconi's office was on the third floor of the Main Building. The escalator was out of order so Sutor and Rhonda took the steps. Sutor was breathing heavily when he reached the third floor landing, and had to pause for a minute. "Back to the gym tomorrow," he muttered, trailing behind Rhonda, catching his breath as she strode down the hall. They came to the last office along the hallway. The door was open, and they stood for a second, looking in.

Dr. Melanie Marconi was cordial. "Come in," she invited with a wave of her hand when Rhonda and Sutor appeared in the doorway.

The place was small and messy. Stacks of papers littered the desk, which was placed perpendicular to the door. Two Apple computers shared space on the desk, one of them a laptop the professor was working on. "Give me a second," Dr. Marconi said, "I have one sentence to go." The shelves above the desk held dozens of books, from a series of *Norton Readers* to *The Best Loved Poems of the American People.* A CD player and a set of small speakers were balanced on the shelves. Paul Simon's *Still Crazy After All These Years* floated through the office. The top of the lateral file cabinet was covered with magazine article reproductions. Rhonda spotted one titled "Gender and Hemingway." On the wall above the file cabinet was a William Wegman poster of his dog, Man Ray. There were piles of papers on the floor, rubber-banded and marked with a designation of class and time. Beside the instructor's green fabric desk chair there was a leather and steel class-room chair. A male student sat in it. He had been dictating a poem to the professor when the officers arrived.

"Done!" the professor exclaimed. She waved her hand in the direction of the visitors, "Jamal, please bring in another chair for our guests. There's one out there in the hallway."

The student mumbled, "Sure thing," and hurried out.

"I'm Melanie Marconi," greeted the professor, rising and offering her hand, first to Rhonda and then to Sutor. Rhonda and Sutor introduced themselves. Rhonda displayed her badge but wished she hadn't. She was feeling insecure, like a student again. Sutor sensed that the professor was looking him over, and he was relieved he had worn an expensive tan and sage silk tie.

The young man quickly returned with an extra chair. The professor introduced him to the officers with, "This is Jamal Jones, one of my best students. He's doing a paper on Toni Morrison."

Sutor offered his hand to the student. Rhonda smiled and said, "I liked her novel *Jazz*." Rhonda sat down, but Sutor remained standing as he surveyed the room.

"Me too," Jamal acknowledged, looking at the professor. "Dr. Marconi didn't. We were just arguing about it."

"Debating," Dr. Marconi corrected. "I think her work is overrated."

Jamal laughed, "She disagrees with the Nobel committee—the cohort effect at work. Dr. Marconi is still enthralled by the poet Auden. She dates herself by her taste in literature."

Rhonda smiled in agreement, "I like Auden. The poem about Prospero freeing Ariel is my favorite."

"I am that I am, your late and lonely master. Who knows now what magic is." Dr. Marconi said the words in a soft and loving tone, as if they'd been written for her. "It's one of my favorites too. Makes me cry when I read it."

Sutor looked at Rhonda in amazement. "I'm in over my head," he admitted. He felt uneasy in a room full of people so much better educated than he—and two of them women; and one of them his subordinate. Sutor had tried his hand at college after returning from the Marines but one year at Villanova University was as far as he had gotten. He had survived his one English class by getting a girlfriend to write his papers. He had never understood what *The Old Man and the Sea* was about, other than fishing.

Jamal excused himself. "Nice meeting you both," he said to the guests. "Thank you, Dr. Marconi."

"Goodbye, Sweetie," the professor said. "Look both ways before you cross the street."

Jamal laughed and left the office.

"He has a one in eight chance of getting murdered in his lifetime," Dr. Marconi remarked. "I worry. He's the brightest kid I've ever taught. I'm trying to get him a scholarship to Penn—affirmative action. It's getting harder, given the political climate of the country." Melanie spun her desk chair around to face her guests. She crossed her legs, allowing a ruffle of her black slip to show. "This affirmative action thing is still polarizing. In my parents' day there were quotas against Jews and other minorities— they could hardly get into Harvard, Yale, or Jefferson Medical School—but they overcame the quotas by the excellence of their work. They became indispensable to any university that wanted quality teachers or scholars."

"They didn't overcome the quotas by excellence alone," Rhonda interjected. "Some did it by changing their names and pretending they weren't Jewish." She was feeling uneasy with the conversation, given how she had become a Lower Merion police officer. "You're absolutely right," Dr. Marconi asserted. "My mother's six brothers had four last names between them." She laughed out loud, a giggly sound that made Sutor think of his mother again. "It's a pain in the neck to invite them anyplace."

Rhonda missed the levity in the professor's tone. "Nevertheless it helped them," she said. "But what's a kid like Jamal to do? He can change his name; but he'll never be accepted, no matter how excellent his performance." She was thinking of herself as much as the student.

Dr. Marconi became serious again. "That's why, even though I'm opposed to affirmative action, I'm using it on his behalf. But because of affirmative action, no matter how good he is, Jamal will never be seen in the same way as a white counterpart who rises through the ranks in traditional fashion."

"Like Toni Morrison," Rhonda said. "Her Nobel Prize will never carry the same prestige as Pearl Buck's."

Professor Marconi nodded, "Unfortunately, true."

Sutor was silent throughout the dialogue between the women. He realized he knew very little about Rhonda, although he had worked with her for many years. She was smarter and more informed than he had noticed. It occurred to him that he knew nothing about her private thoughts. Maybe the high school sweetheart he had decided not to marry had been right about him: he was not relational; he didn't connect with people; he knew nothing about women. It wasn't something he'd thought much about but, lately, he'd been feeling isolated from those around him, more so than usual. He'd felt alone in the past; but, while there had been a career to build and the boys he grew up with to watch basketball games with, it hadn't mattered that much. Now that the career was constructed and the boys were taking their own boys to basketball games, the aloneness was catching up with him.

He redirected the conversation by saying, "Dr. Marconi, we're here to talk to you about police business." He hoped he hadn't sounded abrupt. "We'd appreciate you giving us a few minutes of your time." This was better.

Dr. Marconi was direct, "What do you need?"

"We want to know what you know about the death of Miriam Lavin."

"I don't know anything about it," Dr. Marconi answered. She looked up at Sutor, and he was drawn in by her hazel eyes and dark lashes.

"How did you feel about her? We saw you at the funeral." He liked the professor's looks. She was a little plump and rounded, somewhat motherly looking but very pretty. She had a ton of red, curly hair, which she piled carelessly on top of her head with a ribbon. Huge silver earrings dangled among side curls. She was wearing purple again, this time in a shawl that covered her shoulders. Her black skirt was ankle length, reaching below a pair of black leather boots. "Girly, girly," he called women like that— and girly, girly is what he liked.

"If you saw me at the funeral, then you know how I felt about her."

Sutor hadn't expected such forthrightness. "You're glad she's dead?"

"Yep." She paused to wave at a student who was passing by in the hallway.

"Why?" Rhonda inquired, jotting down the professor's answers.

"She was evil."

"What do you mean?"

"She killed my father," Dr. Marconi declared. "Murdered him." There were two framed photos on the desk. Melanie picked up one and handed it to Rhonda. Rhonda looked at it and passed it to Sutor. It was a photo of a middle-aged couple, the woman, an attractive blond in a silver gown, the man, handsome in a black tux. "My parents, at my wedding, fifteen years ago. My mother died of a heart attack not long after this picture was taken, and my father was murdered two years ago."

"What do you mean?" Rhonda asked as casually as she could, considering the professor's accusation.

"I mean Miriam Lavin killed my father. She murdered him in his bed. Two years ago, on February 11th."

"Who knows about this?" Rhonda wondered.

"Everybody," Dr. Marconi asserted. "Everybody who knew them as a couple. Miriam hated my father and waited for an opportune time to kill him."

Sutor closed the office door. He placed the photo back on the professor's desk and, when he did, caught a glimpse of the second framed shot: a dark-haired man sitting in a lounge chair, a baby asleep on his shoulder.

"Tell us about it," Sutor suggested.

"What's to tell? Miriam hated my father and got rid of him."

"How'd she do it?" Rhonda inquired.

Professor Marconi explained that her father, Morrie, had been ill with lung cancer. He had been on a respirator and feeding tube for some time. Against doctor's orders, and knowing Morrie had been aspirating food into his lungs, Miriam brought him home from the hospital. "My father's nurse called at five o'clock to tell me that he seemed very ill. Miriam had made him a big piece of chicken for dinner, but he wouldn't eat it. He seemed weak and disoriented. He wanted to go back to the hospital. I got hold of Miriam and told her to call an ambulance and get my father back to the hospital. Miriam agreed to do this. I called an hour later and the ambulance had not arrived. Miriam said Dad was doing better. I asked her to put him on the phone. She said he was sleeping. I again insisted that she take him back to the hospital. Miriam attacked me verbally. She asked me why I wasn't the one cleaning my father up when he went in his pants or threw up his food. She was bitter and angry and fed up with Dad. I got a call from Miriam at 4 AM; it woke me from a sound sleep. She said, 'Melanie, your father fell out of bed. He's dead.' There was a self-satisfied tone to her voice, like she'd gotten something over on me. I asked her if she'd called 911. She said she was about to do it. When the emergency squad got to the apartment, my father was dead."

"What do you think happened?" Rhonda asked, writing feverishly.

"She pulled his plug," Dr. Marconi declared.

"Do you have proof?" Sutor questioned.

"I heard the owl scream and the crickets cry," Melanie observed.

Sutor didn't answer. He was about to ask for a translation but decided to let the quote go.

Rhonda replied, "Lady Macbeth."

"In this case foul is foul," Dr. Marconi replied.

Rhonda continued, "Do you think Miriam's murder had anything to do with your father's death?"

"What do you want me to say?" Dr. Marconi inquired.

"I'm just wondering if there's a connection."

"What's to be gained?" the professor remarked. "My father is dead. His wife got away with it. It happened two years ago. What's done is done, unless you believe the past is prologue to the present."

"Revenge is a pretty good motive for murder," Sutor observed. Rhonda looked at him, surprised, but he didn't acknowledge her.

Dr. Marconi looked directly at Sutor. "Honey," she asserted, "the worst revenge I could think of in this world is being Miriam Lavin, living in her shoes every day. On the one hand I'm thrilled she's dead; but, on the other, I had hoped she would live a long, miserable life. Maybe a broken hip or two. One of her daughters, the older witch, has cancer. I wanted her to live to see that daughter buried. A couple of her grandchildren are crazy. This would have tortured Miriam in time. This would have been justice. She was no good through and through, and I wanted her to reap the consequences of a life badly lived. I actually put a curse on her like in *The Color Purple*—like Alice Walker: 'Until you do right by me, everything you touch will crumble. Until you do right by me, everything you even dream about will fail.' It's not perfect but it's close."

Sutor shuttered, jokingly. "I'd hate to make an enemy of you," he remarked, laughing.

Dr. Marconi flirted with him, "Sweetie, you're too good-looking to ever be on my bad side."

Same here, Sutor thought.

"Why did Miriam hate your father enough to kill him?" Rhonda interjected.

"He had humiliated her. On the day of their wedding, in front of their friends and relatives, he tried to back out of the marriage. You're not going to believe this, but when the rabbi asked, 'Do you, Morrie, take Miriam to be your lawful wedded wife?' my father answered, 'No, I changed my mind.' Miriam never forgave him."

Rhonda shuffled through her notes. She came to a page, scanned it and said, "But she stayed married to him for years."

"She had an ulterior motive."

"What was it?"

"M-O-N-E-Y. That's what Miriam was about."

"He spent a lot of money on her?" Rhonda asked.

"Not a dime," Dr. Marconi responded. "He was the cheapest son-of-a-bitch who ever walked the planet Earth."

"So where'd the money come from?"

"She stole it during the last year of his life, when he was on the respirator and feeding tube. My father didn't trust her. He got Miriam to sign a prenuptial agreement giving her a life estate in their condo and a small trust fund for taxes, but that's about all. Then he got scared. He sensed that she was smarter than he was. She had been a legal secretary all her life so she knew all the angles. That's why he wanted to get out of the wedding.

"The day before the nuptials, he came to my house and begged my husband to find him a lawyer to get him out of the mess he was in. But Miriam really was smarter than he was. She had given up her apartment and moved in with him. He was trapped. His last attempt to extricate himself from the marriage was in front of the rabbi. It failed. Miriam and her daughters gave him a handful of tranquilizers, held him up, and got him married. Then the scheming began. Miriam and her daughters stirred their pot in the forest. 'When shall we three meet again...?'"

"How much did they take him for?" Sutor asked.

"Every dime he ever made and didn't spend in his life: my son's college trust fund; all of my mother's jewelry and possessions; all of his CD's and Treasury Notes; properties he owned. The only thing she didn't get was the condo, although she did get a life estate to it. I got the apartment, but I was stuck with Miriam in it until she died."

"What's it worth?" Sutor asked.

"Bupkes."

"What's that?" Rhonda inquired.

"In Yiddish, not much—maybe $250,000." She sensed what they were thinking. "Not nearly enough to risk life in prison for."

"If what you say is true, how did Mrs. Lavin manage to pull all of this off?" Sutor interjected.

"She had papers drawn up by her lawyer grandson, the *putz*, Jerome Eisenberg, her daughter Bernice's kid. She carried them into my father's hospital room and had him sign them when my father was seriously depressed and under heavy medication. The CDs and Treasury notes were easy. She had him sign them over to her. Then she signed them over to her daughters and grandchildren. My father's Vanguard fund paid for a granddaughter's wedding. His Ginny Mae bought both her daughters diamond tennis bracelets. She was even at it the day after he died. My father died at 4 AM. At 9 AM she was at the bank forging an endorsement on a check so that she could get his last $10,000."

"Why didn't you stop it?" Rhonda asked.

"I didn't know. I never imagined any of this was going on. I never liked her, but I didn't think she was a thief and murderer. Who would think such a thing? She came off as a devoted caregiver. She fooled most of their friends and even relatives on my mother's side of the family. A few of the nurses at the hospital were suspicious because they saw her browbeating and abusing my father, but it wasn't their place to say anything. It was all done very quickly, within a span of eight months."

"How do you know all this?" Sutor inquired.

"After my father died, as executrix of the estate, I found close to a half a million dollars missing. I hired a top law firm and spent a small fortune of my own money putting the pieces together."

"Did you have any legal recourse?" Rhonda asked.

"No," Dr. Marconi declared. "None whatsoever. As Herman Melville said in *Billy Budd*, we speak of the law here, not justice. There is no such thing as justice in America anymore. Not for anyone. My own lawyer told me to look for justice in heaven; on earth we settle for law." She laughed cynically, "My lawyer is Catholic; he believes in equity in the afterlife. He told me this after he took me for a bundle. There's no justice anywhere. As law enforcement officers, you know this better than anyone."

Sutor did know this better than most, and he felt badly for the pretty woman sitting in front of him. "Did Miriam Lavin finally get her justice, in this life?"

"Miriam Lavin got a bullet to the head. It was a far better punishment than she deserved."

Rhonda and Sutor drove away from the college in silence. Neither was sure what to think about the professor's accusation. If it were true that Miriam killed her second husband, then it opened up a Pandora's box of possibilities.

"We just got a motive," Rhonda observed.

"What motive is that?"

"Revenge."

"After two years? Besides, you and I both know that motive in a murder case has as much importance as a crate of manure. What we're missing is evidence."

"What do you think of the professor?" Sutor quizzed Rhonda. "Gut instinct."

"I liked her," Rhonda replied. "She seemed very open and candid." She looked over at him, "And you? What did you think?"

Sutor stared straight ahead and answered carefully, "Bright girl."

Rhonda laughed, "That's what you noticed?"

"Bright and pretty." He was remembering an old photo of his mother, the one with her long hair tied back with a bow. "A nice girl."

"She's not a girl," Rhonda reminded him. "She's older than you are, by three years."

"How long has she been widowed," Sutor asked nonchalantly.

"Five years."

Sutor did a mental calculation. "Her father is dead two years and her husband is dead five years?" He felt a second pang of pity for Melanie Marconi—bad sign for a cop investigating a murder.

"Maybe Miriam Lavin bumped them both off," Rhonda uncharacteristically joked. She sensed an upbeat attitude in Sutor, and it relaxed her.

Sutor recited the only Shakespeare he knew: "Many a truth is said in jest."

The humor grew darker when Sutor suggested, "Miriam was a real Mrs. Kevorkian. She believed in wife-assisted suicide."

"Only it wasn't a suicide."

"Sounds to me as if the guy was already dead but hadn't closed his eyes."

"It's not over until the second wife pulls the plug."

Sutor returned to the subject on his mind, "The name Marconi? Italian. I wonder what made a nice Jewish girl marry an Italian?"

"What makes anybody marry anybody?"

"There was a picture on her desk—good looking guy."

"How do you know that was him?"

"I'm guessing."

He was also guessing that Melanie Marconi was tired of being alone, if, in fact, she was alone. He felt badly for the husband. Dead, with that pretty wife left behind and needing company. He forced the images from his mind. It was crazy. She could end up a murder suspect. She could end up in prison. The thoughts came back: She could end up being the woman he would like to meet if it wasn't for the fact that he'd already met her while investigating a murder. The circuitous logic of it was troubling, but there was something about the professor that appealed to him, as if the red hair and hazel eyes, like his mother's, weren't enough.

Rhonda pulled together what they knew: "Miriam Lavin was shot and killed at almost point-blank range. Nobody has come forward as a witness; her car wasn't taken; she had her jewelry on her." She looked over at Sutor, "Colin still thinks it was a carjacking."

Sutor wiggled in his seat, sorry he had left his car behind. "She was executed. Miriam Lavin was executed."

"I think you're crazy," Rhonda blurted out. She was surprised and embarrassed by her outburst; but she thought that Sutor, even if he was her superior, made no sense. "Who would execute a little old Jewish lady?"

"From what we hear about Miriam Lavin, this little old Jewish lady needed a touch of executing."

"You seem to be taking the professor's word that Miriam Lavin was a killer. Did you forget about the scientific method?"

"What's that?"

"Proof."

"Let's go get some. Let's find out if Miriam Lavin killed her second husband."

They were on heavily trafficked Walnut Street and Rhonda abruptly pulled the car over to the curb, parking in front of a fire hydrant. She turned sideways to look directly at Sutor. "Bill, do you hear yourself. You've just changed direction. We're not out to prove that Miriam Lavin killed her second husband. We could care less about that. She could have killed both her husbands for all we know. Our job is to find out who killed Miriam Lavin, and why. It doesn't matter what kind of person she was. She was murdered. This is a capital case. Somebody will be put away for a very long time for doing this."

Sutor got defensive. "You don't have to remind me of that, Rhonda."

Rhonda touched Sutor's arm. "I know. I just don't want us to get off track." Then she suggested as softly as she could, "The professor makes a pretty good suspect."

"I'm not discounting her," Sutor maintained. But in his head he was.

CHAPTER SIX

An arrest was made eight days after Miriam Lavin's murder. The accused, an African-American named Wilson Greene, had given Miriam's Visa Gold card to his girlfriend, Janetta, who used it at, of all places, Saks. A saleswoman in the shoe department, recognizing the name on the card, called security, who held on to Janetta until the Lower Merion Police collected her. She quickly gave them her boyfriend's name and address.

Wilson Greene, booked for possession of stolen property, swore he was innocent of murder. He said he found Miriam's wallet by the side of the road, down US 1, about 10 blocks south of Saks, on the Philadelphia side of City Line. Well, not exactly by the side of the road, Wilson confessed, "It was in a purse." The purse wasn't actually by the side of the road, either. "Someone threw it to me, from a car window. Just up and sent it my way, like a miracle."

Sutor and Colin came in to question Greene, who was a small and wiry, very dark-skinned man in his 40s. His hair was closely cropped; and he spoke so softly, he could barely be heard. He had given up his Miranda rights a few hours earlier.

"What did you do with the purse?" Sutor asked, pulling a chair up close to Greene in order to hear him.

"Kept the money and the keys," Greene whispered, "and gave the bag and the rest to Janetta." He kept his head down when he talked, and his hands shook.

"How much money?" Sutor inquired. He pulled out a stick of gum, unwrapped it, and offered it to Greene. Greene refused the treat, so Sutor carefully wrapped it again and stuck it back in the pack. Sutor, who had been a cigarette smoker since adolescence, had switched to gum just before the Lavin murder. Gum wasn't doing the job for him.

"About $200."

"Why did you keep the keys?"

"I figured on robbing the house. I was gonna wait awhile and then do it."

"How'd you know what house the keys belonged to?"

"Kept the driver's license."

"Where's the handbag now?" Sutor asked.

"Janetta has it."

"What else was in the handbag?"

"Keys, lipstick—stuff."

Colin had been standing behind Greene. He came forward and asked, "What were you doing on City Line?"

"Walking," Green whispered.

"Walking where?"

"To Philly. I was hitching home."

"Where's your car?

"Don't have one."

Sutor leaned close to Greene. "We think you tried to get yourself some wheels last week, Wilson. A big, gray Cadillac, driven by a little old lady whose handbag you stole."

Greene's eyes widened. He looked up at Sutor and began shaking his head from side to side. He held his hands up in front of his face, palm sides out, in an attempt to ward off the accusations. "No way, man. I didn't take nothin' from no old lady. You can bring her in here right now. I'm not the one that robbed her. She'll tell you...."

"We can't bring her in, Wilson," Sutor interrupted, "because she's dead. Shot dead and robbed. Robbed of her handbag, Wilson. Robbed of her wallet. Robbed of her credit cards. Shot dead and robbed. And there's somebody in this room that's got the stuff she was robbed of."

Wilson Greene began to tremble and cry, "Man, it wasn't me. I told you, I found the stuff. Came right down from heaven. A gift from Jesus. I'm telling the truth. A car goes by and out flies the purse."

"What kind of car?" Colin asked.

"I don't know. Red. Not really red but sorta red. You know, red like wine."

Colin interjected, "What kind of gun do you own?," an assumption he took for granted.

"Don't have none," Greene insisted.

"Never had a gun?" Colin asked forcefully. "Give me a break."

"Had one once. Gave it to Janetta so's she can protect herself."

"Where's the gun now?"

"At Janetta's. She lives with her mother. It's in the bedroom drawer under a towel. She keep it hid from her girl.

She seven. Don't want her to get hurt playin with it."

Sutor chuckled to himself at the masterful way the pair had hidden a deadly weapon. No way in hell a seven-year-old could figure out how to lift a towel to get her hands on a gun.

"Let's go," Wilson," said Sutor. He handcuffed Wilson. "We're going for a ride."

Sutor and Colin drove Wilson Greene to 54th Street, where Wilson showed them exactly where and how Jesus had thrown the handbag to him from the reddish car. He said it had been about 9:30 last Friday night. He knew it was 9:30 and Friday night because he came out to Wynnefield every Friday to eat dinner with his girlfriend Janetta. Janetta Nickelson cleaned house for a lawyer couple who stayed in town on Friday nights, leaving Janetta to care for their 6-month-old son. Every Friday night she made Wilson dinner at the house, then they watched TV. He always left just before the lawyer couple came home. He knew when they were coming home because they always called to check on the baby and give an approximate time for their return. Wilson Green had more explanations for his Friday nights than the crew of "20/20," whose show Wilson missed that particular night because, he noted, he had left the house just before it came on. He had walked to City Line, only a mile from the lawyer couple's house, because it was easier to get a lift into Philly from there.

Sutor and Collins drove Wilson Greene back to jail. "Is Janetta alright?" Green asked as he was placed in a holding cell until he could be moved to the county prison. "Can I talk to her? I gotta talk to her."

Sutor told Greene he could call his lawyer but not his girlfriend. Greene pleaded with Colin, "Tell Janetta I love

her. Don't mean to get her in trouble." Colin assured
Greene he'd relay the information.

Sutor and Colin picked up a search warrant and, with
the cooperation of the Philadelphia police, raided the
Nickelson house, scaring the hell out of Janetta's mother
and the three grandchildren she was tending. The house
was a two-story wooden row, in disrepair on the outside
but compact and neat within. The grandmother was
compliant and the children polite. "We're looking for a
9mm automatic," Sutor informed the grandmother, who
sat on the couch with the children huddled around her,
"and a few other things. We'll try not to make too much of
a mess." Colin and the Philadelphia cops were already
going through the second floor of the house.

"I don't know nothin' bout a gun," the grandmother
declared. "I never seen a gun in this house." She was no
more than 50 years old, dressed in black knit pants and a
gray sweatshirt with Temple University written across in
red. One of her sons had attended the college, where he
had earned straight A's and competed in chess; but he had
been killed during his junior year when he made the
mistake of wearing a new black leather jacket on the Broad
Street Subway. The sweatshirt had belonged to this son;
wearing it made her feel close to him.

A cute little girl spoke up, "There's one in my Mama's
bedroom. It's in the drawer next to the bed."

"How do you know?" Sutor asked, offering each of the
kids a piece of gum. They looked at their grandmother
and, after she nodded her approval, they all accepted.

"We play with it sometimes," admitted the child. "We
always put it back," she quickly explained.

The grandmother looked shocked. "Take it away!" she ordered Sutor. "Get it out of the house!" One child in the family dead of a gunshot wound was enough for her.

"We'll do that, Ma'am," Sutor responded.

Colin came downstairs with the 38 Smith & Wesson in a plastic bag. Another hour was spent searching the house, but nothing else of importance turned up.

Sutor thanked the grandmother, handed over the rest of his gum pack to the kids, and said goodbye.

Rhonda and Sutor went to see Janetta Nickelson, who had been arrested and charged with theft and possession of stolen property. She sat alone in an interrogation room at Philadelphia police headquarters, a heavy set woman in her early 20s, lighter-skinned than Wilson, round-faced and pleasant looking, with hair braided into cornrows and decorated with red beads. Rhonda sat across the table from Janetta and informed her that she was being considered an accessory to murder. When asked if she wanted to see a lawyer, Janetta insisted she didn't need one. Like her lover, she began to cry in terror. She confessed to having had in her possession a half dozen credit cards belonging to Miriam Lavin, two of which she had used without repercussions. She had assigned a Visa and a Sears card to a sister; the wallet and handbag had been gifted to her Mom. Janetta Nickelson was a very generous girl but not charitable enough to share a murder rap with Wilson Greene. "He and I been together about two years. I knows that man. He never killed nobody. He don't mind stealing a little bit—he stole some liquor from the house I clean; but I made him put it back so I wouldn't lose my job. He says he found that purse, he found that purse. He give me the wallet and tells me I could do what I wants with it."

Janetta leaned forward, squinted her eyes and offered her special brand of morality, "If I thought he killed that white lady, I wouldn't have taken the wallet and cards. I'm not the kind of person use the stuff of a dead person. No, no. Not me. Alive is one thing. Dead, no way."

"How'd you know she was a white lady?" Rhonda asked. Looking at Janetta, she felt an odd combination of contempt, sorrow, and guilt. There but for the grace of God, she thought. She imagined that Janetta had been brought up, like herself, in poverty, by a church-going single mother. The only difference, maybe, was that Rhonda was an only child. Her mother had never had anything to do with men again after the father of her child, a junior high classmate, started running around with a neighborhood girl. The mother had been converted to the Jehovah's Witness faith just after Rhonda was born. She worked hard, prayed hard, and raised her daughter to believe that with God's help there was nothing she couldn't accomplish. Rhonda, now a Baptist, looked at Janetta Nickelson and suspected it would have taken a hell of a lot of intervention from Jehovah to save this woman from ending up exactly where she was—a suspect in a murder investigation.

"'Cause you makin' such a fuss over it," Janetta observed, displaying a degree of logic. "If it was a black lady, you don't be bothering."

"Is there anything else you want to tell us?" Rhonda asked. "Anything you think would be helpful in clearing you?"

"Wilson's a good man," Janetta maintained. "We getting married. He didn't kill that lady; he's scared of his own shadow. Always with me; I takes care of him." She asked Rhonda to deliver a letter to Wilson Greene for her, which Rhonda agreed to do. Janetta then requested some paper and a pencil so she could write the letter. Reaching into her briefcase, Rhonda took out one of her legal pads and a pen and handed the items to Janetta.

"Let me know if you need anything else," Rhonda said, aware of how easily she could have been in Janetta's place.

The interviews with Wilson Greene and Janetta Nickelson added up to a disappointing conclusion. "Romeo and Juliet didn't do it," Sutor observed to Rhonda as they left the suspects in their respective jail cells and headed out for a late dinner. "Greene didn't kill Miriam Lavin." They walked across the police headquarters parking lot to where Colin was leaning against Sutor's new black BMW sedan. The car was Sutor's chief indulgence in life and whenever possible he left his township issue vehicle behind in favor of his own car. He justified the expenditure by proclaiming he never took vacations and, therefore, deserved to spend money on what he called his "German sweetheart." Driving the car, even if from his office to home, made him feel as though he were in a right and safe place, away from the world of men and crime. He kept a blackjack under the driver's seat and a second gun in his glove compartment just in case this wasn't true.

"How can you be sure?" Rhonda asked.

"He's too stupid; and so is she." Sutor disarmed the car and opened the passenger side door, holding it for Rhonda. Colin settled into the back.

"Nice wheels," Colin complimented, "24-valve, six-cylinder, good traction in winter. Trade you even up for the Corvette I'm renovating in my garage."

"Deal," Sutor said as he closed Rhonda's door. He walked around the back of the BMW, stopping for a second to wipe an imaginary fingerprint clean before stretching himself comfortably into the driver's seat.

"Stupidity never stopped anyone from becoming a murderer," Colin suggested as Sutor checked the rear- and side-view mirrors of his manly toy. "In fact, that's one of the criteria."

"Are you implying there are no smart murderers?" Sutor inquired.

"Are there?"

"Thousands," Sutor stated.

"Name one," Colin challenged.

"I can't," Sutor replied, immediately relaxing as he shifted the car into drive and slid it out of the parking lot.

"Why not?"

"Because they got away with it." He pulled on to Lancaster Avenue and let the car cruise. "Hundreds of people get away with murder every year in this country. A grandmother trips and falls down the basement steps, a husband is accidentally shot while on a hunting trip, a bottle of heart medicine gets lost when a wife needs it most. Happens every day, courtesy of smart people."

"How do they live with themselves?" Colin wondered. He believed in Satan, and hell and damnation, and shuttered to think of what happens to these uncaught murderers after their deaths. "How do they get up in the morning?"

"Easily," Rhonda interjected. She took a more pragmatic approach to life. "They never give it another thought. They're too busy spending the loot they inherit from the murder."

"What loot?"

"It's for the insurance, or the Treasury notes, or the real estate," Sutor declared. "That's why they do it."

Colin crossed himself. "Wilson Greene is a piker by comparison. He killed for a wallet and some credit cards."

"Wilson Greene didn't do it," Sutor asserted. "Miriam Lavin wasn't killed for her handbag. I think Greene did find the handbag by the side of the road. If he had killed for it, he would have taken the money and thrown the rest of the evidence away. I don't think he would have given the wallet and cards to Janetta if he'd killed for them."

"Maybe he's a junkie and only wanted the cash," Colin suggested.

Rhonda turned around to look at Colin. "He's not a junkie. And if he were, he'd have stolen the jewelry too. He could have pawned it. And while we're at it, I don't think either Wilson Greene or Janetta is stupid. It's the height of arrogance to think that of people who have had less opportunity than some of us, although I won't mention any names." She looked at Sutor to see if he realized that her defense of the suspects was really identification with them.

Sutor missed it completely. "Miriam Lavin was robbed, but she wasn't killed for her possessions," he maintained "The killer didn't take her car, and that would have been easy to do. The killer didn't take her necklace or pin. The killer threw the handbag away, with her money and wallet in it. What does that tell you?"

"The killer must have expected that Greene would find the handbag and then be charged with murder," Rhonda said.

"What does that tell you?" Sutor repeated.

"I'm not sure," Rhonda admitted.

"Like I said before, Miriam Lavin was executed," Sutor declared resolutely. "I knew it from the start," he added boastfully. Colin stuttered, "Executed! Why? Who would... How...?"

"The insurance, the Treasury notes, or the real estate," Sutor suggested. "The three musketeers of murder."

"I don't believe it," Colin argued. "I think it was something else."

"Name it," Sutor challenged.

"Maybe revenge. Miriam's stepdaughter hated her."

"And admitted it," Rhonda remarked.

"Either scenario," Sutor noted, "money or revenge, it was an execution."

"Where do we go from here?" Colin inquired.

"Rhonda and I follow the three musketeers," Sutor said. "You're the car man. Go back to Greene. Get more on the car. It's too crazy a story not to have some truth to it."

Colin concurred, "The insurance, the Treasury notes, the real estate, and the car. We should come up with something."

"And the hate," Rhonda added.

"And the hate," Sutor agreed reluctantly.

CHAPTER SEVEN

*S*utor sat behind his desk reading the autopsy report on Miriam Lavin aloud to Rhonda, who sat demurely in a chair beside him, a stack of papers in front of her. One shot, 9mm, probably a Beretta judging by the shell casing found at the crime scene. The bullet had crashed into Miriam's frontal lobe.

"Thinking, reasoning, and problem solving," Rhonda commented. She told Sutor the story of Phineas Gage, an infamous textbook character who lost frontal lobe functioning after an explosion rammed a pole through his head. "He became a vagrant on the railroad, and his brain now sits in a medical school somewhere."

"Miriam Lavin should consider herself lucky," Sutor remarked.

Colin came into Sutor's office wearing a NASCAR cap, on backward. "Listen to this," Sutor related, frowning at Colin's attire. "The shot was angled up, and it came from a distance of about 10 feet. Miriam had a large bruise on the left side of her neck and a broken collarbone. She wasn't shot at close range, yet her injuries indicate a direct physical attack. Were there two people in on this? Did one hold her while the other shot her? Judging from the direction the bullet took, whoever shot her must have been crouched down."

Colin was engrossed in a report of his own. Still clinging to his carjacking theory, Colin felt vindicated as he read a computer printout detailing Wilson Greene's criminal record. "Two arrests," he smugly informed Sutor, "one for theft and one for assault and battery."

Sutor put the autopsy report aside and reached for the printout. "How long ago? Was he convicted?"

Colin hesitated before replying, "Back in 1980 and 1981. Six months probation and two dismissals."

Sutor looked annoyed. "For Christ sake," he muttered. He'd been in a lousy mood for the past week and had been snapping at everyone in the station. He had turned his back on gum therapy that morning just before reaching for his first cigarette since going cold turkey.

"What's your problem with Wilson Greene?" Colin argued, also agitated. He felt he wasn't being taken seriously as a detective, cap on backward or not.

Sutor threw the autopsy report across the desk toward Colin, then pulled out a photo of Miriam Lavin that had been lying on a table in the coroner's workshop. "Go talk to Greene again and, when you're done, come back and tell me if you think he did this," he insisted, shoving the photo in front of Colin. "You want to solve this case overnight? Well, I got news for you. Six months from now we'll still have our heads up our asses." Sutor was rarely crude, and Colin took this minor vulgarity as a sign that his boss was getting flack because the case wasn't going well. He was wrong.

Colin started to say something but changed his mind. He knew it was nearly impossible to talk to Sutor when the boss got an idea in his head. Colin assumed it was because Sutor was mostly German, but it actually was the result of Sutor's confidence in his own instincts.

"I know this murder is a bought and paid for job," said Sutor. "Somebody wanted this woman dead, somebody close to her. Maybe it was the stepdaughter, but I doubt it. She's too honest about hating the old lady."

"Maybe that's her angle," Colin suggested. "She admitted to hating her stepmother to throw us off guard. A real killer wouldn't be so candid."

Sutor frowned disagreeably, "Go have another talk with Greene." Then he casually added, "I'll go see Dr. Marconi again. Maybe there's something she forgot to tell me."

"Yeh," Colin agreed, "like where she hid the murder weapon."

Sutor was not amused.

Colin drove to the county jail. Wilson, now booked for robbery, hadn't been able to come up with $500 to get himself released on bail. That was fine with Colin, who wanted Wilson nearby for a while if only to make it look to the press like the police were on to something.

Wilson was brought to an interrogation room. He was wearing an oversized prison uniform because they didn't have one to fit his small frame. Although he was being represented by a public defender, he agreed to talk to Colin alone.

The detective spread out samples of the shades of red used on cars during the last five years and instructed Wilson Greene to find the one that looked like the car from which Miriam Lavin's handbag had been thrown. After examining the colors for a half hour, Wilson whispered loudly, "Like this," as he pointed to a color that did indeed looked like wine, if one was in the habit of drinking a French, raspberry-flavored Merlot. He immediately reconsidered, "Sort of like this." He looked closer, then suggested, "Darker, maybe."

Next, Colin spread out his treasured collection of *Car and Driver*, and told Wilson to take his time looking through the magazines for a car that matched the wine-red one he had described. Wilson looked for another half hour before pointing to one. "This is the car. The color, too," he said, handing Colin an issue featuring GMs. On the cover was a photo of a burgundy-hued Chevrolet Malibu.

"Are you sure?" Colin asked. "You can take more time, as much as you need."

"Don't need more time."

"Good," Colin declared, patting Wilson on the back. "You just may get out of here in your lifetime."

Wilson, encouraged by Colin's joke, admitted, "I miss Janetta,"

"Speaking of Janetta, my man, we found your 38 at Janetta's house. You own any other guns?"

"No, sir."

"Wilson, I want you to think carefully. On the walk to City Line, did you see anything unusual? A person maybe."

"Didn't see nothin'. I told you that before. I told the other cop, too. Nothin' and nobody."

"Give me your route again. Where did you walk from? What did you pass?"

"Didn't pass nothin'," Greene maintained. "I walked down the street from the house Janetta works at, kept goin' straight, came to where that chicken place is. Thinkin' I'd like to get me some chicken and here come the bag. I picks it up."

"And then what?"

"I buys me some chicken with the money in the bag."

Colin continued, "About the purse. After you had your chicken snack how much money was left?"

"About 200."

"You pocketed the money and gave Janetta the purse, is that right?"

"Yes."

"What else was in the bag?"

"Just some lady stuff. A brush, I think. A comb, tissues—just stuff."

"What else was in the wallet?"

"I didn't look. I took the money and give the wallet to Janetta."

"You said you took the driver's license."

"Yeh, I forgot the driver's license. I didn't take the credit cards." Greene stopped to think. There was something else, but he couldn't remember what it was.

"Concentrate," Colin advised. "Relax and concentrate. What else was in the wallet?"

Greene suddenly brightened. "It was nothing," he related. "A piece of paper with a telephone number on it. It was with the money."

"What did you do with the piece of paper?"

"Nothing. I think I threw it out."

"Is it possible you didn't throw it out? Maybe it's still in the handbag or the wallet."

Greene shrugged. "Could be anywhere; could be nowhere."

Like this case, Colin thought. "Could be that it's still in the wallet or somewhere in your room." Colin stood up.

"Maybe," agreed Wilson.

"Let's go find it," Colin declared.

"You mean I'm getting out of here?" Greene asked, elated at the thought.

"You and me are getting out of here, for a little while. You're gonna help me."

"Then I'll get out of here?" Greene suggested hopefully.

"Maybe," Colin said, eager to win Greene's cooperation. He was starting to think Sutor was right about this suspect. He seemed too slow to plan a carjacking, although how much brain power it takes to pull an old lady out of her car and drive off with it is a question open to debate. There was something guileless about Wilson Greene. He seemed to be one of those docile black men who daily works hard at a menial job, stays at home after work, and faithfully attends church on Sunday, except that Greene did none of these things.

"Do you believe in Jesus?" Colin asked. He had a sense about Wilson and wanted to test this feeling.

"Lord, yes," Greene responded. "I be praying to Jesus since I got put in here, and I'm just sitting here waitin' for Him to get me out. He's takin' His time; but, I suppose, He got more important things to do than come down here after me."

Colin hated to admit it but Sutor was right. This guy didn't kill Miriam Lavin.

"He'll be here soon enough, Wilson," Colin commented as walked out of the interrogation room. "Stay put."

Colin called Rhonda and asked her to go to the evidence room and check the handbag and wallet they had confiscated from Janetta's house. He waited until Rhonda called back to report that the handbag and wallet were empty.

Colin drove Wilson Greene home to the small room he lived in over a North Philadelphia bar before the county had begun putting him up. Police had searched the room earlier, looking for a gun and anything connected to the Lavin case. They had come away with nothing. But they hadn't been looking for a piece of paper with a phone number on it, and they might have passed it by.

"Oh, Lord," Wilson cried out when he saw the carnage left by the inquiring police. The few belongings he had—mattress and blankets, some dishes, a teapot, a broom, toiletries—had been tossed around like pieces of garbage. The only three shirts he owned had been balled up and thrown in the corner sink, where a steady drip of water soaked them.

"Shit," Colin exclaimed. "I hope that phone number isn't in a shirt pocket." He picked up the shirts one by one and searched the soaked pockets.

"Not here," Colin said, disappointed.

"Maybe my pants," Wilson suggested. "Over there." He pointed to a clump of brown fabric laying half under a chair.

Colin reached down and picked up the pants. They were brown corduroy, with two pockets in the front and two in the back. "If you believe in Jesus, you'd better pray to him now," Colin advised Wilson.

Wilson began praying aloud. "Please, Lord Jesus..."

"Yes!" Colin shouted. "It worked already." He held up a torn piece of paper, "This it?"

"Thank you, Jesus," Wilson whispered.

"I have to take you back now," Colin informed Wilson. He felt badly for the fellow because of the room mess, and he would have preferred to stay and help him clean up. A social worker, maybe that had been his true mission in life—in any other family but his own.

Wilson began to cry, "I miss Janetta. I want to stay here."

Colin patted Wilson on the back. "I'll see what I can do to get you out on your own recognizance," he pledged. "That means you'll have to promise to show up for your robbery trial. I'll tell the judge how helpful you've been and maybe you'll get a break."

"I'll pray for you," Wilson declared.

"Never hurts," Colin said before driving Wilson back to the county jail.

Within days the charges against Wilson were dropped and he was released. Janetta was picked up and charged with theft for using Miriam Lavin's credit cards.

CHAPTER EIGHT

Melanie Marconi opened the unlocked front door to her house, shook her head, and called out to her son Jesse, "Sweetie, I'm home." She dropped her bulging cloth briefcase on a bench in the vestibule and carried two large, brown grocery bags through a long hallway and into the kitchen. A massive German shepherd bounded up the basement steps and jumped up on her, causing the grocery bags to topple onto the kitchen counter. Melanie hugged the dog and let the animal lick her face as she picked up the phone and dialed Jesse's cell phone number. "Hi, Sweetie. I'm home. Please turn down your music and come downstairs for a minute." She unlocked a door leading to the backyard and opened it. "Go out, Gertrude," she instructed the dog, holding the storm door ajar for the animal to pass through.

The large and open kitchen had a Victorian cottage look to it. Glass-fronted white cabinets ringed the room, each shelf stacked with collections of stoneware: hand-crafted pitchers, teapots, and bowls were among the dozens of pieces grouped behind the painted doors. Dishes were piled in the sink; stacks of mail and mail-order catalogs littered a massive pine kitchen worktable. There were newspapers piled on a stool and a basket of laundry sat next to the refrigerator, unfolded clothing strewn in it. It was the kitchen of a working mother.

Melanie pulled milk, bananas, grapes, strawberries, a loaf of Italian bread, a bag of coffee beans, and half dozen Styrofoam containers from the grocery bags. She thanked God for Thursdays because it meant the neighborhood farmers' market was open though the weekend; dinner was pre-made and ready through Sunday. She had never gotten the hang of cooking, probably because her mother, who had a slight talent for it, never shared even the most elementary of culinary secrets with her daughter. Melanie's mother had preferred to cook alone, eat alone, watch television alone, and essentially live alone, which, remarkably, she managed to do even though she had a husband and child sharing a house with her.

Melanie was a different kind of mother, as she had vowed she would be. She always wanted to be with Jesse, and she took pains to eat dinner with him every night of the week that her work and his activities allowed, either in neighborhood restaurants or from the brown bags. She reasoned the making of a meal wasn't half as important as the sharing of it.

The grapes and strawberries were dumped into a ceramic colander. Melanie placed the colander in the sink and turned on the water. She picked a clean glass out of the dishwasher, filled it with water, and gave each of the African violets on the windowsill a drink. The purple was her favorite, so she offered it an extra swig. From the window Melanie could see the wood-fenced backyard and all the evergreens Richard had planted in the eight years they had lived together in the house. The azalea plants were wilted from the winter cold, the trees above them were bare, the rabbit hutch was empty, and a green tarp hid the gas barbecue grill. Melanie thought of Auden's poem in memory of Yeats: *He disappeared in the dead of winter: / The brooks were frozen, the airports almost deserted, / And snow disfigured the public statues; / The mercury sank in the mouth of the dying day. / O all the instruments agree / The day of his death was a dark cold day.* She blinked back tears and returned to washing the strawberries.

Jesse appeared at the kitchen entrance. A muscular 5'9", he filled the space in the doorway. He was dressed in jeans, a 76ers sweatshirt, and the kind of boots Admiral Byrd might have used on his trek to Antarctica. The kid wore two earrings in his left ear and a gold Star of David around his neck. "Hi, Mom," he offered, nonchalantly. Seeing the containers, he asked, "What's for dinner?" as he walked over to the sink and gave Melanie a kiss on the cheek. He sensed she was upset but didn't say anything. He hated it when she got in this mood because he vividly remembered a time when she had been happy, and he desperately longed for those days again.

He tried hard not to think about what had happened to his father: shoveling snow off the driveway, dead of a heart attack in seconds. Sometimes, in his sleep, Jesse heard his mother's endless screams, and the frightening howl that had come from her throat when the paramedics told her it was too late. He was only ten when it happened, asleep in his room, but he knew even then that the only thing capable of bringing his mother to her knees would be the news that something terrible had happened to Richard or himself. "I'm here in my bed," he remembers thinking, "so it must be Dad."

Melanie turned off the water. "I brought you chicken cutlets," she said, touching Jesse's arm for a second but pulling her hand away before he could make an adolescent retreat. She longed to hold him the way she had when he had been five or six, when he had liked his hair stroked and his back rubbed. "Do more, Mommy," he'd plead, and she'd thank God, and do more. Now it was an unsaid, "Do less, Mommy"—less kissing, absolutely no holding, not much talking, and no more time together than if they were neighbors. A blond-headed girl from school, named after a store, had taken over the job Melanie had savored from the day it had been thrust upon her. Maybe it wouldn't be so bad if there were still Richard to cuddle with; but it was becoming increasingly, alarmingly, heartbreakingly clear to her that both the men in her life were gone.

"Can I go over to Austin's tonight?" Jesse asked. It was a city, not a store. "She says she'll help me with my French."

"It's a school night," Melanie answered. "I thought you were doing all right in French."

"I could use some help," Jesse suggested. "Just for a little while."

"How will you get there and home?"

Jesse gave his mother a beseeching look.

"I can't, Honey. I'm having a visitor."

"Who?"

"A police sergeant. He's investigating Miriam's murder. He'll be here soon so we better get through with dinner. You'll have to make it another night."

"I'll walk," Jesse argued. "It's not far."

"Not a good idea," Melanie stated. "It's dark out, and cold."

"So what. I'm a kid. Dark and cold mean nothing to me."

"No," Melanie insisted, "I don't want you to walk."

Jesse became angry, as she knew he would. "You're being ridiculous," he yelled, his face turning red. "Nothing's going to happen to me."

"I'm sure that's true, but I would rather you stay in tonight. "

"Give me one good reason," Jesse continued. Melanie referred to her son's temperamental relentlessness as his "Italian side," the part of him most like Richard. He had also inherited his father's height and large build, the dark, curly hair, and an ability to play the piano without relying on sheet music. Jesse had a wonderful singing voice and an aptitude for mimicking foreigners. He was incredibly funny when he wasn't in a grouchy mood, which wasn't often since puberty had commandeered his mind and body. When Melanie looked at Jesse, she saw almost nothing of herself in him, and that was a relief to her.

"Jesse, it's late already. Almost seven o'clock. By the time we finish dinner and clean up, it will be eight. Sergeant Sutor is coming about then. I understand you want to visit Austin, but it's not a good idea tonight."

"Why? Give me one good reason?"

"I just told you why; I don't want to repeat myself." Melanie turned her back on Jesse. She opened two food containers, took two plates from a rack over the stove, and scooped pasta salad onto each of them. She placed a chicken cutlet next to the salad on one plate and a crab cake next to the salad on the other.

"How about if I walk one way and you pick me up after the guy is gone?"

"Jesse, enough!" Melanie pulled two cloth napkins and some flatware from baskets under the worktable and handed them to Jesse. "Please, set the table." She opened a drawer on the side of an English pine table tucked against the kitchen wall and took out two quilted placemats. "Set the table and sit down, please." She went to the refrigerator. "What do you want to drink?"

Jesse slammed a kitchen chair against the table. "You're not being fair," he yelled.

"I think you're not being fair," Melanie replied softly. She knew that trying to out yell a teenager was a losing proposition, so she worked hard at staying calm and controlled when in a confrontation with Jesse. "Have some orange juice."

"I'm going anyway," Jesse announced resolutely, plopping down on a chair.

"Sweetie, you're not going anywhere so cut it out. You're being difficult tonight, and I'm getting really angry with you. I'm tired, I have papers to mark, and I have this character coming over to pick my brain about a murder I care nothing about. Please, don't make my life any more difficult."

Before sitting down, Jesse laid out the napkins and flatware. "You make my life miserable," he muttered.

"I'm sure I do sometimes," Melanie admitted, as she brought the plates over to the table and then went back for the glasses of juice. "Bon appétit," she declared, pleased that she and the girl with the city name knew at least two words in common.

William Sutor pulled his "German sweetheart" into Melanie Marconi's driveway at precisely 8 PM. He was impressed by the house: Pennsylvania farmhouse in style, all white and shuttered with a porch leading across the front and rounded to the back left side. It was located in Penn Valley, an exclusive section of Lower Merion Township. Spotlights shot on automatically as Sutor's car passed strategic points along the driveway and, by the time he drew up to the garage to the right of the house, the place looked like Yankee Stadium on baseball nights.

He pulled up behind a teal green Honda CRV and a dark purple Camaro convertible. A dog barked furiously from behind the house as Sutor got out of his car; but, other than that noise, the surrounds of the driveway seemed desolate. Houses on either side were visible through trees and bushes, but they were too far away for any neighborly interactions to transpire. Sutor wondered if Melanie Marconi ever got apprehensive living out of earshot of other people. He had grown up in a twin home in one of the township's working class sections, where a family disagreement in any house on the block became the neighborhood topic of conversation for a week. As a kid, Sutor had liked knowing who among his neighbors was a drunk or wife beater, pregnant out of wedlock, or talking to Jesus in the attic. He had liked the noise of the street; when it was too quiet he couldn't sleep. Noise is what had made him decide to become a cop.

Sutor had called before showing up at the Marconi home, an unusual action for him. He preferred to catch people unaware when he questioned them, before they could get their guard up or secure their attorney's advice. He informed Melanie Marconi of his impending visit, and he wasn't sure if it was because he wanted her to see him as a well-mannered guy or because he wanted to warn her. He even asked when it would be convenient for her to talk. Did she prefer her office or her house? Before work or after? Either time and place were all right with him. Melanie suggested he come at dinnertime, perhaps join her and her son for a bite to eat. It was Sutor who had been thrown off center.

Sutor had agreed to meet with Melanie after dinner, a safer time he told himself, both professionally and personally. He had stopped home after work to shower, shave, and change into a gray wool suit that worked well with his gray-flecked brown hair. He unconsciously straightened his tie and rang the front door bell. The bottom half of the windows leading to the porch were shuttered closed, so he couldn't tell if there was movement in the house.

"Door's open! Come on in!" Melanie invited through the house intercom.

He pulled open the storm door and stood there another minute, off balance again. An ornate silver mezuzah, nailed to the doorframe, caught his eye. He turned the brass handle on the heavy oak front door and pushed against it. It opened into a small center hallway decorated with a quilt, baskets, and an antique spinning wheel.

"I'll be right there," Melanie called from the kitchen doorway.

Sutor waited in the hallway, feeling awkward. He had come to interrogate a possible murder suspect only to find himself fidgeting in the vestibule of the suspect's house wondering why the hell he had stopped home to change his suit before confronting her about the death of a woman she admittedly loathed. He noticed Melanie's briefcase on the bench and ran a finger over the handle of it. On the wall above the bench was a *ketubah*, written in both Hebrew and English, announcing the marriage of Melanie Lavin and Richard Marconi: *I am my beloved's and my beloved is mine*. An elaborate needlepoint pillow on the bench read *Shalom*. Sutor began to feel this visit was not one of his better ideas.

Melanie came into the hallway. "How are you, Sergeant?" she smiled and extended her hand. She was wearing a long black sweater over a pair of jeans, and her hair was tied back with a purple and black scarf. In the dim hallway light, dressed so casually, she looked ten years younger and even prettier than when he'd seen her in her office. Without her shawl, he could see that she had a solid, rounded figure. He preferred a little plumpness in women past 40, and a few lines about the eyes, symbols of life having been experienced.

"Doing OK," Sutor replied, shaking her hand. He held out the Dunkin' Donuts box he had with him, "For you and your son, a variety."

"And a box of questions for me," Melanie remarked, accepting the donuts. "Thanks, this is really sweet of you."

Sutor couldn't recall the last time he had been called sweet. He was grateful to Rhonda for recommending he stop and pick up something on his way over. Rhonda had suggested it would illustrate his fine deportment, and maybe throw Melanie off guard. Melanie's comment told him that she had no intention of being thrown off guard by chivalry. She was acutely aware that this was not a social visit, despite the offering. It was good that he had been reminded of this too.

"How'd you know I have a son? Checking up on me?" she teased.

Sutor didn't answer. She was a step ahead of him again; and, he figured, by answering he'd end up having to run to catch up.

Melanie ushered Sutor into the living room, "Make yourself at home. I have coffee brewing—Sumatra and French roast mix; it's strong. Cream and sugar?"

"Sugar only," Sutor replied. He wasn't a coffee drinker, but he figured he'd tough it out.

She read his mind, "I can make you tea if you prefer."

He did, in fact, prefer tea, like his mother had, but didn't mention it. "Coffee will be fine."

"I'll be right back."

The living room was startlingly beautiful, furnished in an eclectic mix of Victoriana and American country. Melanie had started a fire in a cast-iron stove fireplace insert. Additional light came from an intricate Tiffany lamp, an original, Sutor guessed correctly. The couch was hunter green velvet framed in mahogany. There were books everywhere: on the built-in oak shelves that lined two walls, piled high on the coffee table, on the floor beside the chair, and on every one of the deep, wood windowsills. An oil painting of a large purple rose was strategically displayed above the fireplace.

Sutor surveyed the bookshelves, packed with hardbacks: Anais Nan, Krisnamurti, Colin Wilson, Joseph Campbell. He hadn't the faintest idea who these authors were. He moved on to an end table where a bunch of paperbacks were stacked: Witold Rybczynski on houses, Andrew Solomon on depression, Germaine Greer's *The Change*, a pile of novels by Anne Tyler and Peter Taylor. There were books spread out on the coffee table: Richard Dawkins' *The God Delusion*. Something called *It's Easier Than You Think*, about being a Buddhist. He picked up a book about death and mourning, parts of which were underlined in pink magic marker. He randomly chose a paragraph: *The perceptual or emotional defense mechanism most often experienced by the bereaved is dissociation. The external, reality-based world is often removed or rejected from working, ongoing consciousness.* Melanie must have scribbled the note next to this: "O, grief hath changed me since you saw me last, / And careful hours with time's deformed hand / Have written strange defeatures in my face."

He wasn't sure what either of the passages meant, but he felt as though he was eavesdropping and put the book down. He walked toward the fireplace to get a better look at the painting above the mantel. There were books on the mantelpiece also. One in particular caught his eye—a thick paperback titled *Getting Even: The Art of Revenge*. He picked it up and began to leaf through it. It was a do-it-yourself justice manual, categorized into revenges suited to every-day life. A couple of pages were turned back. One piece suggested writing a letter to the editor of a local paper championing racial supremacy or pornography and signing it with your enemy's name and address. Another advised the pouring of instant pudding into the gas tank of an enemy's car. Petty stuff. There was no mention of a 9mm bullet aimed at the thinking and reasoning part of the brain.

Melanie appeared, holding a tray with two cups of coffee and a plate of the donuts on it. She gestured toward the oil painting above the fireplace, "Do you like it? The artist is Joseph Raffael. I bought that painting 30 years ago,

when his work was affordable. I love the purple colors."
She held out a cup.

"This room is amazing," Sutor observed, quickly
closing the book. He took the coffee cup from her and
balanced it on the book, "Thank you."

"My husband was very artistic; he was in the advertising
field. He had impeccable taste and a passion for antiques. I
like early American, Shaker, and American Folk; and he
liked turn-of-the-century Victorian. So we compromised
by mixing and matching. This room is my favorite; it's part
of a new addition to the house. It has a special feel to it,
doesn't it? Works with the furniture."

"Yes, it does," Sutor concurred, unsure of how history
and architecture and house goods relate to each other. He
thought of how his parents' house had looked when he was
a child: mismatched furniture that really didn't fit. Now he
was grown up, still living in the family home, taking care
of his father. The place—and his taste—were in dire need
of repair. A month earlier he had sprung for a new bedroom
chair. It had come in a box, and he had to put it together
himself. This was not something he thought to mention to
a woman who owned lamps and vases autographed by the
people who had made them. Sutor sat down on a tapestry-
covered chair angled by the fireplace; Melanie moved to
the couch.

"I'd introduce you to my son, Jesse, but he locked
himself in his room. He's mad at me; I won't let him out
to visit his girlfriend," she sighed. "He's testosterone
driven right now. It should pass in another 50 years."

"I remember those days," Sutor said, although that
wasn't quite true. His father had exerted more control over
him than any old raging hormones. His endocrine glands

had stopped secreting the minute his old man walked into a room.

"I'm dying of curiosity," Melanie volunteered, returning to the business at hand. "Who killed Miriam?"

"We're not sure," Sutor acknowledged as he turned *Getting Even* over so she could see he had it.

"Any suspects?" she wondered, ignoring the book.

"We're working on it." He sipped his coffee and waited uneasily. He longed for a cigarette but assumed the absence of an ashtray anywhere in the room meant smoking would not meet with the homeowner's approval.

"I expect so." Melanie held out the donut plate, but Sutor shook his head no. Melanie broke off a piece of a donut and began nibbling on it. As if reading his mind again she remarked, "You're a smoker. It's OK to smoke in my house." She reached into a bookshelf and pulled out an ashtray.

Sutor declined the offer. "How do you know I smoke?"

"Just a feeling. My husband was a smoker and you remind me a little of him."

He was flattered by the comparison to her husband, a man he knew nothing about other than he'd lived with this woman. Sutor asserted, "I'm trying to quit, for the eighth time."

There was a long silence while Melanie drank her coffee and Sutor played with his spoon. Melanie didn't offer any further help that would get him to the point of his visit, and Sutor was reluctant to bring up the subject that, ostensibly, led him to this house in Penn Valley.

Finally, Sutor gave in and admitted, "You know I'm here on business, so we might as well get started. There are a few questions I'd like to ask you about your relationship with Miriam Lavin."

"Shoot," Melanie declared, an interesting choice of words given the subject matter.

"Where were you the Friday night Miriam Lavin was murdered?

"I was with a friend."

"Are you sure it was two Friday nights ago?"

"Positive. I'm with my friend every Friday night. I come home from work, have dinner with Jesse, and then go visit my friend."

"What's her name?" Sutor took a notebook and pen from the inside pocket of his suit jacket.

"Harold Rosenberg."

Sutor blushed. "Sorry," he said, feeling an odd combination of embarrassment and a tad of jealousy, which made no sense to him. "What time did you get home that night?" What in the world made him believe there wouldn't be a man in her life? A woman like her, alone for five years. He felt like a fool, or a man who had been without a woman long enough to forget what pretty girls do when the sun goes down.

"I didn't get home." She wasn't in the least self-conscious about telling him this. "I stayed with Mr. Rosenberg."

"All night?"

"Yes."

"Do you remember what time you did get home?"

"Ten in the morning. I always get home by 10:00 on Saturdays. Jesse has a piano lesson at 11:00; I drive him."

"Was Jesse with you during the night?" It was a silly, prying question, but he couldn't help wanting to know.

"No. He spends Friday nights at his friend Brian's."

"Where does Mr. Rosenberg live?"

"Center city; Rittenhouse Square; on Delancey Place."

"Is there anyone who can vouch for you being in town when Miriam was killed?"

"Mr. Rosenberg can, but I'd rather you didn't bother him with questions."

"Why not?"

"I'd just rather keep him out of this thing. I don't want him to worry about anything."

"Why would he worry?"

"He just would."

Her concern about her Friday night friend seemed strange to him. Would the guy be hesitant to back her up? Is he a married man stepping out on his wife once a week? He reached over and placed his full cup on the table in front of Melanie, allowing the book to become more visible. Melanie acknowledged it and laughed, "Jesse loves that book. It appeals to his adolescent meanness."

"Does it appeal to your adolescent meanness?" Sutor asked.

Melanie laughed, "No question about it. Unfortunately, the deeds in that book are too overt for me. I prefer subtlety when I get even."

"It's been said that when a person seeks revenge, he digs two graves: one for himself." It was one of the few quotes Sutor knew—he'd heard it on a quiz show the day before.

"It's been said wrong. Injustice grates on the soul. It robs people of their just sleep. The best tranquilizer for injustice is a good dose of vengeance."

"Did you want to get even with Miriam?" She had told him so during his office visit, but he wanted to see if she had grown more cautious with her statements.

"Desperately," she admitted, obviously not worried in the least.

"What was your plan?"

"I was working on it." She pointed to the book he was holding, "I wanted it to be a lot more hurtful than sending a pizza to her apartment in the middle of the night."

"A bullet to the brain is pretty hurtful," Sutor reminded her. It was hard for him to believe that a woman who draped afghans across the arms of chairs could feel such venom. He wondered if her candidness was intended to point him in another direction. A real murderer would be reticent to admit how much she hated the victim. Perhaps.

"Not painful enough for me." There was a hardness to her voice he hadn't heard before.

"You knew Miriam well, Dr. Marconi, and you knew what kind of person she was. Who do you think killed her?"

"You want me to speculate? Miriam had a lot of money, stolen from a dying man. It was money that rightly belonged to me. It wouldn't have done me any good to kill her since I won't benefit a dime. I have no real motive, other than hate, which isn't worth a bushel of beans financially. Somebody in Miriam's family now gets my father's money. One of those lowlife, thieving cretins did it. You'll see."

Sutor asked for a rundown of everyone in the family. Melanie gladly gave her opinion of each and every one of Miriam's children, grandchildren, in-laws, friends of in-laws, and anyone else even remotely related to the Herzelman family, including people who might have inadvertently passed them on the street. "All scumbags, down to the last man, woman, and child."

The phone rang and Melanie picked up a remote receiver laying on the end table, answering it while still agitated. "Yes," she said harshly. "Sorry, dear," she apologized into the phone. "How are you tonight?" Her tone changed dramatically, becoming soft and loving. "Can I call you back in a few minutes?" She stood up. "Sergeant Sutor is here. Remember I told you about him?" She paused and Sutor saw a worried look on her face. "Don't be concerned; everything's fine. I'll call you back." She grew more upset as the caller spoke. "OK, Honey. Yes, in a few minutes. Don't fall asleep yet." She hung up.

Sutor wanted to say, "Mr. Rosenberg, I presume," but he held his tongue. Melanie volunteered nothing, but she seemed anxious to get rid of him. "Anything else, Sergeant?"

"Oh, I almost forgot," Sutor responded. "Do you know anyone who drives a burgundy Malibu, four-door, a fairly new model?"

"Not off hand," Melanie shook her head. She moved around the room as she talked to him, disconcerting Sutor, who couldn't concentrate while watching her flit from the fireplace to the window and back to the fireplace.

"Can I help you with anything else, Sergeant?"

There were a few things he could think of in response to her question, but he kept them to himself. "Do you own a gun, Dr. Marconi?"

"Yes," Melanie admitted.

"I'd like to see it."

"It's in the vestibule," she responded, heading out of the living room. "Come this way," she instructed, prompting him toward the front door.

She walked with him into the hallway and out to the vestibule.

"It's right here," Melanie volunteered. She reached into the briefcase she had left on the vestibule bench, pulled out a 25 caliber Raven, and handed the gun to Sutor.

"A Saturday night special," Sutor observed. "Where'd you get it?"

"Every teenager in America owns one," Melanie answered. "A friend gave it to me."

"Is it licensed?"

"No. Is that why you're here? To arrest me for carrying a concealed, unlicensed weapon?"

"Why do you have it?"

"I work in the city. I travel to and from the city. I live alone. In that order."

"Do you know how to use this?" Sutor inquired.

"With deadly accuracy," Melanie declared, "and with little hesitation if need be."

"Not a good idea," Sutor commented, concerned that she would blow a hole in herself. "What if your son got hold of it?"

"Jesse doesn't know about it. He never goes in my briefcase. I practice at a range on Spring Garden Street. You can check it out. I know how to use a gun."

He didn't know what to make of her, this pretty lady filled with sorrow, a deadly aim, and a lover. She made no sense to him. But neither had his mother, who had stayed with a man she hated her entire adult life. Or any of the women who had taken him into their beds over the years knowing he had no real interest in them. He felt closer to Rhonda than any woman he had ever known; and, yet, he couldn't bring himself to tell her about his insane attraction to Melanie Marconi. Even standing in front of Melanie, he wasn't sure what it was about for him. She seemed so removed from the world, disassociated, like the grief book said, that he couldn't grasp enough of her to wrap his feelings around with any clarity.

"I'm here if you have any more questions, Sergeant. Call me anytime."

Sutor gave Melanie back her Raven. "Thank you for seeing me," he replied politely, hating to leave.

"Come anytime," Melanie invited, touching his arm as she opened the front door. The sensation of her went through his suit jacket and shirt and onto his skin. "I appreciate your thinking of Jesse."

"My pleasure. I hope to meet him one day, when his hormones die down."

Melanie laughed, "You should live so long."

Sutor walked out onto the porch. The sound of the dog barking filtered to the front of the house. "Take care." The spotlights popped on as he headed down the path toward his car. He turned to look back at Melanie, but the door was already closed. He was disappointed that she hadn't been interested enough to watch him for a moment or two.

Sutor got into the BMW, started the engine, and pulled slowly out of the driveway. As he turned into the street, the spotlights went out, plunging the house into darkness. He pulled over to the side of the road, reached into his pocket for his cell phone, and dialed his office number. He knew

Rhonda was working late. "Rhonda? Anything more on the car? Did you check with New Jersey? No, not much more than we had before. I'll see you in ...."

He saw the lights of the Marconi house spring on. He glanced at his car clock: 8:40. "I'll call you back, Rhonda, can't talk now. Stay put. I'll call you back."

The Honda drove past him, traveling at a high speed. He quickly pulled out behind it and followed the car as it headed east and picked up the Schuylkill Expressway leading to Philadelphia. Fifteen minutes later Sutor was in the city, watching as Melanie pulled into the private driveway of an elegant, four-story townhouse. He saw her get out of the car and half run across a brick courtyard leading to the house. He watched as she hurried up a flight of steps to a railed landing, fumbled with her keys, turned the lock on the front door of the townhouse, and walked in, letting the door close behind her.

Sutor sat in his car for a half hour, listening to the radio, staring at the residence, and trying not to imagine what was going on inside. He fooled with the radio buttons, looking for his favorite jazz station. The reception in town was poor, only Kenny Rogers came in clearly: *This woman, she's tearing my world apart. This woman, don't know what she's doing.* Sutor was furious with himself for being attracted to this woman. It guaranteed to complicate his job, his life, and his sleep. *This woman, don't even know her name. This woman touches me and I lose control.* He didn't understand it. Many women had been attracted to him over the years; but, after short dalliances, he lost interest in each of them. Not one had been a murder suspect, burdened with an adolescent, and racing to the arms of another man in the middle of the night. *She goes walking by, and the city lights, and the city lights they make you blind.* Sutor flipped off the radio, pulled out of his space, and headed home—to his father's house, the mismatched furniture, and a murder case that was no closer to being solved tonight than it had been the day it occurred.

Sutor sat in his car in front of the house he'd lived in from the day he had been born. The house, in an area of the township once known as Hungrytown, was only a couple of miles from Melanie's place, but it might just as easily have been on Mars for the differences it represented in life assumptions. Hungrytown had a new name—Narberth—but it was still a working-class enclave shared now by the Irish Catholic descendants of the domestics that founded it and the Jewish and WASP newcomers who sought to fix up the rundown houses and shops and turn the area into something resembling a New England village.

The shutters on the stone twin had been painted a half dozen times over the years, and each time the color had been the same: hunter green. His mother had wanted something more cheerful, red at best, but light blue as a compromise. Sutor, as a child, had wanted red, for his mother. After she died, he didn't much care what color the shutters were. The Sutor side of the twin was well kept and orderly. A hedge around the front garden was trimmed evenly; rose bushes had been mulched for the winter and covered with canvas; the grill was protected with a precisely tied green tarp. A log holder on the porch displayed four rows of evenly stacked wood, each piece cut into a two-foot length.

Sutor turned on the radio again and hit a button that tuned in the jazz station. An old rendition of Herbie Mann's *Summertime* came on: *Your Daddy's rich, and your*

Momma's good looking. Sutor chuckled to himself. His Daddy, Henrik during his youth in Germany, but now Henry Sr., was indeed well off. He had owned a nursery business that that grown heartily over 40 years as Philadelphia's western suburbs developed and expanded. Although he railed against "those bastard Jews" whenever he was in a sour mood, the Jewish newcomers to the area had been responsible for most of his business success as they sought to decorate their properties with the rhododendron and Japanese maples they could have bought for a third off his price if they had been willing to drive a half hour into the country. Henry's "big money," as he called it, had come from the sale of his prime property along Montgomery Avenue, now the busiest shopping strip in the township, a piece of land he originally had bought from a farmer for a price that wouldn't buy the kind of car his son now drove.

Sutor's mother, Louise, had been good looking. Neither the money nor her looks had done anyone in the family any good. His father clung to the belief, "You don't appreciate things unless you earn them yourself," the traditional motto of parents seeking to justify their own withholding. "I put a roof over your head and fed you, didn't I?" Henry Sr. reminded his two sons at every complaint from them about his stinginess. Henry Jr. had answered, "It's the law, you had to," before packing his bags and heading west, leaving his younger brother to carry on the family fight on behalf of their now-dead mother. If there was anyone on earth that needed Melanie Marconi's revenge book it was Bill Sutor.

There were lights on in the attached twin, and Sutor could see a man and a woman walking around in the dining room. They were putting dishes in a breakfront cabinet while taking caressing and kissing breaks. It looked a bit ludicrous to Sutor. The woman was gray-haired and heavy set, and the man would have been gray-haired and heavy-set if he had any hair at all or lost 40 pounds. In the 20 years this couple had lived next door to him, Sutor had done nothing more than nod hello to them if they happened to leave their house the same time he left his. Henry Sr. hadn't done even that, even though the house partners had come to his wife's viewing and dropped off a plate of homemade sugar cookies afterward.

Sutor felt something creeping through him but couldn't identify what it was. It wasn't a feeling of anything, but rather the absence of a feeling of anything. The people next door had once given him sugar cookies, and he had attached no meaning to this act of kindness. He had brought Jesse Marconi a box of donuts, and the boy's mother had seemed genuinely pleased by the gesture. He didn't really know what all this giving of food meant, and that made him sad.

Sutor rooted around in his glove compartment until he found an old pack of Marlboros. There were two cigarettes left. He pressed the car lighter. The neighbors were dancing now. Sutor moved his car a few feet back to get a better look and watched as the pair slow danced around the dining room table. What could they possibly be dancing to? He lit one of the cigarettes and took a long, appreciative drag on it. He tried to imagine himself in his neighbors' place. He knew who he'd dance with if, by some miracle, he learned how to dance. He'd missed his high school prom because his father had determined that paying money for his son to party with a bunch of rowdy, spoiled kids was nonsense. Sutor also had missed his senior year class trip and the Lutheran Church outing to Cooperstown, for similar reasons.

The neighbor lady raised her dancing partner's tee shirt and began kissing his enormous belly. She moved her mouth up his chest, onto his neck, and, finally, onto his lips. Sutor could see the man run his fingers through the woman's straggly hair. The man kissed the woman on her forehead, eyes, nose, and lips, then unbuttoned her blouse and pulled it back and down her arms. Unhooking her bra, he pulled it forward and watched as her huge breasts tumbled out before him. The man and woman began to dance again, slowly and in step, her head resting on his shoulder.

Sutor imagined Melanie Marconi dancing with Harold Rosenberg right now, in that gentrified townhouse. Harold was taking her blouse off; she was kissing Harold's stomach.

The half-naked neighbor couple put their arms around each other, walked over to a table positioned under the front window facing Sutor's car, and turned off the light.

Sutor lit his second cigarette with the butt of the first. He'd have to go into his father's house whether he wanted to or not. Henry Sutor, formerly Henrik, awaited him.

CHAPTER NINE

"Nobody has a kind word to say about her." Rhonda sat on the edge of Sutor's desk, her legs crossed, reading to him from a legal pad perched on her knee. "The doorman at Valley Forge Towers says Miriam Lavin never gave him a Christmas gift. She had a series of housekeepers —six in four years. The manicurist at Saks says, and I quote, 'She was a miserable bitch.' The only person I found who liked her is her lawyer, Alan Kaplan, who I spoke to on the phone. He represented her in numerous law suits."

Sutor found himself focused on the tiny roses woven into Rhonda's black mesh stockings. "Who'd she sue?" Women and their stockings, something he'd never thought much about before. He wondered how many kinds there were out there in the world of female legs, and he made a mental note to notice in the future.

Rhonda pulled a sheaf of papers from her briefcase. "Here are copies of court filings on Miriam's behalf. She charged Methodist Hospital with failing to order an X-ray of her first husband's head after he fell down the stairs. She sued a moving company for damages after they moved her furniture into the Valley Forge apartment—she said they chipped her armoire. She was part of a class action suit having something to do with power lines. She even took the Valley Forge tenant's association to court because they wouldn't let her keep Morrie Lavin's wheelchair in the lobby. There are a few incidental cases against stores and individuals; a fall on her hip here, charges of fraud there. And here's the best one yet: she sued Alan Kaplan for malpractice."

"I thought you said Kaplan liked her?" Sutor interjected.

"That's what he told me."

What were the outcomes of the cases?"

"She lost against Methodist when three emergency room nurses testified that Miriam was abusive to them and took her husband out of the hospital before they could order the X-ray. The moving company settled for $500. The suit against the power companies is pending. Morrie died, and the wheelchair case died with him. She picked up a few bucks, nothing big, from a couple of stores."

"Who represented her in her suit against her lawyer?" Sutor asked. "It's hard to get one lawyer to testify against another."

"Jerome Eisenberg—her grandson."

"What happened?"

"They lost."

Sutor reached for Rhonda's notes. "What do you think? Does this expand our list of suspects?"

"There's nothing here," Rhonda observed, "unless an angry nurse from 15 years ago bumped Miriam off."

Sutor flipped through the pages. "If she'd go to all this trouble over this minor stuff, I'll bet there's something bigger out there we're missing."

"I checked out Melanie Marconi's story," Rhonda continued. "Miriam did rob Morrie Lavin blind, most of it legally. There were a few slip-ups, though. Morrie died at 4:10 AM. Miriam was at his bank the same day. She cashed in one of Morrie's CDs—a big one. The bank issued a check in Morrie's name, not knowing he was dead. Miriam forged Morrie's name on the endorsement and collected the money. Because Morrie was dead by then, that check belonged to his estate. His estate was Melanie Marconi. She's Morrie's only child."

"Did he leave Melanie everything?" Sutor's voice lowered slightly when he mentioned Melanie's name. He looked away from Rhonda and began fiddling with a Wandering Jew, its plant shoots twirling across his desk. A Wandering Jew—apropos, he thought.

"Yes, except for a trust fund to be set up for his grandson Jesse's college education."

"How much?" Sutor asked, nonchalantly pulling off a withered leaf. He had a half dozen plants on his desk; and, though he tried to distance himself emotionally from the years he had worked with his father, he still had a weak spot in his heart for a good looking *Acer palmatum*, his favorite kind of Japanese maple tree.

"A half million, plus a hundred Gs from the trust fund."

Surprised, Sutor looked up. "How much did she end up with?"

"Nothing."

"Not a dime?"

"Doesn't seem so."

"How about the trust fund?"

Rhonda shook her head, "If I'd known Miriam Lavin, I would have killed her myself, just on principle."

Sutor stood up, "Who gets Morrie Lavin's money now?"

Rhonda shrugged. "Don't know. Miriam's daughters, I suppose."

"Don't suppose," Sutor demanded. "Get a copy of her will."

"If Miriam was as obsessed with money as it appears, there's a good chance her daughters and grandchildren are too," Rhonda suggested. "The apple doesn't...." She stopped short, "Oh, my God." Rhonda slapped herself on the knee, "How could I miss it? It was one of Miriam's daughters. They must have known their mother had the money she stole from Morrie. They're probably the heirs to it. One of them was waiting for her in that parking lot."

Rhonda's theory was too farfetched for Sutor. "Can we return to the planet Earth now?"

"It was one of Miriam's daughters. I'd bet my life on it."

"Don't bet your life on it, Rhonda. I'd hate losing so competent a partner."

"I'll take that chance," Rhonda said with certainty. "Greed and murder is their legacy—like mother, like daughters."

"Rhonda! You're being ridiculous! There isn't one shred of evidence pointing in that direction."

"Anastasia or Drusilla, which daughter?" Rhonda insisted.

Sutor laughed, "You're not giving up, are you?"

"As an old psych professor of mine once said...."

"Spare me," interjected an exasperated Sutor, who had no respect for psychology or psychologists, even though he knew little about either.

"You're leaving a large boulder unturned," chided Rhonda.

Sutor relented. "OK, you want to check out the daughters, go to it. Get their bank statements over the past two years. You want to look under rocks, be my guest. Let's see what you find."

"Worms," Rhonda suggested, "wiggly, crawly worms." Rhonda had planned to get her graduate degree in family therapy, and the subject of disturbed families held a keen interest for her.

Sutor laughed and reached for his jacket. "Come on," he said.

Rhonda jumped off the desk. "Where to?"

"You want worms, I know just the place." He held the office door for her, "You drive. It's in the city."

Alan Kaplan's office was on the 20th floor of the 1701 office complex in Philadelphia. Located a block from City Hall, it was one of the most elegant buildings in town, home to such high-end stores as Tiffany's and Restoration Hardware, and the most prestigious law firms in the city. Rhonda and Sutor announced themselves to a pretty receptionist, waited a half hour until Kaplan was free, and then followed the woman down two hallways decorated with tasteful scenic oil paintings of Philadelphia landmarks, including Betsy Ross's house and Independence Hall. Sutor saw that the receptionist was wearing stockings with seams up the back. His mother had worn stockings like that, and he had assumed they had gone out of style when she had. It was good to see that some things don't change.

Kaplan's office was bright and open, with a window facing Market Street; it was representative of Kaplan's place within the firm of Kidwell, Ditcher, Peplau and Brim, all deceased.

Kaplan, a small, stout man, not much past 40, sporting a bow tie and matching suspenders under an expensive silk pin-stripped navy suit, greeted Rhonda and Sutor at the office door, shook Sutor's hand only, and ushered his visitors to two chairs facing his desk. Instead of moving behind his desk, Kaplan pulled up a third chair and faced his guests directly. He offered tea or coffee, a cigarette, some jelly beans, and a commentary on the weather. Rhonda accepted coffee and Sutor requested tea because Rhonda had convinced Sutor that eating or drinking with people softens them up by putting them in a social mood.

Kaplan got up and walked over to a credenza near the office door. "Sorry, no tea," he observed, pouring coffee from a stainless steel pot. "In the old days I could order a secretary to make tea. Can't do that anymore. Damn shame." He looked at Rhonda, "Cream or sugar?" She declined both. Kaplan handed Rhonda the cup and sat down again. He himself wasn't drinking or eating.

"What can I do for you?" Kaplan asked. "I think I told Detective Robinson everything I know when she called me."

"Let's go over it again," Sutor suggested. "You represented Miriam Lavin."

"Many times," Kaplan replied.

"In the Methodist Hospital case," Sutor continued, "she blamed the emergency room people for her husband's death."

"Yes," Kaplan answered.

"You lost."

"Yes, I did."

"How come?"

Kaplan shrugged. "It happens."

"Miriam sued you," Rhonda reminded him. She liked Kaplan's outfit, thought it added an independent element to what appeared to be conservative surroundings. She also liked his bluntness and seeming lack of egoism—and he poured a nice cup of coffee.

"It happens," Kaplan said again. He wasn't particularly social, either. And he wasn't about to volunteer any details of his dealings with Miriam.

"Why did it happen, Counselor? Why did you lose, and why did Miriam sue you?"

"She was unhappy with the verdict. She thought I handled her case incompetently."

Rhonda flipped through her notepad. She stopped, read a section, and chimed in, "Clearly you're not incompetent, Mr. Kaplan; editor of the Law Review at Penn; graduated at the top of your class; brought into this firm even before graduation. You won one of the largest malpractice cases the city has seen, the one where the doctor went on vacation before telling his patient she had a tubal pregnancy. You wouldn't have taken Miriam's case if you didn't think you could win it."

"The case was a winner," Kaplan replied.

"What happened?" Sutor asked.

"She got greedy. Turned down a very good settlement offer because she thought she could con a jury. She lied on the stand. The jury threw her out and me with her."

"So why'd she sue you?"

"Why not? She wouldn't take responsibility for doing something I told her not to do. She was out for money, and she was going to get it somewhere. I was the mark."

Rhonda looked back to her notes. "Her grandson, Jerome Eisenberg, represented her, and he lost."

Kaplan laughed, "You get what you pay for."

Sutor inquired, "What can you tell us about Eisenberg? What kind of lawyer is he?"

"Obviously, he's not as good as you," Rhonda suggested, "but is he OK as an attorney?" If food and drink wouldn't do it, maybe praise would. "Have you beaten him in other cases?"

"Don't flatter me," Kaplan commented, flattered anyway. "Jerry Eisenberg is a *putz*; anyone could have destroyed his case. I went up against him three years ago in Wilmington, Delaware. The judge almost put him in jail for contempt because he was so hostile and argumentative in the courtroom. Eisenberg was a classmate of mine at Penn. He never cared much for the law—he wanted to be an English teacher—but his family wouldn't have it. I think his father threatened to withhold his college tuition if he didn't agree to go to law school. The old lady, his grandmother, was slipping him money, and she would have cut him off too. He spent the money on booze and hookers, and there was never enough. Like a good boy, he went to law school."

Kaplan, a man who had sued a bunch of cute little emergency room nurses on behalf of a women he knew to be a liar, continued, "Eisenberg never had any respect for the law. He thought the best thing about it was that it was a tool by which lawyers could get rich. Jerry and Granny made a living off the law. What did it cost them? A few pieces of paper? A little time?" He chucked, "I could sue you two right now if I wanted to. Believe me, there's something I could think up that might stick legally. You threatened me—your word against mine—albeit a pain in the ass, but it could be worth a few bucks; the township you work for might not want to be bothered with it."

"This is what Eisenberg does?"

"Over and over, with a little help from the late granny."

Rhonda ran down the cases involving Miriam.

"Tip of the iceberg," Kaplan stated. "You're looking at Philadelphia only. Go into Montgomery County. Try Delaware County. Try fucking Alaska for all I know." He looked at Rhonda, "Forgive the language."

"Any idea who killed the late granny?" Sutor asked. "Care to speculate?"

"Anyone who knew her," Kaplan declared.

Rhonda interjected, "You told me you liked her."

Kaplan laughed. "I did," he acknowledged. "She was a tough old broad." He picked up a handful of jelly beans and began munching on them. "She was relentless— money, money, and more money, from anyone who had it. Gotta give the old girl credit."

Sutor didn't understand the admiration. "What was it all for?" he inquired, philosophically. "She was in her 70s. Why did she want to spend her last years this way, in one courtroom after another? I've been in a lot of them in my time, and they're the last places on earth a sane person would go voluntarily."

Kaplan was offended. "Many sane people love courtrooms. Take me, for example." He raised his eyebrows at Rhonda and wiggled them in an imitation of Groucho Marx.

"I mean normal people," Sutor responded, trying to regroup but making it worse.

Rhonda came to the rescue, "He means lay people rather than attorneys."

"Yes," Sutor quickly agreed. "Why would Miriam need money so badly that she'd be willing to spend her last years in litigation?"

"It's simple," Kaplan explained. "Where do old ladies with blue hair go to get the attention age and their husbands deny them?"

"The hairdresser," Sutor suggested, dating himself. He thought of Miriam Lavin on the floor of the Saks parking lot, every lock in place.

"Come on," Kaplan urged. "Attention. Money. Excitement. Where would you go?" He addressed Rhonda, "What do you do on Saturday nights when you want to have a good time?"

Rhonda couldn't remember the last time she had had a good time, so nothing came to her mind. She took a guess. "I'd visit friends."

"Come on," Kaplan urged. "Think."

"I don't know," Rhonda admitted.

Kaplan chuckled, "The casinos. They woo lonely and insecure people into their webs by offering free meals, a bed, and room service. People like Miriam Lavin, vain and self-centered, they think all the fuss is about them. They haven't a clue that it's all a scam, a great legal train robbery. Only the train is made up of people's lives—their mortgages, their marriages, their kid's college fund, their careers, their retirement accounts. The casinos take it all, not just the gold but also the engine, the passenger cars, and the caboose. Yet people like Miriam are always ready to go on another train ride."

"I take it you don't gamble," Rhonda said, suddenly feeling depressed at the thought of her dull life.

"On the contrary," he maintained, "I've given up more than my share of dead presidents to the crap tables." He leaned forward to be sure he was heard. "But I never gave them the farm," he noted. He took Rhonda's hand in his and teased her with a Southern accent, "And I never killed nobody to pay up my debts."

Sutor thought about what Kaplan had said. "Do you know for a fact that Miriam Lavin frequented the casinos?"

"Saw her there with my own two eyes, many times."

"She lost a lot?"

"Enough to warrant a suite; more than I ever got. My losses stay in the hundreds; I get dinner for two at a McDonalds. The late Mrs. Lavin was a high roller."

"She had that kind of money?" Sutor asked.

"Not enough to pay my bill—she stuck me like she did everyone else she owed—but enough to sit at the black-jack tables night after night. The woman was an addict."

"Where do you think she got the money?"

"Anywhere she could."

Rhonda inquired, "Do you think she was capable of killing her husband?" She avoided Sutor's gaze because she had lectured him about putting Miriam on trial instead of her killer.

"She was capable of anything."

"What was her relationship with her daughters? Do you know?" Rhonda asked, unable to give up on her family legacy theory.

"The older daughter is Miriam's clone: mean, arrogant, greedy. She doesn't need the money—her alcoholic husband is vice president of a prominent chemical company. The younger one is better looking but stupid. If either of them did it, I'd be surprised."

Kaplan looked at his watch, "I have a very important client to see or I'd take you both to lunch. The Voyager Club. It's private. Mostly lawyers and politicians meeting to cut deals that rob the taxpayers." He looked directly at Rhonda and winked. "They hate women and blacks there."

He stood up to signal their meeting was over. "I have an idea," Kaplan suggested to Rhonda. "Saturday night, want to try your luck at the blackjack tables with me?"

Rhonda wasn't sure what Kaplan meant? She stammered, "What..."

Sutor didn't like where the conversation was going. He rose and extended his hand to Kaplan, "Thanks for your help."

Rhonda stood up also.

Kaplan shook Sutor's hand and turned again to Rhonda, "Atlantic City. We'll take in a show, shoot some craps, my treat all the way."

"I don't think so," Rhonda replied, amazed at the offer. "Thanks anyway." She felt female and pretty for the first time in years, and these senses scared her to death. Of all people, this hotshot lawyer Kaplan; this white, Jewish guy. What's wrong with this picture?

"I'm not married if that's what you're worried about," Kaplan assured Rhonda. "Divorced, two kids, but single as they come. You must be too, because you're not wearing a wedding ring. Women always wear wedding rings—victory signs."

"Married or not," Rhonda replied, "I can't go out with you."

"Of course you can," he insisted as he grabbed her left hand and kissed the back of it.

Kaplan turned to Sutor, who was not amused. "You're her boss. Is she mixing business and pleasure to go out with me? I'm not a suspect, am I? So why can't this pretty lady go out with me?"

"I'm not involved in this," Sutor muttered, annoyed and amused. "Rhonda's a big girl. I don't interfere in her private life."

Kaplan turned back to Rhonda, "Saturday at six. We'll be down the shore by 8:00, take in a show, and have a bite to eat. OK?"

"I can't Saturday."

"When?" Kaplan pressed.

"No," Rhonda declared, emphatically. She was feeling overwhelmed and wanted to flee. Her college lover had been as persistent as Kaplan, and he had nearly ruined her life. She imagined what Kaplan's reaction would be if he found out about her fatherless daughter, Carly. "I'm not available."

"It's because I'm Jewish," Kaplan joked, "and white. That's it, isn't it? You can say it; I won't be offended."

"No, it isn't," Rhonda responded, defensively.

"Why then? I'm relatively attractive; I'm a gentleman, especially with lady cops who have guns; I've got a few dollars to spare. So what's the problem?"

"I'm just not available," Rhonda insisted. "Right now, anyway." She was shocked at herself for adding this. It left an opening she hadn't intended to create.

"OK," Kaplan acquiesced, "but when you get available, give me a call." He took out a business card and wrote on it. "I put my home number on the back. When you dump that guy you're going with, call me. Or you can fax me; here's that number; or better yet, e-mail me; ignore the office e-mail and contact me directly. I'll put my personal e-mail address down too; I'm AK Law. Easy to remember. Here's my personal cell phone number." Kaplan added the information to his card. "Call me any time," he added, handing the card to Rhonda. He added, "You can text message me, too."

"Thanks," Rhonda said, taking the card and putting it in her jacket pocket.

Kaplan walked Sutor and Rhonda down the hallway. He pushed the elevator button; the doors opened immediately. "You're not going to solve this one," he commented to Sutor. "Too many people hated that lady."

"That alone makes it easier," Sutor replied, following Rhonda into the elevator. "It wasn't a random killing."

Kaplan called to Rhonda just as the doors closed, "You stay in touch, Sweet Thing."

They sat in the police car and talked. Sutor recounted, "Kaplan said, 'I never killed nobody to pay my debts.' Who does he think did it? What debts?"

"He was speculating," Rhonda suggested. "He didn't mean anything by it."

"He was implying," Sutor argued. "He said Miriam was a big casino customer, but he also implied that the person who killed her was too."

"He didn't imply anything. He was talking about himself."

"You didn't hear it correctly. He said someone killed Miriam in order to pay off his debts."

"You're crazy. He didn't say that at all."

"He knows more than he's telling us. He unconsciously slipped when he said the killer had casino debts."

"You mean all we have to do is find out who in the Herzelman family has casino debts and we've got the murderer? Then it's simple. Miriam had the debts, so I guess that means she shot herself from across a parking lot."

"This is serious, Rhonda," Sutor insisted. "What Kaplan said is important. You're not taking it seriously."

"You're not taking me seriously," Rhonda complained. "You're so anti-psychology that you can't accept any information not obtained in a traditional way. I think its one of the daughters. If you understand the motivation behind a crime you're better able to solve it."

"Motivation, my behind. If there's one thing I've tried to drill into your head, it's forget motivation and go after the evidence."

"What's wrong with looking at both. Aren't you interested in understanding a crime as well as solving it?"

"Nope."

"Why not?"

"I'm not interesting in dissecting things."

"Where's your intellectual curiosity?"

"Beaten out of me the day my father caught me looking at his *Playboy* magazines when I was 12."

Rhonda knew it had come long before that. "Open you eyes, Sergeant. There's a whole world waiting for you out there."

"That's what I'm afraid of," Sutor responded, seriously.

Rhonda started the engine of the car. "Where to?" she asked.

"Atlantic City," he said. "Where else?" He patted her arm and added sarcastically, "We'll take in a show, shoot some craps; my treat all the way."

She felt like smacking him but, instead, she headed for the Benjamin Franklin Bridge, into New Jersey.

CHAPTER TEN

$\mathcal{S}$utor sat at the dining room table and laid out every piece of evidence compiled about the Lavin case. The table was a heavy, dark mahogany piece, covered with a lace cloth, a relic from his maternal grandparents' house. A matching breakfront held his mother's china and glassware, none of it noteworthy to him until recently.

What made his brother Henry know enough to get out, move west, marry, and have kids, make a life for himself? Sutor had not been his father's favorite, so how had he gotten stuck with the old man? It had been the brother who got to play high school football while Sutor worked sorting azaleas and rhododendrons so his father could attend his namesake's games. Henry Jr. got a car when he turned 16, a beat up contraption but, nevertheless, a drivable vehicle. It was the brother who drank too much, wrecked the wreck, was arrested, and got bailed out and defended by his proud father for "doing things that normal boys his age do."

"I'm the one who unpacks the lawnmowers and stacks the soil and goes out to get him lunch," Sutor had complained to his mother over and over during his childhood. His mother had advised him, "You won't win his love no matter how much mulching you do." Sutor hadn't understood what his mother was telling him, and, for this reason, he was still sleeping in a bedroom with pictures of baseball players on the faded wallpaper.

It was almost 10:00 PM on Friday, his least favorite night of the week. He was three weeks into the Lavin case, and one day less than a week since he'd last seen or spoken to Melanie Marconi. There were six legal-sized expansion folders on the table, each divided into six pockets. Within the pockets were manila folders containing the facts that had been compiled about the murder. The manila folders held specific details about the Lavin case; they were labeled alphabetically, from *Autopsy* to *Vehicles*. Under *Autopsy* there were folders for *Medical Personnel, Wounds*, and *Findings*. The divider on Melanie Marconi held folders on her background, Sutor's interviews with her, and her friendships, this last an attempt to find a place for Harold Rosenberg. Like Rhonda, he jotted notes on legal-sized pads of paper in a clear, concise print.

Sutor first reviewed the murder itself, from the moment Fromma Friedman found the body through the grim details of the autopsy report. He considered every theory, from Colin's insistence that the murder was a carjacking gone awry to Rhonda's view that Miriam's daughters were the murderers. His fear that the killing rested with Melanie Marconi stayed in his head rather than on a note page.

Sutor went over Rhonda's Atlantic City notes. Miriam had racked up significant debts at Bally's over the years, and had paid them all. She was a good customer; she had been consistently complimented to dinner, and once in awhile to an overnight suite.

Sutor reread Wilson Greene's account of the handbag that had sailed through the air and into his arms on the wings of God.

Sutor got up, went into the kitchen, and made himself a pot of tea. It occurred to him to switch to coffee so that he might have something in common with Melanie Marconi. Talk about grabbing for straws. Could a relationship be based on this? Stranger things than a Sumatra and French roast mix attracted people to each other, he was sure. Sutor hated to think of Melanie as a murderer, but his review of the case brought no one else to mind. She was the only one with a motive to kill the old woman, and she had certainly hated her stepmother enough to put a bullet in her head.

Sutor began again, going over and over his files, sure there was something here he had missed. He studied the notes about Fromma Freedman, this time reading the words out loud, hoping that he might hear something he hadn't picked up visually. "Fromma Freedman came upon the body at 9:30. She knew the victim. The victim bought a nightgown from her. The victim was her last sale. This means Miriam Lavin left the store close to 9:30, closing time." Sutor repeated his words. What was wrong here? He went through the notes again. Then he picked up the phone and called Rhonda. She was home, sound asleep, and not happy to hear from him. It was almost midnight.

"Mrs. Freedman lied," Sutor shouted into Rhonda's ear. "Miriam Lavin couldn't have been her last customer of the night. Miriam bought perfume just before 9:00. She bought the nightgown before she bought the perfume.

Fromma Freedman waited on Miriam Lavin before 9:00. If this was her last customer, then she left the store early, which means she might have seen something she didn't tell us about. If she had left work when she said she did, there would have been a lot of other people in the parking lot. Why wasn't anyone else heading for a car? The store was closing; people had to leave."

Rhonda responded groggily. She had been putting in 16-hour days on the Lavin case while trying to get her schoolwork done. Tonight she had specifically gone to bed at 9:00 to make up for her lost sleep. She snuggled into her flannel sheets and mumbled an answer.

Sutor continued, "If the murder was committed at 9:30, just as the store closed, someone in addition to Freedman would have seen something."

Rhonda slid further down under her covers. She muttered sleepily, "I shop at Saks once in awhile. At 9:30 there's an exodus from the hair salon in the store."

"Why was Fromma Freedman the only one in the lot at 9:30?" Sutor asked. He drew the face of a clock on his note sheet.

"Maybe it was a slow night," Rhonda suggested.

"It wasn't 9:30," Sutor insisted. He was already into the file labeled Saks, pulling out copies of charge card receipts. "At 8:20 Miriam bought dishes on the third floor; at 8:56 she charged perfume on the first floor." He frantically shuffled the receipts but couldn't find what he was looking for. "The woman in the china department said that Miriam came back to pick up her dishes after they were gift wrapped. This would have left her a little under a half hour to linger in the store before heading for the parking lot."

Rhonda interrupted, "I interviewed the people who waited on Miriam in the china and perfume departments. Both said she was in a hurry. I think she picked up the dishes and left the store. Probably about 9:00."

"Here it is!" Sutor exclaimed. "According to the Saks computer records, she bought the nightgown at 8:32. Fromma Freedman waited on Miriam an hour before she was killed."

Rhonda was drifting away. "What difference does it make?" she murmured. "The woman bought dishes, some perfume, and a nightgown. It has nothing to do with her murder."

"It makes a lot of difference. If Miriam bought the nightgown at 8:32, how could she have been Fromma Freedman's last sale of the night? What was Mrs. Freedman doing for the next hour before she discovered the body?"

"Maybe she was in the lady's room. I don't know. Who cares?" Rhonda was testy and too fatigued to care. "Maybe Fromma killed Miriam. Maybe Miriam said something to annoy her. Everyone else hated her, why not the lingerie saleslady?"

"Very funny. Get dressed, Rhonda. Fromma Freedman isn't telling us something. We're going to interview her again."

"What?"

"Right now! We're going to Mrs. Freedman's house. The woman is lying."

"Do you know what time it is?," Rhonda protested.

"We'll surprise her," Sutor urged. "We'll knock her off balance by showing up in the middle of the night."

"Can't we knock her off balance tomorrow?"

"Tonight," insisted Sutor. "I'll come by and pick you up."

Rhonda became immediately alert. "Don't you dare! I'm not going out tonight! It waited this long, it can wait until morning!" She had no intention of letting Sutor come to her house, now or ever, especially with Carly asleep in the next room. Her illegitimate daughter was the last thing in the world Rhonda wanted the man in charge of her career to know about.

"It's not that late. I'll come get you."

"No!" She sat up in her bed, her panic covering the sudden chill.

"Are you sure?" Sutor missed the tension in her voice.

"I'm sure. I'm definitely sure."

Sutor acquiesced. "We'll go tomorrow then," he said.

"No, I'll go tomorrow. I'll talk to her alone—woman to woman."

"OK. Sorry I woke you. Go back to sleep."

Rhonda hung up wondering if Sutor was losing his grip on the case. She lay awake another hour contemplating her secret life with her secret child and her secret shame.

Sutor hung up convinced that he was about to crack the case. He stayed up until almost dawn reviewing the Lavin murder files and wishing he hadn't missed out on a good portion of his own life.

––––––––––––––––––––

Rhonda knocked on the front door of Fromma Freedman's French style, stucco mansion in Villanova, at the western end of the township, shortly before 8:00 AM, expecting to find the lingerie saleslady up and dressed before she left for Saks. The detective had pulled her unmarked police car into a circular driveway large enough to serve as a landing site for a small plane.

Mrs. Freedman called through the intercom, "Who is it?"

"Rhonda Robinson, of the Lower Merion Police Department."

Mrs. Freedman was dismissive. "I can't talk to you now, " she declared. "I'm late for work."

"I'm afraid you don't have a choice, Mrs. Freedman," Rhonda replied loudly. "I advise you to open the door and talk to me."

There was no response for five minutes, then Fromma Freedman appeared in the doorway of the house. She addressed Rhonda through the storm door, unconcerned that the temperature had dropped substantially during the night and the woman before her was speaking through a cloud of cold air. Mrs. Freedman was dressed in a way that ensured her customers that she worked for recreation rather than need. The diamond pin on her red wool suit jacket cost more than Rhonda made in a year, and both Mrs. Freedman and Rhonda knew it. Mrs. Freedman thought such things gave her privileges other people didn't have. "You'll have to excuse me; I can't talk to you right now; I have to get to work."

"Saks doesn't open until 10," Rhonda reminded her. Part of the reason Rhonda had gone into law enforcement was to counter the powerlessness she had felt all her life, but a piece of her still knew that the Mrs. Freedman's of the world would always look down on her, if even from their jail cells, as occasionally was the case. Rhonda understood how much the lives of people on the Main Line were form rather than substance, and she appealed to this vanity in her approach. She took a cue from Colin and threatened to plaster the Freedman family name on the front page of the *Main Line Times*, "right above the horse show people." She wasn't wearing gloves and she could feel her hands molding to the handle of her briefcase.

Mrs. Freedman turned her back to Rhonda and called out loudly, "Sam, come here! I need you!" When there was no answer Mrs. Freedman yelled out again. "Sam! Now!"

Rhonda heard a slight thumping noise. An elderly man, clutching a walker, appeared behind Mrs. Freedman. "This is my husband," Mrs. Freedman told Rhonda. "He's an attorney." It was the ultimate threat from a Main Line madam.

Sam Freedman was a couple of inches shorter than his wife and a lot of years older. "What's the problem?" he asked.

"This officer wants to question me about something I don't know anything about—the Miriam Lavin killing," Mrs. Freedman told her husband. "I have better things to do with my time."

"Answer her questions," Sam Freedman directed, his voice low and his tone abrupt. He used the walker to edge his wife aside. "Come in, Miss," he ordered Rhonda. "It's cold out there." He let go of the walker with one hand and opened the storm door. He turned to his wife and instructed, "Tell her everything you know." He rotated his walker around and started to walk away. "Don't leave anything out," he ordered as he turned his back to his wife, "unless you killed Miriam Lavin."

"And what if I did?" Mrs. Freedman remarked sarcastically. She had been married for almost 40 years, and she was still trying to get her husband's attention. Sam Freedman figured he'd done his husbandly duty by letting his wife buy a six-bedroom house after all the kids were out and they didn't need the space anymore, so what the hell else could she possibly want from him.

Without answering, Mr. Freedman disappeared, the sound of his walker fading as he moved toward the back of the house. "Offer her a seat and a cup of coffee," Mr. Freedman called out. "Be a *mensch*."

Rhonda got a sense of how real power worked from that tiny exchange. Sam Freedman may have been old and ailing, but, clearly, he was in charge of his household. And he had more sense than his family gave him credit for. He knew his wife; he wasn't fooled into thinking she was with him for anything other than a luxury roof over her head, an unlimited line of credit on her American Express, and the social position his career had offered her. That had been OK with him during all the years he had kept a series of mistresses, but, in his old age, it was a bitter existence. Nevertheless, he was a lawyer; he understood how to make a deal, and this was the best one he could get. Rhonda, ever the psychologist, knew exactly why Mrs. Freedman went to Saks five days a week: to be with people like herself.

Reluctantly, Mrs. Freedman ushered Rhonda into the kitchen. It was a gray and black extravaganza—sleek, state-of-the-art, and the last place on earth anyone would go to enjoy a meal. Not so much as a side chair reflected the French style of the house; and it occurred to Rhonda, who had a good eye for design, that if there were laws in the township concerning architectural integrity, Mrs. Freedman would be in prison for life, which in most respects she already was.

Mrs. Freedman, noticeably annoyed, pointed to the kitchen table, a marble slab surrounded by black lacquered chairs. Rhonda sat down and pulled a notepad from her briefcase. Mrs. Freedman did not offer Rhonda a cup of coffee, but busied herself changing items from one handbag to another that better matched her outfit.

"Lovely house," Rhonda commented, attempting to soften Mrs. Freedman's edge. "Reminds me of Monet's home at Giverny, the outside, that is." She couldn't resist adding, "I visited Giverny two years ago and still think about the gardens. You might enjoy a visit there if you like French design."

"I like whatever my decorator brings to my house," Mrs. Freedman responded, believing she was showing her superiority to Rhonda.

"I'm surprised," Rhonda lied. "You seem to me to be a woman of creativity. I should think you know as much as a decorator." She imagined God was going to strike her dead that very moment for her corruption.

"I probably do," said Mrs. Freedman, succumbing to Rhonda's flattery. "Actually, I picked out most of the things in the house myself."

Rhonda had had enough of silly banter. She hated to waste time on nothingness, which is what she considered any kind of small talk. Rhonda knew that chitchat often paid off handsomely in the law enforcement business, but she avoided it whenever possible. She ended the small talk with, "Mrs. Freedman, I have some questions to ask you about the Miriam Lavin murder case."

"I answered to everything I know. There's no more. I don't know why you're hounding me."

"You seem to be having difficulty talking about what you saw, Mrs. Freedman. Why is that?"

"I didn't see anything, so why should I be having trouble?" She remained standing near the six-burner stove, which looked untouched by human hands.

"I think you did see something."

"You can think what you want, but you're wrong."

"You lied about leaving Saks at closing time. You left long before that. You admitted that Miriam Lavin was your last sale of the night. Computer records show that she bought a nightgown from you before nine o'clock."

"So maybe it was before nine o'clock. What difference does that make?"

"That leaves you with a half an hour to kill. If you really left the store at 9:30 the parking lot would have had more people in it. You left earlier than that, didn't you? You didn't find that body at 9:30; you found it closer to 9 o'clock."

"So what? So what if I left work a little earlier than usual? I don't need the money. I don't have to work, you know."

"Why did you lie about the time you found the body? What did you see?"

"I didn't see anything," insisted Mrs. Freedman, indignant that this lowly policewoman should be sitting at her kitchen table questioning her.

Rhonda turned psychologist. "It seems to me that you are worried about getting involved in a murder case. What's bothering you so much about it?"

Mrs. Freedman became angry, "Do I need such publicity? The papers will talk about my family, my husband, and me. You saw my husband. He was once the head of a big law firm; an important person in Philadelphia—a friend of the mayor, a box at the stadium . He had a stroke two years ago that aged him 20 years. Nobody knows how bad it was. We don't go out anymore. Nobody sees him."

Rhonda felt sorry for the woman, not because her husband was infirm, but because she thought his importance as a person was diminished because of it. "He seems like a nice man. I should think anyone would be pleased to spend time with him."

"It's embarrassing. Nobody wants to be around people who have lost their purpose in life."

"Why don't you let his friends and colleagues decide that for themselves?"

"I know them," Mrs. Freedman maintained. "They don't like sad stories."

Rhonda, who knew nothing but sad stories, suggested, "Perhaps it's time for different friends."

Mrs. Freedman looked at Rhonda as though she were an alien, "Different friends?"

Rhonda changed the subject, realizing the woman was beyond hope. "I understand now why you didn't tell the whole truth, Mrs. Freedman, so let's just get everything out on the table so we can solve this awful crime and you can get on with the life you want. We checked the Saks records. Miriam Lavin left the store about 9:00. Your last sale was just before that time. You left early too, didn't you?"

Mrs. Freedman nodded yes.

"What did you see?"

"I told you, I didn't see anything."

Rhonda was forceful, "Mrs. Freedman, what did you see? I'm not leaving here until you tell me the truth."

"A car," Mrs. Freedman admitted.

"What kind of car?"

Mrs. Freedman shrugged, "What do I know from cars? A car; I saw a car."

"What was the car doing?"

"It was sitting there. And then it drove off."

"Sitting where?"

"Near my parking space—near the handicapped section of the lot. You know, I am within my full rights to park in handicap—my husband and his stroke. It gives me the right even though I don't have a special license plate."

"What color was the car?"

"I don't know. The parking lot doesn't have many lights."

"Concentrate for a minute. Can you remember anything about the car? Try to remember the color."

Mrs. Freedman looked up at her kitchen ceiling. She focused her thoughts for a minute and said, "An unusual color. Maybe purplish"

"Purplish? You mean wine colored?"

Mrs. Freedman repeated. "Sort of purplish." She shrugged, "I'm not sure."

Rhonda helped her out. "Like a burgundy maybe?"

"Could be. Yeh, I guess so. Yeh, that's it."

"Any idea about the year?"

"New."

"How do you know that?"

"It looked like the car my husband was going to buy for my son, against my advice, I might add. He never thinks enough is enough when it comes to the kids."

"Do you know what kind of car it was?" Rhonda asked again.

"No."

"But it looked familiar?"

"It looked like my son's car-to-be, which for all I know he already owns."

"Would you please ask your husband what kind of car he and your son were looking at?"

"I don't want to bother him," Mrs. Freedman responded, which, of course, wasn't true since she had already dragged him out for her own purposes. "He's not well."

"Is your son around?"

"Thank God, no," Mrs. Freedman declared.

"Call your husband in here, Mrs. Freedman," Rhonda directed.

Mrs. Freedman called out to Sam, again twice. Sam thumped his way to the kitchen. He ignored his wife, looked at Rhonda and inquired, "What's the problem here?"

"The year, make, and model of the car you were planning to buy your son."

"Which son? I bought all three of them cars."

"Which son, Mrs. Freedman?" Rhonda asked when the women offered no assistance.

"The last one," Mrs. Freedman answered.

"Does he have a name?" Rhonda probed.

"Stephen," Mrs. Freedman acknowledged, grimacing.

"He's looking at a Corvette," Sam Freedman stated. "It's loaded—GPS system, satellite radio, the works." He seemed to be taunting his wife, particularly by taking a seat at the kitchen table.

Rhonda wasn't sure if he was joking or not. One never knew with these people. "A Corvette?" She was paying off her Saturn over five years while she busted her ass at work and in school, and this guy was buying his kid an expensive sports car just for being alive.

"I said that to annoy my wife," Sam Freedman admitted. "Some kind of sports car. I don't know for sure. We looked at 50 cars; one was a Corvette. My son doesn't know what he wants." Sam Freedman looked at his wife and remarked coldly, "Gets that from his mother."

"Thank you," Rhonda said. She addressed Mrs. Freedman again: "Did you get a look at the driver of the car the night of the Lavin murder?"

"A woman was driving. I didn't see her clearly. I only saw her for a second, driving away from where my car was parked. I didn't think much of it then, and I don't think much of it now."

"Did you hear anything? A shot, maybe?"

"No. I had just come into the parking lot and was walking toward my car."

"Did you notice a license plate number?"

"Of course not. I would have told you if I had, wouldn't I?"

"How many people were in the car? Anyone besides the woman?"

"Just the woman."

"Think carefully, Mrs. Freedman. Did you notice anything distinctive about the woman? Her face? Her clothes? Did you recognize her?"

"I didn't notice anything."

"She drove past you, didn't she? You must have seen something."

Mrs. Freedman insisted, "What else can I tell you?"

Rhonda asked a question she hated: "Was she white or black?"

"White. Definitely white."

"Are you sure?"

"Sure I'm sure."

"What makes you so positive?"

Mrs. Freedman picked her handbag up from the kitchen counter and got out her car keys. She ended the interview with, "How many black women do you know who have red hair?"

Sutor praised Rhonda in a halfhearted way. A burgundy car. A woman. Red hair. Good work. He sent Rhonda to Saks to show Mrs. Freedman a photo of Melanie, an old shot Colin had obtained from a Temple University yearbook. He instructed her to check around the store while she was there: show the photo to the security guards, salespeople, janitors, even customers. See if anyone else recognized Melanie Marconi. Then he sat back and waited in his office for three hours, worried every second of the delay.

Rhonda returned to say that Mrs. Freedman couldn't swear to it, but the woman in the photo sure seemed to be the woman she saw in the parking lot. No one else at the store recognized Melanie's face. "Mrs. Freedman isn't the most reliable of witnesses," Rhonda commented.

"She's all we have," Sutor asserted.

"What now?" Rhonda wondered.

Sutor stood up abruptly and reached for the suit jacket perched on the back of his desk chair. "I have somewhere to go."

"Where?" Rhonda asked.

"I'll tell you later. It may turn out to be nothing." He put the jacket on and straightened his tie.

"Do you need me along?"

"No."

In the years she had worked with him, Sutor had never left the office without telling her where he was going. She sensed his destination was important, and probably outside the boundaries of police propriety. "I can help."

"Not this time," Sutor insisted.

William Sutor knew the way to his destination in center city Philadelphia because on at least four occasions over the past month he had made the same journey, had parked down the street from Harold Rosenberg's townhouse, and had waited for an opportunity to see what that man looked like. Sutor imagined he would be an LL Bean kind of guy, dressed in khaki pants and a chambray shirt, and driving one of those Polo green Jags.

Sutor surmised that either Rosenberg was a recluse or he left the house disguised in a long blond wig, because no matter what time of day Sutor spied on the Rosenberg residence, no one who looked like the kind of guy Melanie would take for a lover came or went from the place. What mystified Sutor most during the course of his surveillance was the number of men and women, in addition to Melanie Marconi, who visited the Rosenberg home. As a child Sutor had lived in isolation from his peers because of his father's political views, and he had entered adulthood having never learned the art of friendship. It was difficult for him to understand how or why Harold Rosenberg had so many pals. "I'd better go talk to Howard Hughes," Sutor said out loud as he pulled into the brick-paved courtyard of Rosenberg's townhouse.

The house looked deserted. Through sheer white drapes Sutor could see an open expanse of living and dining room combined. He rang the bell. One of those crazy houses without walls, he observed. No privacy. The guy probably had $200 cooking pots, Sutor surmised, inherited wealth, no doubt. His grandmother probably left him the house, with the walls where they belonged. He's a stockbroker, maybe a lawyer. They're the only guys that make the kind of money that allows them to turn a whole house into one room. Sutor rang the bell a second time. He peeked through the drapes again and saw a elderly, gray-haired woman walking toward the door. "Can I help you?" the woman asked, through a small opening held together by the door chain.

"I'd like to see Mr. Rosenberg," Sutor replied, showing his police identification. "I'm William Sutor. Lower Merion Police."

"He's not up to seeing anyone," the woman said.

"I'm here investigating a murder. I have to talk to Mr. Rosenberg."

"I don't think it's a good idea," the woman demurred. She was pale, thin, and haggard looking, and the black sweat suit she wore was a size too large.

"I must insist, Madam. Please don't make me leave and come back with a warrant. It's a waste of my time, and Mr. Rosenberg's as well."

"Mr. Rosenberg has no time to waste," the woman commented. She closed the door, unlatched the chain, and opened the door again. "Come with me."

"May I ask who you are?" Sutor followed behind the frail woman who walked with a slight shuffle.

"I'm Mr. Rosenberg's mother."

They walked though a keeping room kitchen—filled, as Sutor predicted, with $200 pots—and up two flights of stairs carpeted with Orientals, through a sitting room decorated in hunter green leather and floor-to-ceiling beige silk drapes, and into a dimly-lit bedroom. "Honey, this police officer wants to talk to you."

Harold Rosenberg was lying in a king-size cherry wood poster bed; he was semi-awake. A handmade quilt, like the one Sutor had seen in Melanie Marconi's house, covered his body, which Sutor estimated to weigh no more than 100 pounds. A tube leading to a bag of liquid balanced on a pole protruded from a port in Rosenberg's chest. One leg stuck out from the blanket; it made Sutor think of an Easter chicken he had raised as a child, before his father gave it to a neighbor to eat. Rosenberg's face was hollow and grayish, his hair was disheveled, and he needed a shave. "AIDS," he announced to Sutor, "end stage." He motioned for his visitor to sit down on a chair placed a few feet from the bed.

Sutor struggled to keep himself from gasping. As far as he knew, he had never seen an AIDS patient up close, or even far away, for that matter. He thought nobody died of AIDS anymore, unless they lived in Tanzania. He had no idea that 17,000 people living in the United States had died of the disease the previous year.

Sutor took a seat a good ten feet from the bed, and introduced himself from across the room, "I'm a sergeant with the Lower Merion police department, investigating the murder of Miriam Lavin." He handed his card to Mrs. Rosenberg, and she passed it on to her son, who was too weak to hold on to it.

"He's tired," Harold Rosenberg's mother explained. "Please ask him your questions as quickly as possible."

"I'm very sorry to bother you," Sutor said, trying not to touch anything in the room, including the arms of his chair. "I have some questions to ask you about Melanie Marconi."

"What about her?" Rosenberg asked, trying without success to lift his head.

"What's your relationship to her?" Sutor wanted to get this one out of the way first.

"She's my best friend."

Sutor estimated Rosenberg's age as at least ten years younger than Melanie's. "How long have you known her?"

"Many years. Her husband was a friend of mine too." Rosenberg seemed to smile. "I'll be seeing Richard soon."

"Did you know Miriam Lavin?"

"The bitch? Unfortunately, yes."

"Do you have any idea who might have killed her?"

"Sure." Rosenberg replied. He began to play with a tube near his waist, and Sutor got a quick peek at a bag attached to the end of the tube. "A colostomy," Rosenberg informed him. "I have cryptosporidiosis, a parasite is eating away at my gastrointestinal tract." He pointed to the bag of liquid, "That's my TPN—total parenteral nutrition. Everything you can imagine is in that bag. A hearty meal once a day."

Sutor's stomach felt queasy. "Who do you think killed Miriam Lavin?" he inquired, desperate to change the subject, get the information he needed, and get the hell out of there.

"Anyone who knew her."

"Anyone specific?"

"She was a *chozzer*," Rosenberg commented.

"What's that?"

"You don't know what a *chozzer* is? Poor thing. You're not Jewish, are you, Honey? A *chozzer* is a pig. Miriam married Morrie and stole all of Melanie's mother's stuff: her jewelry, her clothes, her furniture, everything. Who the hell would want the crap from someone's previous wife except a pig?" He paused for a minute. "Thank God that won't happen around here when I'm gone."

"I hope not," Sutor concurred, feebly.

"I know not," Rosenberg asserted. "My friends aren't *chozzers*."

"Can you account for Melanie Marconi's whereabouts four weeks ago, on a Friday night?"

"She was here. She's always here on Friday nights. It's her night to stay with me. There's a schedule: my friend Ed has Monday; Judy has Tuesday; Mom has Wednesday; my Aunt Dot has Thursday; Melanie has Friday. On the weekends, people work it out. My friends don't want me to be alone when I croak."

"Do you live alone?" Sutor was looking for collaboration.

"My partner died two years ago."

"I'm sorry," Sutor responded, then added, "Is it possible Dr. Marconi left the house while you were sleeping?"

"Sure," Rosenberg admitted.

"Would you have heard her leave?"

"Probably not. My little arsenal knocks me out," he remarked, pointing to a row of bottles. Sutor couldn't make out the labels from his place across the room, and that was fine with him.

"So you don't know if she was here all night that Friday."

"She didn't do it," Rosenberg declared. "She wouldn't jeopardize her son that way. Too risky, even if she wanted to do it. It was done by someone who had nothing to lose."

"What do you mean?" Sutor asked, wondering if Rosenberg was trying to tell him something.

"It wasn't Melanie. I know that for a fact." Rosenberg pointed to a desk near the window, "Hand me that syringe and needle, would you? I need a shot of Ativan. Dying is very anxiety provoking."

Sutor hesitated until Rosenberg explained, "They're wrapped up; completely sterile. You don't get AIDS by passing unused needles, just used ones that have been infected."

Sutor reluctantly stood up, walked over to the desk, and picked up a syringe and needle. He handed the dying man the items he wanted. Recognizing that Rosenberg was incapable of driving, Sutor asked, "Do you keep a car on these premises?"

"Jag. Green." Rosenberg's voice was weakening.

"I assume you were home the night of the killing."

"Assume away."

Sutor felt an overwhelming need to flee the Rosenberg house, walls or no walls. He stood, "I won't keep you any longer. I appreciate your seeing me."

"The first and last time," Rosenberg noted, stretching out his arm for a handshake.

Sutor forced himself to come close to the bed, and extended his hand. "I wish you well," he said, reminding himself to wash his hands at the very first opportunity.

"Too late for that, Sweetie." Rosenberg fumbled with the syringe, while Sutor averted his eyes.

"Take care," Sutor mumbled, feeling stupid for the remark.

"I'll walk you down," Harold Rosenberg's mother offered.

Rosenberg's mother and Sutor walked though the house together, the mother silent. "How long does he have?" Sutor inquired.

"A month or two; tonight if he's lucky."

"Does Dr. Marconi come every Friday night?" Sutor asked. "Could she have missed one night, a month ago, on a Friday?"

Rosenberg's mother glared at Sutor. "Melanie never misses her night; I never miss mine; my sister never misses hers; and everybody does what he or she has to do. It's clear you don't know much about the people who have AIDS or the people who care for the people who have AIDS."

Sutor ignored the accusation. "Thank you for letting me talk to your son," he said uneasily as they reached the front door.

Rosenberg's mother turned her back to Sutor and walked away without answering. Sutor let himself out.

The encounter with Harold Rosenberg had so unnerved Sutor that he sat in his car for a few minutes trying to make sense of the scene inside the house and any relationship it might have to the murder of Miriam Lavin. Had Harold Rosenberg been bedridden a month earlier? How close was he to Melanie Marconi? Close enough so that he would have helped her pull off a crime such as murder? Would he have done her such a favor before he died?

Sutor shook his head to clear it. He lit a cigarette, his tenth of the day. The thoughts he was having were crazy. Rosenberg's mother was right: he knew nothing about AIDS sufferers or the people who took care of them. He also knew little about the murder of Miriam Lavin, and his failure in this regard was pushing him toward implausible theories. On one hand Sutor was overwhelmingly relieved to discover that Melanie Marconi was not meeting a lover when she drove into town, but on the other, he didn't know if her Friday night rendezvous guaranteed her innocence.

Sutor started his car and began to back out of the courtyard. A horn beeped loudly as someone swung around him and pulled to his right in the driveway. The driver of the arriving car, a blond in his 30s, smiled at Sutor and gave him a wink. Sutor was too distracted to notice the flirtation. The car was a late model Malibu, in a deep burgundy hue.

Chapter Eleven

"Coincidence," Colin declared, as he bit into a corned beef special and sent a string of coleslaw onto his bright yellow shirt. His Mickey Mouse character tie already bore the remnants of a previous lunch, probably a pizza, but one could never be sure when it came to Colin's diet.

Rhonda concurred, "It's a popular car and a nice color." She handed Colin a napkin. Her lunch was a tomato and lettuce salad, another concession to her career after she had read that overweight women are less likely to be promoted in their jobs than thin women. Colin could be a pig and a slob, and he'd still move up the old-boy's police department ladder. Old boys is what Rhonda considered most of the men she worked with, except for Sutor, who acted like a grown-up man by never once saying anything off-color or condescending to her. Until lately that is, when Sutor had begun acting a little strange.

Sutor wasn't a believer in coincidence, and he said so.

"You should read Carl Jung's essays on synchronicity," Rhonda advised. "He believed in the simultaneous occurrence of two meaningful but not causally connected events. In other words, same things occur in time and space, but they are not the result of the same causal activity."

"Jung never had to solve a murder," Sutor observed. He sipped on a black-and-white milkshake—another man not worried about his waist and career. He asked Rhonda if she had the *Philadelphia Inquirer* with her.

"So what's your theory, Dr. Einstein?" Rhonda inquired, avoiding Sutor's question, "since you don't believe in the study of the human mind." Her one luxury in life was reading an intact morning paper at some point during the day, and she hated loaning it out before that time because she generally got it back with a section or two missing.

"I rely on the physical world for answers," Sutor replied. "The physical world is what we have to take to a jury. You know, like a gun, a car, a suspect, in that order."

"How about a motive first?" Rhonda insisted. "Why would Rosenberg do it for her?"

Colin spoke up, while munching on a pickle, "Because he's dying of AIDS, and he's mad."

"Jesus Christ," Sutor exclaimed. "You've been hanging around Rhonda too long."

"I talked to the guy in the burgundy Malibu," Sutor said. "He's a friend of Rosenberg's; one of the caregivers; comes on Wednesdays and Fridays; leaves when Melanie Marconi arrives after dinner." He asked Rhonda for her newspaper again, adding, "just the real estate section."

"Did you ask him about the night Miriam was killed? Did he leave on time?" Colin questioned.

"He's not sure. On one of the Friday nights last month, he left his car in Rosenberg's garage overnight. He had a date and got picked up."

"Talk to his date. Maybe she'll remember which night it was," Colin suggested.

Sutor and Rhonda looked at each other and they burst out laughing simultaneously. "His date wasn't a she. It was an unidentified he," Rhonda advised, reluctantly handing Sutor her newspaper.

"The blond bombshell isn't talking," Sutor informed them. "His date was a married doctor from the suburbs." He reached across the table and picked from Colin's plate of French fries; Rhonda sipped on her diet Snapple.

"I don't think a woman who takes care of her dying friend could kill someone," Colin said with authority. He was a firm believer in saints and angels; and, since hearing about her relationship with Rosenberg, he was convinced Melanie Marconi was one or the other.

"I hear Ted Bundy was nice to his mother," Sutor commented. "Find out if Harold Rosenberg ever bought or registered a gun," he instructed Colin, "particularly a 9mm Beretta. Check Philadelphia and all the surrounding counties."

"Maybe you could trick Melanie Marconi," Colin suggested to Sutor. "Tell her you know she borrowed the Malibu on occasion."

"What's that proof of?" Rhonda asked. "Melanie's a smart woman. She'll admit to driving the car. 'So what?' she'll say. 'I went to the store and back. Harold needed something.'"

"We'll never pin her down," Colin was convinced.

Sutor instructed Rhonda, "Colin will do more checking on Harold and the car, and you need to go back to that lawyer and find out more about Miriam."

"I talked to Alan Kaplan an hour ago," Rhonda announced, surprising them both.

"Did he ask you out?" Colin teased.

Rhonda glared at Sutor, who immediately defended himself, "I only said that Kaplan was very taken with you. That's all." He offered her a piece of a chocolate chip cookie, which she declined. "And who can blame him?"

Rhonda reproached Sutor: "Do I put your personal life on the street?"

Colin laughed out loud, "Personal life on the street! I don't even know how old you are, Rhonda. I don't know if you even have a personal life. I work with a ghost. Here I go and tell you every detail of my miserable married-with-children life, and you never tell me anything. Come on, give us the scoop on Kaplan."

"There's no scoop on Kaplan; and, if there was, you'd be the last person I'd tell."

Colin put his hand on his heart and declared, "I'm hurt."

Sutor interrupted, "What did you talk to Kaplan about?"

"Distribution of Miriam's estate; Morrie's money."

"We know who got it: Bernice Eisenberg and Susan Ganardo."

"The demon daughters," Colin joked.

"Right," Rhonda confirmed. "The girls got the certificate of deposits and money market funds and some stocks. But there was insurance, too, and a trust fund. Beneficiary: Miriam's beloved grandson, the attorney, who is also the executor of her estate. Kaplan is the attorney hired by the grandson to oversee the estate. It's odd that Miriam had sued Kaplan and yet Eisenberg hired him."

"How much are we talking about?" Sutor asked.

"Half a million split between the daughters, $300,000 in insurance, a $100,000 in the trust fund. The grandson came out with more than either his mother or his aunt."

"So the lawyer grandson got $400,000—a good chunk of change but not a fortune. He can't retire on it. Does he need the money?" Sutor inquired. "He must make a nice income on his own."

"He does well," Rhonda concurred, "in the six figures. He's got a wife who does even better. She owns a company that develops software programs used in hospitals and medical offices all over the country. We're talking assets of twenty million in the company. They live in Chester Springs, an hour west of the city, where they have a full-size tennis court and their own lake."

"What kind of cars do they drive?" Colin wanted to know.

"A red Mercedes convertible and a gray Volvo." Rhonda laughed, "No burgundy Malibu. It's not going to be that easy."

"A city car and a country car," suggested Colin, who felt he knew everything about people by the vehicles they drive. "A rich folks' car and a politically correct car. They can't decide who they want to be in life."

"He doesn't strike me as a red Mercedes type," Sutor observed.

"Who's *not* a red Mercedes type?" Colin asked. He drove an old Ford station wagon because of the kids, and he dreamed of the day they would be grown and gone, and he could trade in his family tank for a small, sleek rocket.

"I'm not," Rhonda insisted.

"You wouldn't trade in that secretary's car you drive for something more luxurious if you had the money?"

"Don't insult my car."

"I'm not insulting your car. You know I love anything that sits on four wheels. I'm just saying that cars tell us a lot about people. Look at Bill here, with his fancy machine—conservative and dull."

Rhonda tapped Sutor on the hand with her straw, "Can you believe how this guy pegs you?"

Sutor wasn't listening. He was staring at a page of the paper and marking it with circles.

"Bill," Rhonda called to him, "what are you looking for, another car?"

Sutor looked up, "Colin, find out if the grandson ever rented a Malibu. Get on the car. Devote all your time to it. It's the key to this thing."

"The guy's rich," Colin said. "He didn't have to kill the old lady."

"His wife is rich," Rhonda reminded Colin.

"Same thing," Colin replied. "What a husband has belongs to the wife and vice versa."

"In your family, maybe, where nobody has anything."

"The car," Sutor repeated to Colin.

"I'm on it."

Sutor turned his paper around so Rhonda could see an ad he had circled. "How's this look?" It was an advertisement for a one-bedroom apartment.

"It's in an all-black neighborhood," Rhonda observed, without elaborating.

Sutor asked, "Where should I live?"

"I thought you lived with your father?" Colin interjected. "Who'll take care of him if you leave?" He couldn't imagine anyone breaking away from a family member in need.

"I'm not leaving," Sutor volunteered, "I'm just looking."

"Leaving starts with looking," Rhonda commented.

They finished their lunch small talking about the relative merits of living home with parents or moving out on one's own. When the waitress brought the check, Sutor grabbed for it.

"Not fair," Rhonda protested. "You got it last time."

"I'm in a good mood today; take advantage of it. Next time it's on you."

Colin offered to take care of the tip. He left $3 on the table, which Rhonda added to in memory of the days when she had waited on tables.

Colin's unmarked township car was parked in front of the deli. Rhonda patted its hood and advised, "Pretend it's a Mercedes."

Disgusted by having to go home to a station wagon capable of carrying a refrigerator, Colin sidestepped the issue and, instead, inquired, "Can I ask you one important question, Rhonda?"

"Sure."

"How old *are* you?"

CHAPTER TWELVE

*J*t was Melanie Marconi's idea that they meet over lunch after Sutor called her at the college and asked if he could come into town to talk to her. "I have an hour break at 1. I'll be at the Lighthouse Café, near the college. You're welcome to join me."

He wanted to say no; he wanted to keep things on a professional level, meet in her office or his, have a colleague within hearing distance to protect him from what he might say if he were free to say anything at all to this woman who he thought about whenever he was thinking about companionship or murder, depending upon the time of day. Instead, he answered, "One o'clock—that'll be fine."

He was there first, waiting at the bar having a beer and a cigarette when she came in, hurried and flushed from the two-block walk from her office, her red hair ruffled from the wind and curled behind a flowered silk scarf. He put out his cigarette and offered her a drink; she told him Kir on the rocks and let him order it. They small talked for a while, about the college, Jesse, and her dog, Gertrude, who was having hip problems. Sutor said his mother once had a dog, but he, personally, wasn't fond of animals. Melanie commented, "Remind me not to get involved with you. I think something is terribly wrong with people who don't like animals."

"Maybe I just haven't met the right dog," he joked, trying to regroup. Melanie laughed before inquiring if he was married. When he told her he wasn't, she teasingly questioned, "You haven't met the right woman either?"

A blond hostess informed Sutor that his table was ready. She put their drinks on a tray, and led them there. Sutor held Melanie's chair while she got comfortable, hoping his good manners made up for the dog faux paux.

"Thank you," Melanie acknowledged, as she took her drink from the hostess.

The decor of the restaurant was nautical: shell and net hangings, a tropical fish tank, and photos of lighthouses adorned the place. "I love this restaurant," Melanie told Sutor. "My dream was to live on water. I almost made it, twice." She shook her head in disappointment and a strand of hair came loose from the scarf. "It's not in the stars."

"What's keeping you from it?" Sutor asked. He wanted to lean over and touch the strand of hair.

"Death."

"Whose death?"

"My husband and I were planning to buy a Carver, Command Bridge, about 38 feet. When he died, I couldn't afford the boat on my income alone. Then, when my father died, I assumed there would be money for this indulgence. There wasn't." She twirled the straw in her glass and stared into the swirling liquid. "Tragedy and evil: killers of dreams." She took off the scarf and her hair tumbled around her face.

"How long has it been since your husband died?" Sutor probed, even though he already knew.

"Five years."

"It must be hard raising a teenage son alone."

"It might as well have been yesterday." She looked away from him, toward a print of a lighthouse in Maine, where she had often vacationed with Richard.

"Maybe, in time, you'll get your boat," Sutor suggested, wisely not mentioning that he hated anything related to water, except taking showers.

"My time for boats has come and gone. My next order of business is to get my son through high school and into college. He's my priority."

"What about a social life? You have to make time for yourself." He was prying but trying to be subtle about it.

"A single parent can't have a social life and raise an adolescent." Now, at least, he knew his competition was her son not another man. From his personal experience of sons and mothers, he would rather it had been another man. "Jesse would go crazy if I began dating, and rightly so. He's devoted to memories of his father. In his eyes, to accept another man would be an act of blatant disloyalty."

"What if you met someone you liked?"

"I'll worry about it when the time comes," Melanie replied, then changed the subject with a smile: "Tell me about your dreams, Sergeant Sutor."

"I don't have any," Sutor lied.

"Of course you do."

"They're secret," he confessed.

"Wishes are supposed to be secret, not dreams. Dreams must be shared if they are to come to fruition."

"I dream of catching Miriam Lavin's killer." It was the only way he knew to get back to the official reason for this meeting. It broke the spell, and he was sorry.

"How is that going?" Melanie asked. "Any suspects?"

"Many suspects, some promising leads," Sutor acknowledged.

"Sounds like you have very little."

"We have too much and too little." He paused and forced himself to continue, "That's why I'm here. I want to ask you a few more questions."

He was hoping she would say, "OK, that'll be fine," but, instead, she suggested they order lunch. She looked at her watch, "I have to be back in 40 minutes."

Sutor signaled for the waitress again. They both ordered chicken salad sandwiches; Melanie added cappuccino and Sutor asked for any kind of herbal tea.

"I visited Harold Rosenberg," Sutor confessed.

"I know," Melanie admitted, unconcerned.

"He gave you an alibi for the night of Miriam's murder."

"That was sweet of him."

"I admire you for helping to take care of him."

Melanie dismissed the praise with a wave of her hand, "I stay one night a week. It's not much to do for a dying friend. I wish I could be available more often, but I have Jesse at home."

"Friday is your night?" Sutor inquired.

"Isn't that what Harold told you?"

"Are you always there on Fridays?"

"Just about," she responded, leaving him an opening for suspicion.

"You've missed some Fridays?" he suggested, wondering if she was baiting him.

"Not that I can recall; but, of course, Harold's been ill for two years. How far back are you asking about?"

"The past four Fridays."

Melanie put a finger to her head. "Let me think. The last four Fridays I was definitely at Harold's."

"All night?"

"No doubt."

"Who relieves you?"

Melanie realized that their frivolous banter had turned into a serious interrogation. "Do I need a lawyer?" she wanted to know.

"We have a witness who saw someone driving a burgundy Malibu in the Saks parking lot the night of the murder. Do you know anyone who has a car like that?"

"I don't know one car from another," Melanie stated before asking again, "Should I call my attorney?"

"Think of the color. Do you know anyone who drives a burgundy car?"

"I don't pay attention to such things."

He didn't for a moment believe that a woman who drove a purple Camaro and a teal Honda CRV didn't know about cars and colors. "A woman was driving the car. A redheaded woman."

Melanie laughed. "A redheaded woman in an almost-red car. There can't be too many of them around. Your crime sounds near to being solved—your dream is coming true." She was making fun of him and he deserved it.

"Sorry," he acknowledged, "I sound stupid. So I'll ask you directly: Were you in the Saks parking lot the night of Miriam Lavin's murder?"

"If I was there, you'd figure I killed her, wouldn't you?"

"I'd consider it."

"You're already considering it. I'm your prime suspect."

Sutor lied, "One of many."

"Look me in the eyes and tell me you don't think I did it," Melanie challenged him. She leaned forward, her chin on her elbow, and stared straight at him.

Sutor avoided her gaze. "It could have been any number of people."

Melanie surprised him with "You're looking in the wrong place. And you're looking at the wrong motive."

"How do you know that?" He couldn't help looking into her eyes. He couldn't help wanting to believe her.

"Take my word for it."

"You know who did it, don't you?"

"I know as much as you do," Melanie assured him.

The waitress brought their food to the table. While they ate, Melanie asked Sutor questions about his life and career. He was torn between thinking she was purposely distracting him from his investigative goal and believing she was interested in him personally. He admitted to being a workaholic and he confessed to having a limited social life. Melanie reminded him that life was short and death was long and he mustn't confuse work with living. He didn't tell her that if it weren't for his work, he'd have nothing at all to do.

"After my husband died, I asked Hal Rosenberg what I should do with the rest of my life. He said, 'Live.' I'm passing that advice on to you."

Sutor desperately wanted to reach over the table and kiss Melanie, softly, on the cheek. Instead he probed, "Are you living?"

"I'm afraid not," Melanie admitted, stirring her Kir with a small straw. "I don't know where to start."

"You have a lot of good years left," Sutor noted.

"There aren't enough years left in the universe to make up for Richard's death and Miriam Lavin's life," Melanie declared bitterly.

"You could marry again," Sutor suggested. He hated to admit it to himself but he was relieved Harold Rosenberg was who he was, even with his deadly disease. "You're a very attractive woman." He wanted to kick himself for what he knew was a typical male come on.

Melanie scoffed at his compliments, "Hagsville, Honey. After 40, the ball game's over for women. We don't want to face it so we get facelifts and tummy tucks and vacation in goofy places where they make you touch your toes and eat wheat germ. After 40 the last thing a woman needs is a new marriage. That just brings her someone else's problems: offspring problems, prostate problems, conflict of interest problems. What menopausal woman needs that?"

Disappointed, Sutor persisted, "What do women need after 40?" He was surprised by the degree of her cynicism even knowing what she had been through during the last five years.

"A large bank account, a good job—preferably both. Loyal, noncompetitive friends, both male and female. A place of one's own and a dog and cat. An interest in gardening or traveling or some such thing. If really lucky, sex once in awhile with one of the friends, nothing serious, mind you."

Melanie looked at her watch. "I have to go," she said abruptly, quickly downing her cappuccino. "We'll talk again in a couple of weeks. Hopefully your dream will have come true, and the darling person who put an end to Miriam Lavin's life will reveal himself." She added mischievously, "Or herself."

Sutor realized he had asked very few questions about the Lavin murder, and he tried to sneak in a few more. "You're keeping something from me. Why?"

"Because I'm your prime suspect."

Sutor signaled for the check and, when the waitress laid it on his side of the table, he waved Melanie away when she reached for it.

"I invited you here," Melanie asserted. "It should be my treat." She put her scarf back on.

"Next time," Sutor replied, knowing he would never go for such an arrangement when a woman was in his company.

"Thank you for meeting me. I assume we'll talk again soon. But I'll be away for awhile," Melanie volunteered, "at a conference at the TradeWinds in St. Petersburg Beach. I'm leaving Thursday."

The news momentarily upset Sutor; he didn't like the idea of her not being near. They walked out of the restaurant together and parted company on the sidewalk.

"Enjoy Florida," Sutor called after her. "Go boating."

She turned and waved from the corner, "I'll try."

As Sutor got into his car, it occurred to him that Friday nights with Harold Rosenberg weren't guaranteed. If Melanie could pass up next Friday night for a conference in St. Petersburg, then perhaps she had missed an earlier one in order to confer one last time with Miriam Lavin.

CHAPTER THIRTEEN

Colin traced the phone number on the paper he had retrieved from Wilson Greene's pants pocket to the home phone of an Allison Long. "Imagine this," he announced to Rhonda, "she's a legal secretary in the law offices of Cardozo Rossen Leonard, the firm that employs Miriam's grandson, Jerome Eisenberg." Colin emphasized that Cardozo Rossen Leonard was housed in the 1701 Building, where Alan Kaplan also had his offices. "Something's finally happening."

Rhonda was not convinced the phone number would lead anywhere. She was increasingly worried that her first murder case would end up stalled, along with her career.

Colin drove into Philadelphia, to a high-rise apartment complex overlooking the Delaware River in the exclusive Society Hill section of town. Allison Long lived on the 23rd floor; her corner unit viewed the water from every angle. Even Colin was able to figure out that her secretary's salary didn't cover the cost of the place. He stood outside Allison's apartment for a few minutes rehearsing what he was going to ask her. Wishing Rhonda were with him, he knocked tentatively.

Allison Long answered the door dressed in a red leotard that revealed an expertly done pair of breast implants. She reminded Colin of his wife, a head taller than he was, dark-haired, dark eyes, pretty, and no doubt able to touch the floor with the palms of her hands without bending her knees. He desired her sexually on sight—another similarity she had with his wife—particularly after she blocked the door with her long, lean body and inquired in a sultry tone, "What do you want?" He showed his badge and asked to come in.

"Should my attorney be present?" Allison wanted to know.

"What makes you think you need one?" Colin inquired, keeping his eyes on her face.

"I work in a law firm. My boss stresses that no one should talk to the police without a lawyer present."

"Maybe I'm here to sell you tickets to the circus on behalf of the pension fund," Colin suggested. "Would you need a lawyer for that?"

"I hate the circus," Allison answered. "I hate clowns, and I've known a lot of them." She was quick and smart; a minus as far as Colin was concerned. She hesitated, then acquiesced, "Alright, come in."

She barely stepped aside, forcing Colin to rub against her slightly as he passed into the apartment. She smelled of sweat and perfume, and he inhaled deeply as a whiff of a musky scent drifted up his nostrils. She slid in front of him and led him down a hall into a vast living room, where she directed him to a black leather sectional that spanned two walls of the room.

Coming from a house decorated in Lazy Boy loungers, Colin was fascinated by the ultra-modern look of Allison's apartment. The floors were covered in a sleek, beige Berber. The only wall that wasn't a window with a view held a large, original painting of something black, white, and squiggly that had no resemblance to anything living or dead in the universe. On the teak coffee table in front of a brown, soft leather couch were dozens of little glass figures; Colin spotted a rabbit, a swan, a couple of birds, and a frog. There was a massive flat-screen television in the room and an elaborate stereo setup. Chris Isaac was singing unrequited love songs from tiny speakers set up high on the stark white walls.

Allison sat down on an exercise mat in the middle of the floor and leaned back on her elbows, keeping her legs straight out so that every line and curve of her perfectly toned body were visible. Her toenails were painted a bright red, and one toe on each foot had a gold ring on it. She wore a diamond ankle bracelet on her left leg. Colin had trouble keeping his eyes off her nipples protruding through the thin fabric of her exercise outfit.

"What can I do for you?" Allison inquired, coolly.

"Did you know a woman named Miriam Lavin?" Colin asked.

"No." Allison looked straight at Colin and fluffed her long hair.

"Did you ever hear of her?"

Allison sat up. "Nope."

"Do you know a lawyer named Jerome Eisenberg?"

"He works at my firm, in a different department. I'm in labor law, he's in medical malpractice."

"Miriam Lavin was his grandmother. She was an elderly woman found murdered a few weeks ago."

Allison shrugged, "Too bad for her." She pulled up her knees and wrapped her arms around them.

"Allison, we found your home phone number in Miriam Lavin's wallet. Do you have any idea why?"

"Not a clue."

"Are you sure?"

"Of course I'm sure?"

"You never met her and you never met her grandson?"

"I didn't say that. I never met her but I've been in her grandson's company on occasion: at a Christmas party that just passed; in a meeting once. I know him to say hello to."

"Have you ever been out with him socially?"

"He's a married man," Allison answered indignantly. "Most of them are in my firm. I'm single. Why would I hang around with someone who's married? Besides, did you ever meet a lawyer socially? Jerks. They treat their secretaries like shit, and their wives too. They're always stressed to the max and carrying on about something or other. And they're cheap. Do you know what my asshole boss gave me for Christmas? A bottle of bubble bath—cheap bubble bath at that. The women lawyers are as bad as the men, believe it or not. Are you married?"

Colin ignored the question and asked her what kind of car she drove. "A Mercedes convertible, blue with a beige interior," she volunteered, offering to take him for a ride in it.

"You must do pretty well at that law firm," Colin observed.

Allison laughed. "I work a lot of overtime."

Colin resumed his line of questioning, asking her where she had been on the Friday night of the murder. She said she hadn't a clue, it was so long ago; she didn't even remember what she'd done the night before, which Colin doubted from the expensive look of her apartment. Colin asked her a few more details, mostly about her job, the firm and the people she worked with. She insisted three times that she didn't know Jerome Eisenberg or Alan Kaplan. And she surely didn't know Miriam Lavin. When it became clear there was nothing he was going to learn from Allison, Colin got up, leaned down, and gave her his card. "Call me, before it's too late," he warned her.

She took the card. "Want to stay awhile?" Allison proposed. She was laying flat on her back on the mat, her hands raised behind her head, her legs slowly rising, stretching sideways in a V. "We could exercise together."

"Another time," Colin murmured, feeling his heart rate increase without the benefit of a treadmill.

"See you," Allison remarked, adding, "Forgive me for not getting up," as she slowly closed her legs and lowered them.

"No problem. We'll talk again soon."

"About what?" Allison responded, rolling onto her stomach. "There's not another thing I can tell you."

Colin let himself out of the apartment and stood in the hallway a minute to catch his breath. He was feeling so aroused as he hit the hallway elevator button that his face turned red when the doors opened and there were two middle-aged women on board.

Colin stopped at the business office to inquire about Allison's rent payments. She paid in cash, a dead giveaway that it was someone else's money. He speculated that the

Mercedes had been bought with cash also, not a difficult leap. He asked to see the rental records. She had been living at the ritzy high rise for a little less than a year. Her application showed her previous address to be an apartment on 21st Street, at the other end of town. Colin questioned the office manager, a bald and chubby middle-aged man, about Allison's personal life. Has she ever been seen with a man? Who brought the rent payment in? Were there any problems concerning this tenant?" The office manager said that Ms. Long came in on the first day of each month and paid the rent with 30 100-dollar bills. She was seen with any number of men, no one in particular. She was a wonderful tenant: quiet, unassuming, polite to the staff. A pretty girl, the agent confirmed. "Always a pleasure to see her."

"Jerome must have gotten tired of being around ugly women," Colin observed. He was back in his favorite place, the deli, devouring an Italian hoagie in revenge for the breakfast of granola and raisins his wife had served him in hopes of prolonging his life, if not his marriage.

"What makes you so sure she's involved with him?" Rhonda asked, a tuna sandwich in her hand. She had decided to be frivolous about her weight for a change.

"I feel it. Call it instinct. Intuition." He opened a bag of potato chips and offered some to Rhonda.

"You haven't got an once of instinct or intuition in your body," Rhonda remarked, waving away the chips.

"What makes you say that?" Colin challenged.

"You have to be unblocked to be in touch with those forces."

"Unblocked from what? What do you mean?"

"Unblocked as in unaware. Unblocked from all the

crap you have clogging your consciousness. I know you, Colin. I know that you hate being a cop. I know that your family put a foreclosure sign on your life before you had a chance to figure out how you wanted it to go. Be a cop, like dear old dad. End of story. Not, be a car mechanic, which would have served you better. Get married early, have children, like all the other men in your clan. Done deal. So you make jokes about your wife and kids, and talk about cars all day to avoid facing how miserable you are."

"How do I get unblocked?" Colin persisted, uneasy at having a conversation that was disloyal to his family.

"You go inside—deep inside—into what's called 'the dark side of the moon,' the unconscious, where truth is hidden." Rhonda knew her undergraduate degree didn't qualified her to diagnose so much as a dog running in circles biting his tail. She hoped he wasn't going to ask for professional advice.

"And then what happens? I leave my family and drive off into the wilderness in a reconditioned Mercedes?"

"Maybe, but not realistic. Your Catholic guilt would do you in. And it's irresponsible to jump ship once you bring kids into the world."

"So you're saying I'm fucked," Colin acknowledged.

"Probably."

"Are you there?" Colin probed. "Are you in touch?" She never looked very happy to him so maybe she was as blocked as he was.

Rhonda nodded. "I strive everyday of my life to get to a higher plane of existence, one that transcends the woes of the everyday world we live in. I work at trying to understand other people's points of view. I try not to be prejudiced. I work on having patience and tolerance. It's a struggle everyday to stay above the trivialities of everyday life."

"I'm stuck," Colin admitted, jabbing his fork into his dessert, "just like this cinnamon bun. So what the hell can I do anyway?"

"Enjoy where you are," Rhonda suggested, "just like you're doing with that cinnamon bun."

"What do you mean?"

"If you can't fight and you can't flee, flow. You have a wife and you have children, and they love you and rely on you. Instead of complaining about them, take them into your heart."

"You know, for a black woman, you're pretty smart." Colin declared, in a non-joking way.

Rhonda felt suddenly sad. Here was Colin—her partner, her lunch companion, a man she knew would do anything he could to help her if she ever got into trouble on the street. When she had been sick with the flu, he had called her every day and offered to bring her food. When the car she had before the Saturn had broken down, for two weeks Colin had given her his station wagon to drive so she could get to night school safely, while he took public transportation to and from work. He had invited her to his home for Christmas dinner last year and, when she refused the offer, had called her on the phone and sung "Jingle Bells" into the receiver.

Yet, truth be told, he was a racist. He thought she was smart—for a black woman. In the end, it didn't matter much to her. Rhonda, the eternal psychologist, had trained herself to distinguished between beliefs and behaviors. "I don't care whether people like blacks or not," she once announced in a black history class, to the chagrin of a black professor, who was postulating a view of black supremacy based upon skin pigmentation, "as long as they don't act on their feelings. If I can get the job I'm qualified for and buy the house I want, what the hell difference does it make whether someone likes me or not because of my race?" The professor had insisted she was a fool, and he had acted on his feelings by giving her a grade lower than she deserved. Thus, Rhonda learned the hard way how similar people are, at best and at worst, no matter what their color.

"If I'm so smart, how come I haven't figured out who killed Miriam Lavin?" Rhonda argued, changing the subject.

"You will," Colin assured her. "And when you do, I'll take half the credit."

Rhonda laughed and indulged herself by reaching for one of Colin's potato chips. "One third of the credit—we have to cut Bill in."

"You can take all the credit if we fail."

Rhonda reached for another potato chip. "No chance of that. This black woman is going to make you all look like morons."

CHAPTER FOURTEEN

*S*utor made a number of calls to a pal in the Tampa police department, ostensibly to discuss a carjacking and killing in Tampa that bore a slight similarity to the Lavin case. It was a stretch that he hoped no one in Lower Merion would notice. By a slick manipulation of his friend, Sutor wrangled an invitation to come down to Tampa for a day or two and help out with the case.

Over the years Sutor had learned something from Rhonda about the male ego, and he certainly wasn't above using this information when it came to getting close to Melanie Marconi, in a place far from home. "You'd better call John Handler, the superintendent, and check with him," Sutor suggested, adding a compliment for insurance: "You're the best there is in the homicide business. I'll pick up some pointers about this case from you while I'm there." For double insurance he mentioned he hadn't been fishing in years. Did his friend still run around in that little old Boston Whaler, and could he still drink everyone in the department under the table?

When police superintendent Handler called him in and instructed him to go to Tampa, Sutor, ever cooperative, declared, "I'll leave tomorrow." Once on the plane, he questioned his own sanity. In over 20 years on the force, he had never done anything even remotely unethical. He insisted on paying full price for his meals at area restaurants, sent money in to cover his parking tickets, and filed reports when people tried to slip him advance payments for things he might some day do for them. He hated the graft, bribery, and tax evasion scams that characterized the lives of many of the township's wealthiest citizens, and he wondered if these neighbors slept well at night or if they tossed and turned in fear that their illegal deeds would catch up to them, as they had with Miriam Lavin. He surmised that Miriam had slept well, warmed by her stolen nest egg, and he assumed Miriam's killer was sleeping well now, hopefully not in the Sunshine State.

Sutor rented a car at the Tampa airport and drove to a nearby Marriott, where he washed up, ran a razor over his face, changed his shirt and tie, and called his police pal to tell him he'd be by the next day. Following a map he had picked up at the airport Avis counter, he drove out to Route 275 and headed south across Tampa Bay toward the Gulf of Mexico, and Melanie.

He knew he was taking a chance—she might be with someone - but he thought that possibility was remote since, aside from Harold Rosenberg and her son Jesse, there was no evidence of a man in her life. A pretty woman, a gay guy with AIDS, and a 15–year-old boy: a weird trio if he'd ever seen one. Why didn't she have a real man in her life? Her husband was dead long enough for her to have moved on. On second though, how long is long enough?

His mother was dead 20 years, but it was still too brief a time for him to think of her with fond memories rather than pained sorrow. It was simple: Melanie hadn't met a man capable of helping her look forward. Maybe he was that man, he fantasized, chuckling at his own inflated view of himself. He was as bad as Rhonda said all men are. Still, there was hope.

St. Petersburg Beach is a small enclave settled mostly by immigrants from Boston, Washington, and other eastern cities whose populace had grown sick of hard winters and harder crime. Jobs are scarce and those that exist are of marginal status. Other than in the hotels, there are few restaurants that serve food more sophisticated than fried, baked, or sandwiched grouper. Past ten o'clock at night there is little activity on the main drag of motels, eateries, and souvenir shops, which is fine for the people who live or visit there. It's a town of aged people, nice people, people who want to hang at home watching situation comedy reruns on television.

Melanie Marconi spent the first week in February in St. Petersburg Beach every year because her professional group, *The Teaching of Literature in Colleges and Universities*, held its annual conference there. Sponsored by the University of Illinois, some of the best professors in the country were called upon to present ideas and techniques on how to convince a semi-literate student population that the great books are the great books, and worth taking a look at if one wants to understand how life works.

Melanie was one of the speakers this year, her topic, *Remembrance of Things Present: The English Curriculum in Context*, an esoteric title for a piece that proposes looking at book choices in a time-related framework. In *The Scarlet Letter* she had her students change adultery to AIDS; *Moby Dick* became the abortion issue with the anti-choice forces represented by Captain Ahab. It was the third time she had presented at the conference so she was well known among her colleagues. Had she never spoken a word in any year past, she would still be infamous for her affinity for lipstick and hair dye, which set her apart from most of her female colleagues, who tended to equate brainpower with blotched skin and graying locks.

In earlier years Melanie had brought Jesse with her to Florida, but since Richard's death she looked forward to the week alone to rest, read, and hang out with grownups. Melanie hated the beach, but she did love to sit at the outdoor cafe of the massively pink Don CeSar Hotel at sunset, listening to sorrowful sounds over the speaker system and watching the sun go down over the water. She came to St. Petersburg Beach primarily for the sunset.

Sutor felt anxious as he paid the toll on the causeway leading to Gulf Boulevard and St. Petersburg Beach. The Don CeSar rose ahead of him and, for a minute, he had second thoughts about his intrusion on Melanie's trip. He mentally reviewed his position: he was a homicide investigator with important questions that couldn't wait. What questions could he ask that couldn't wait? The weeks were passing with an increasing urgency to solve the murder. He'd tell her they were close to making an arrest. She'd never believe it. He'd hint that he was attracted to her. If she seemed interested in him, he'd tell her the truth: that he thought about her more than made sense to him. If she seemed indifferent, he'd tell her he wasn't a man who wanted commitments in life, but maybe they could just be together sometimes. He'd tell her anything she wanted to hear.

Sutor drove down Gulf Boulevard until he saw the TradeWinds Resort. He turned into the hotel parking area, found a spot, said out loud, "Sutor, you're nuts," parked, and got out of the car. In the lobby of the hotel he stopped to look at a white cockatiel in a cage. The bird came over to him and tried to bite his finger—an omen, he thought. Sutor toyed with the bird for a while; it sensed a friend and calmed down. Through the bars of the cage, Sutor could see across the lobby. He spotted a familiar face but couldn't remember where he had seen it before. The face stood out because it was black while every other person in the lobby, including everyone on the staff, was white. Who the hell is that guy? I've met him before, but where? The black man walked across the lobby and through French doors leading to a flower-bedecked courtyard. Sutor quickly followed. The black man scanned the listings on a number of doors facing the courtyard, found the room he wanted, and entered it. Sutor followed. He found himself stuck in a lecture: *Penis Envy in the Writings of Victorian Women.* The speaker was dressed like Emily Dickinson: a buttoned-up, high-necked white blouse, and long gray skirt. Her light brown hair was pinned up into a bun.

Sutor took a seat on the back row where he had a clear view of the black man, who chose to sit close to the front of the room where he could hear the speaker better. It clicked! The student he had met in Melanie Marconi's office the first time he and Rhonda had visited her! What was his name? What the hell was he doing at the conference? Emily Dickinson had just begun her talk about Emily Dickinson when Sutor got up and quietly exited the room.

The desk clerk gave Sutor Melanie's room number, 4026, after Sutor showed him his police badge. The clerk didn't notice that it wasn't from St. Pete. Sutor walked to a bank of house phones and dialed. It was close to three o'clock and he expected to leave her a message saying he was downstairs and wanted to talk to her. He was startled when she answered the phone.

"Bill Sutor here," he said. "How are you?"

"Fine, thanks. How are things on the Main Line? Any more granny murders?"

He wasn't thrilled about being made fun of. "The old ladies are OK, last time I noticed. Only I'm not on the Main Line; I'm downstairs in the lobby." He was quick to explain that he was on an important case in Tampa and had come over to talk to her about the Lavin case since he was so close by. "I don't have much time. Are you able to talk?" He was dying to see her and the sooner the better.

"I can meet you in an hour if you can wait. I'm finishing up some work."

She wasn't anxious to see him or she would have come right down, Sutor thought. "I have to meet someone about the case I'm working on, but I'll be back at 4." Taking the biggest gamble of his life, he asked, "Are you free for dinner?"

"Yes, I am."

"Good," Sutor declared. "I'll see you in a little while."

With an hour to fill, Sutor inquired as to the best place in town to eat. The hotel concierge suggested an Italian restaurant in nearby Redington Shores. It was the same place raved about in a guidebook of the area he picked up at a bookstore on Gulf Boulevard where he went to kill the hour. He called the restaurant and made a reservation for seven o'clock. This would give him time to spare to sit with Melanie over drinks and pretend they were a couple.

He got back to the hotel at 4. As he walked into the lobby, he could see her through the open door to the courtyard; she was sitting on a bench among the pink and white begonias, reading a book. He watched her for a minute and marveled that this middle-aged woman, dressed in a long, pink linen skirt, white button-front tee-shirt, and sandals, her hair pinned up by a spray of silk Lilies of the Valley could make him risk losing everything he had lived and worked for his whole life, namely the job he loved, his security, prestige and, worst, the way he viewed himself as a cop. For the first time in his life, he truly understood how some people are driven to murder.

She glanced up, saw him, and smiled as he came down the courtyard. "Hi."

"How are you?" He stood looking down on her. "Good book?

"Sit down," Melanie urged, moving a white knit shawl from the place next to her and shifting down the bench a little to make room for him. She showed him her book, a small paperback called *Meeting the Madwoman*. "It's about female madness and female creativity as reflected in literature and myth," she explained as she opened to a page and handed him the book. He read an underlined paragraph: *Madness encompasses a wide range of states, from the extreme of insanity to fury, anger, and moodiness. We can recognize it in confusion, frenzy, foolishness, recklessness, and impulsiveness, as well as infatuation, passion, enthusiasm, divine ecstasy, and spiritual awakening.*

"One of my detectives is a psychology major. She'd like this book," Sutor observed. "Tell me more about it."

"It suggests women are being driven mad by a patriarchal culture in which they are neither heard nor acknowledged. The madness is reflected in their everyday behavior. My own mother sat in the dark in her bedroom when I was growing up, her depression a sign of her madness. I have a lady friend who gets drunk into the night and another who goes from lover to lover. A madwoman rummages in the trash cans in front of the college; she refuses offers of money and help. Nuns are madwomen who flee the world of living men to the safer arms of make-believe dead ones. Madwomen live with a hundred cats, or they live locked away in institutions. Madwomen beat their kids and sometimes kill them. Others, like me, overindulge their kids in an attempt to keep them near and assuage their own loneliness. Miriam Lavin was a madwoman, relegated to thief and killer when she couldn't find a place for herself in the world. There are unlimited kinds of madwomen: crones, caged birds, muses, revolutionaries, visionaries."

"Which kind are you?" Sutor asked, a memory of his dead mother crossing his mind.

"I'm Lilith, Adam's first wife, the one before Eve. She chose to live her life alone rather than be treated as an inferior. Because of her independence, she has come down in Jewish mythology as a demon that tempts men into sexual encounters. I'm also like the poet Emily Dickinson: a recluse—same skin as Lilith's."

"A recluse? Don't you get lonely? Especially in a place like this?" He didn't see how this woman could ever be a recluse, with all the men out there wanting to keep her company—proof that he didn't know what she was talking about.

"More than you can imagine," Melanie admitted. "But the price not to be is more than I'm willing to pay. I'm not willing to be part of a world that refuses to hear me." She offered him a gift: "Keep the book and read it. You might learn something about women."

Sutor flipped the pages of the book. He'd be the first to admit he didn't know much about women in general, but he had no interest in filling in that gap in his education. He was interested in understanding one woman only, this woman sitting beside him, and, if it meant reading some crazy book about crones and muses, he'd gladly do it. Beside, if he read the book, he might find out the truth about his mother's madness, and he wasn't sure he wanted to examine that issue at this point in his life. Sutor put the book in his jacket pocket and explained, "I made a dinner reservation for 7. Is there a bar here? Would you like to go for a drink?"

"I'd love to," Melanie replied, "but I have a favorite place in St. Petersburg Beach. Would you like to see it?"

"Anywhere you like," he acquiesced. Sutor picked up Melanie's shawl from the arm of the bench and put it around her shoulders. "Lead the way." He would show her that he was a man who listened to women by taking her where she wanted to go.

"Do you want to drive or walk?" she said.

"Doesn't matter."

They took a long walk on Gulf Boulevard to the Don CeSar and, once there, Melanie led him through the hotel to the waterfront cafe, where they could see the sun setting over the Gulf. The cafe was nearly empty, and they sat down at a round table at the edge of the beach. A waitress approached them and Melanie ordered her usual Kir on the rocks, Sutor a VO and water, straight up.

"Scott and Zelda came here," Melanie observed.

"Who?"

"The Fitzgeralds."

Sutor nodded. Scott and Zelda could be his homely next-door neighbors in the twin for all he knew.

"The writer F. Scott Fitzgerald and his wife, the writer Zelda Fitzgerald. Zelda was a madwoman."

Sutor hid his ignorance with a joke: "If they don't write murder mysteries, I don't read them."

"I apologize for my rudeness," Melanie responded. "English professors assume everyone reads the dated tomes they assign to their captive audiences, also known as students."

"I'm not as much of a reader as I'd like to be," Sutor admitted, deciding not to pretend to be an intellectual.

"That's OK," Melanie replied. "I'm more of a reader then I'd like to be. Teachers, in general, are an inactive bunch; they live through others. History teachers pretend to be Napoleon; they imagine what they would have done at Waterloo and speculate about his relationship with Josephine. English teachers second-guess Hemingway, changing the ending of *A Farewell To Arms* in their minds. That's what all these academic conferences are about—people pretending to live instead of living. You have a real job, in the real world. You're forced to face life every day."

"The worst of life," Sutor reminded her. She seemed melancholy and negative, and he wondered what he could do to cheer her up.

Melanie stared out over the Gulf, her sorrow seeming to travel with the sunset down into the water. She didn't speak again until their drinks came. "I assume you're here to talk about Miriam Lavin's murder," Melanie remarked, lifting her glass in a toast.

Caught off guard, Sutor suggested, "Let's forget about Miriam Lavin for today." He had taken a drastic step, crossed a boundary from which he couldn't return—he had moved from a professional relationship with Melanie Marconi to a social one. Any restraint he had had when he crossed Tampa Bay evaporated in the cool dusk air and among the colors of the sun playing against the water. He felt himself sinking, along with the day, and dove in deeper, "It's too beautiful an evening and too beautiful a place to think about murder." And I'm with too beautiful a woman, he wanted to add.

Melanie didn't let him off the hook. "I thought you came down here to investigate the Lavin case? You wanted to talk to me about it."

He backtracked, "I'm supposed to be in Tampa, helping on a murder investigation."

Melanie looked him squarely in the eyes. "So why are you in St. Petersburg Beach instead of Tampa?"

He gave himself up to her when he answered, "Because you're here."

She put her hand on top of his and looked toward the dying sun. "I'm nowhere," she responded, her voice suggesting a sadness that swam out into the Gulf past the three-mile limit.

"You're here with me," Sutor persisted, wishing it were enough.

She smiled at him. "Yes, I am," she confirmed. "I'm glad you're here."

The sounds of Sade drifted across the cafe courtyard. Well-dressed couples looking young and in love began to fill the tables around them. Scattered bursts of laughter filtered across the patio. Melanie looked out to the sea and quietly recited a poem: *He was my North, my South, my East and West, / My working week and my Sunday rest, / My noon, my midnight, my talk, my song; / I thought that love would last forever: I was wrong.* She turned to Sutor, "W. H. Auden, my favorite poet."

He felt she needed comforting, but he didn't know what for, and he didn't know how to. She was silent for a while until he carefully prompted, "What are you thinking about?"

"My husband."

"You've been here with him?"

"No."

"What were you thinking?"

"I'm thinking how much of all this he missed."

"By dying so young?"

"By being who he was."

Sutor ignored the obvious question. Instead, he asked, "You miss him?"

"I find it difficult to believe I have to spend the rest of my life without him. I imagine the last word I say before I die will be his name."

Sutor felt a stab of pain at the thought that no woman had ever loved him the way Melanie loved her dead husband. "I envy you having such a wonderful marriage."

"I didn't say it was a wonderful marriage."

Sutor was puzzled. He didn't have enough experience with relationships to know that love and happiness were not synonymous.

Melanie had never spoken of her marriage or Richard to anyone because she knew no one would understand her continuing grief five years after he had died, but today, in a place away from where the marriage and Richard happened, it seemed safe to open her wounds to the evening air. She rationalized that what you say or do doesn't count away from home. It's not real, not the sun nor the sea nor the man. It's a mirage that disappears in a few days when real life continues.

"Family stuff was a problem," Melanie said. "He was Italian; I'm Jewish. He was the ancient mariner, with a family albatross around his neck. He killed the albatross by marrying me, but the killing brought him bad luck. I carried my own demons, passed to me by my parents. We should have lived happily ever after. We were crazy about each other, had a wonderful kid, nice house, good friends. He ended up in a grave and I ended up alone."

"I'm surprised you haven't met someone else by now." Sutor decided to take a chance and continued, "You're a beautiful woman. I would think you gets lots of offers of company."

"I'm worn out," Melanie said. "Between Richard's dying, my father's illness, Miriam's embezzlement, Jesse's adolescence, and your investigation of me, I don't have the energy or inclination to get involved with anything or anyone. Anyway, I come with baggage: a teenage son."

"Everyone comes with baggage," Sutor observed. "If it's not a kid, it's job problems. If not job problems, it's drinking. Or a crazy ex-wife. There's always something." He didn't think it prudent to mention an elderly parent awaiting the return of the Fuhrer. "You're just not ready yet."

Melanie smiled. "How does one get ready?"

"She meets someone she likes enough to move on with." He was amazed at himself for saying what seemed to be the right thing. Rhonda often alluded to his lack of psychological insight, but here he was, having a conversation with a bright woman and not looking like a fool.

"I have no time," Melanie maintained. "Hal Rosenberg is dying, any day now."

Sutor didn't answer.

Melanie looked away. "And there's this case to get done with."

He felt uncomfortable, as if he was adding to her misery by investigating the Lavin murder.

"You've been following me," Melanie stated. She pulled her hand away from his.

He decided not to lie. "Yes."

"Have you been following anyone else?"

He changed his mind about lying. "Yes, a few people."

"Why?"

"You know why."

"We're all suspects or just me?"

"Everyone on the planet Earth," Sutor responded, trying to lighten up the conversation a little. "Actually, just the people who hated Miriam, and that turns out to be just about everyone on the planet Earth."

Sutor took her hand back and squeezed it. "I'm sorry about Harold Rosenberg."

She said, "Thank you. Hal and I have been friends for many years, even before Richard died. He was the other man in my life. It was like having two husbands."

"Your husband didn't mind?" He couldn't bring himself to use her husband's first name because he didn't want to make Richard more alive than he was, even dead.

"He liked Hal. The relationship took pressure off the marriage. Now that they're both dead, I'm doubly alone."

"Harold's not dead yet," Sutor noted.

"He's dead," Melanie insisted, tears forming in her eyes. "The life he loved is over."

"Who is it that said, "It's not over until it's over'?"

"I'm going to help Hal kill himself when I get back."

Sutor was startled. "What!"

"He's had enough—too much—suffering. He's bedridden now, being diapered, unable to eat, getting bedsores. His life is over. It has been for a long time now. We bought a book on how to commit suicide and Hal is stockpiling the ingredients. He's going to wait for me to come home before doing it. He wants me there to help him. I promised I would, and I try not to break my promises."

He felt she was testing him, attempting to find out if he was an ordinary man or a cop. He knew what he said now would determine his fate with her. She was going to commit a murder, maybe her second, and this time she was telling him ahead of time. He thought it was wrong of her to assist Hal Rosenberg in ending his life. It was murder.

"What do you think?" Melanie prodded.

"Who am I to say?" Sutor answered. "I'm not dying of AIDS." He preferred not to answer directly.

"You have no idea what suffering is until you've spent time with Hal," Melanie noted sadly. "If I had the courage, I'd shoot him today." She wiped the corner of her eye with a cocktail napkin. "There is no end to losses," she said. "Would you believe that a month ago Hal and I were in New York, at the theater? He wasn't in great shape then, but he got around. This thing he has now hit him out of the blue. It's a parasite that comes from water. AIDS patients rarely die of it anymore with all the new drugs, but Hal's system has been compromised by so many other ailments that he's not able to overcome this, even with state-of-the-art meds."

"A month ago he was out and around?" Sutor inquired. He had discounted Rosenberg as a suspect because of his health; now he was forced to include him again.

"Hard to believe, isn't it?"

Harold Rosenberg, with access to a burgundy Malibu, a short time to live, a best friend cheated out of her inheritance. Would he do it?

"You never know in life," Sutor observed, for want of something more enlightening. Harold Rosenberg was her alibi for the Friday of the murder. She had said she was with him all night. Sutor had assumed this meant Harold was housebound. He figured perhaps Melanie had slipped out on Harold just after 9:00 and was back by 10:00. But Harold was still getting around the night of the murder. Could he have helped her, knowing he wouldn't be around long to answer for the crime? Sutor felt overwhelmed by his speculation. This new information was putting a pall over his perfect evening. He wished a wave would wash up over the cafe and sweep all thoughts of the Lavin case from his mind. But he had one more thing to clarify. "I saw a student of yours at the conference; a black guy; the one I met in your office."

"Jamal Jones."

"I didn't realize they invited students to these kind of things."

"They usually don't," Melanie confirmed. "I wrangled an invitation for Jamal so that he could network with people from other colleges. He's going to go to graduate school after Temple. His interest is black literature, an affirmative action specialty."

"You've taken a real interest in Jamal? Why?"

"He's bright, one of my best students. I've taught him in two classes. He came up the hard way and needs a break."

Sutor made a mental note to check on Jamal. "It's nice of you to help him."

"It's what I do for a living. There are similarities between our jobs: my students come to college criminally uninformed. If I don't get them, you do."

"Is that how you view crime?" Sutor asked. "As an inevitable way of life for ignorant people?"

"It's an inevitable way of life for anyone who wants to get ahead in America. That's why senators and congressman partake, along with corporate leaders, Wall Street brokers, lawyers and doctors, bank robbers, crack dealers, and little old Jewish ladies on their second marriages. Variations on a theme."

"You're successful," Sutor suggested, surprised at her cynicism, "and, to my knowledge, you haven't robbed a bank."

"You call what I do success? If I hadn't been married and my husband hadn't died and left me insurance and Social Security for Jesse, I'd be driving the same kind of car I see pulling into the faculty lot every day: ten-year-old gray Camerys, beat-up station wagons, at best, new Hyundais. Pathetic after 30 years of teaching."

Sutor realized she cared more about her lost inheritance then she had indicated. The money had been important to her, and watching it slide across the blackjack table at

Bally's had to be more than she could stand. "You would have been very well off if not for Miriam Lavin," Sutor suggested.

"No kidding."

"It must hurt."

"Hurt isn't the right word for it."

"What is?"

"It grates."

"Does her death make it easier?"

"It helps, but it's not enough."

"What could be worse?" Sutor persisted.

"I think the worst thing in life that happened to Miriam Lavin was that she was who she was. She had to live every day of her life with a liar, a thief, and a murderer."

The waitress returned with their drinks and a plate of peanuts. Melanie sat in silence, sipping her Kir from a small straw. "Enough about pain and suffering. Let's enjoy the view."

Sutor excused himself. "I'll be back in a minute. I want to tell my contact in Tampa I'll be a little late."

He went into the hallway outside the men's room and called Rhonda. She was out of the office and Colin picked up. "Get me a rundown on a guy named Jamal Jones," Sutor instructed. "Rhonda and I met him in Melanie Marconi's office. He goes to Temple. He's in his 30s, black, close to six feet tall. You can get his Social Security number from the school." He fidgeted with the phone wire, anxious to get back to the table while Colin was long-distance small talking. Sutor answered succinctly. Tampa's fine. Sure. Nothing yet. Colin said there was an envelope for him on his desk with the word *personal* written across it.

"The return address says it's from a Harold Rosenberg. Do you want me to read it to you?"

Sutor, stunned, yelled into the phone, "No!"

"You sure?"

"Leave it there!" Sutor ordered. "I'll be back tomorrow night; I'll read it then." He commanded Colin again, "Don't open that letter! Is that clear?"

Colin muttered, "Alright, alright. I'll leave it on your desk."

"Put it in the top drawer, under my pencil tray. Do it now!"

Sutor waited until Colin hid the correspondence. "See you tomorrow," he said abruptly.

"Sure thing," Colin replied, but Sutor had already hung up.

Sutor sorted out his thoughts before returning to the outdoor cafe. Why would Rosenberg write to him? Did he want to clear his conscience before he died? Did he name himself as the killer? Did he name Melanie? Sutor knew he should immediately drive Melanie back to the TradeWinds, thank her for a pleasant evening, and make it his life's mission to never run into her again unless the meeting took place in a courtroom. The whole idea of this trip had been insane. His loneliness had been so acute that he had let it fog his judgment, and now he was at this desperate point. Was it his loneliness or this woman? Whatever, it was a deadly combination. He walked across the patio vowing to retreat from this mess he was making of his life.

CHAPTER FIFTEEN

*M*elanie was leaning back in her chair when Sutor returned. She had let her hair down and it flowed behind her. She stared over the water and pointed to the sun, just about gone, "Isn't it beautiful?"

"Nice," Sutor agreed. His back ached from the tension of his call to Colin. He became aware of his tender knee joints and the temples of his head were throbbing. The psychic pain he felt over Melanie and the Lavin murder had converted to physical pain and had spread to all the regions of his body. It was not the kind of soreness alleviated by an aspirin or heat pack.

Melanie picked up on his mood change. "Was your friend expecting you tonight?" she asked. "We can take a rain check on dinner if you have to meet him."

He had his out, handed to him like a party gift. His fork in the road, Professor Marconi might say, the one that makes all the difference. Sutor choose the one less traveled. "It's fine; we're meeting tomorrow; it's not urgent.

"I thought you spend all your time on Miriam's murder?"

"There are other things that we're concerned with," Sutor noted, wanting the subject to go away.

"I'm happy to hear that. She isn't worth the effort you're putting in."

"Murder is against the law," Sutor argued, "no matter who the victim is."

Melanie changed the subject. "Enough about murder and enough about me. I don't really like to talk about myself, and I surely don't like to talk about that lowlife my father married." She tossed a peanut into the air in the direction of a little bird. "Tell me about you."

"There's not much to tell."

"That's what men say when they don't want to open up. It's only fair.

"You already told me you're not married but you didn't say whether or not you're divorced." Melanie delved, "Kids?"

"No wife, no ex-wife, no children, no ex-children," Sutor replied.

"Why not?"

"Never got around to it."

"You're not going to get away with that."

"Never met anyone I wanted to marry."

"Why not?"

He wanted to say because he'd never met anyone like her; but, instead, he muttered uncomfortably, "I've been busy."

"I expect women are beating down your door," Melanie commented. "Single. Good looking. Secure job. You're a walking *Philadelphia Magazine* ad." She became suspicious. "Who do you live with? Do you have a companion?" she probed, wondering if Sutor had something in common with Harold Rosenberg.

"I live with my father," Sutor admitted, sensing how ridiculous this sounded. "He's elderly and somewhat infirm," he lied. "I have a brother who lives out West so I was elected to take care of our father." He thought he was losing her, but he was wrong.

"That's very responsible of you. I give you a lot of credit. If I had been willing to take care of Morrie, he wouldn't have gotten bumped off by Miriam."

"I thought we weren't going to talk about Miriam anymore."

"You're right," Melanie acquiesced, and then surprised him by asking, "Are you up for a walk on the beach? We can head back to my hotel this way."

"Whatever you want," Sutor concurred, relieved to be rid of the focus on his life. He signaled the waitress for the bill but, before she brought it, he dropped more than enough money on the table for the drinks and a generous tip.

Melanie picked up her shawl and took off her shoes. "You're not dressed for beach walking," she observed, looking at Sutor's loafers and socks.

"That's OK," he replied, briefly taking her hand and leading her across the patio to an expanse of sand.

They walked almost a ½ mile on the beach, side by side, their hands drawn together but not quite touching. The sun had set and the sky had darkened over the water. The music from the Don CeSar faded. It was chilly and most people had left the beach. Melanie took Sutor's hand in hers and they walked along in silence.

Melanie tired first. "Let's sit down for a minute," she suggested.

She led Sutor to a covered lounge chair in a deserted section of the beach, hidden by umbrellas, beach chairs, and other paraphernalia. She settled down on the side of the lounger and shoved her feet into the sand. Sutor sat down next to her. "Are you cold?" he asked as he took her shawl from her arm and put it around her shoulders.

"God's in His heaven, all's right with the world," Melanie recited.

"Auden again?" Sutor was no longer self-conscious about not knowing poetry.

"Robert Browning."

Melanie took a barrette out of the pocket of her skirt and began to pin up her hair.

"Leave it," Sutor urged, taking the barrette from her hand. "It's beautiful." He picked up a strand of hair and curled it around his finger, leaned in and kissed the ringlet.

Melanie turned toward Sutor and studied his face in the gathering darkness. Her eyes were open wide and they seemed a bit misted.

Sutor placed his hand on the left side of Melanie's face and held it there a minute, staring into her eyes. "You are the most beautiful woman I've ever known," he whispered, his voice cracking.

She continued to look at him, without speaking.

"I don't know what to do about you," he admitted. "I don't know...."

She leaned forward and let her lips meet his in a gentle kiss. He put his arms around her and pulled her closer, returning her kiss first on her lips and then on her neck, cheek, and eyelids. He grabbed onto her hair and used it to draw her lips back to his. Her moan in response excited him beyond anything he had ever experienced. With their lips still touching, she leaned back on the lounge chair and pulled him on top of her. A passing thought warned him to stop before it was too late, but it came and went too quickly to be taken seriously. It had been too late from the moment he first saw her. He sensed he was a doomed man but nothing could have made him care about that at this moment.

She did not object as he unbuttoned her T-shirt and kissed her breasts through her pink lace bra. Slowly he dropped one and then the other of her bra straps down her arms, kissing her shoulders and neck while he freed her breasts. Reaching behind her, he unhooked the bra, letting the shirt and bra fall into the sand while he buried his face in her warm, rounded body. She reached up and tried to loosen his tie but was so overwhelmed by her need for a man—possibly him, she wasn't sure at this point—that she could only lie back on the lounge chair and let him do whatever he wanted to her. She closed her eyes and drifted off into a sea of passion that matched the force of the water hitting the beach in the distance.

Sutor didn't care that she wasn't helping him; he loved that she was giving herself to him without restraint; his only concern was that he do nothing that would offend her. "Do you want to stay here?" he whispered in her ear. She nodded yes and arched her body toward his. While he cradled her in his left arm and kissed her breasts, Sutor ran his right hand down her body until it reached the bottom of her skirt. As he pulled her skirt up farther and slid her panties off, she urged, "Please, you must."

In his wildest dreams, he had not expected this, and he said so. "Sweetheart, I don't have a condom with me." Always a careful man, his mind flashed for a split-second to Hal Rosenberg's AIDS, a pregnancy, Melanie's age, menopause, the loss of his job, a loss of control, and a few things he couldn't quite grasp, until Melanie repeated, "You must," and every rational idea he'd every had in his life evaporated into desire for her.

Sutor stood up and quickly undressed, leaving only his shirt on. He glanced around and was relieved they were in such a secluded place. Easing himself on top of her, he slowly slid inside her, praying that he could stay enough in command to somewhat satisfy her. He had no illusions that he could prolong this first encounter; he just didn't want to be embarrassingly premature.

Neither of them endured for long. Within a minute, her whole body began convulsing as her physical being released all the psychic energy she had stored up since her husband's death. Wave after wave of anguish and longing swept through her, beginning in her brain and advancing all the way to her toes, like a tidal wave of despair washing onto the beach and out again to the sea that had given it birth. She clung to him as if her life depended on it, which it did, although she'd never have admitted it. He was overcome as quickly and totally, and was surprised to hear a strange male voice whisper, "I love you."

When it was over neither of them moved nor spoke for a long time. He wondered what she was thinking, but dared not break the spell by asking. Did she know it was he holding her? Was she thinking about her husband? Was she thinking about anything?

He stood and put his clothes on, leaving his socks and shoes in the sand, then sat down on the lounge chair again, close to where her head rested. Her eyes were closed and, for a second, he thought she was asleep. "Sweetheart," he murmured. She opened her eyes and looked at him.

Lightly kissing her on the lips, he reached down next to the chair, picked up her clothes from the sand, shook them out, and helped her into them. "Do you want your shoes?" he asked, tenderly. She nodded.

He gathered up her sandals and put them on her feet, then put on his own socks and shoes, and helped her up. "Should we walk back?" he inquired, feeling like an awkward adolescent after his first sexual experience.

"You sound upset that this happened," Melanie observed, straightening her skirt.

"I'm overwhelmed," Sutor answered, putting his arms around her and kissing her hair. "I wish we could stay here like this forever."

"Far from the madding crowd. It's like having one's own little world."

"Do you want to go back to the cafe?"

"It's too far; my hotel is closer," she suggested, pointing ahead to the lights of the TradeWinds.

"Are you hungry?" Sutor asked.

"A little."

"I made a dinner reservation but I think we missed it. We could go out near here and get something to eat."

"We could get room service."

"Whatever you want," Sutor concurred.

They walked to the TradeWinds, arm in arm. Sutor wished Melanie would say something, tell him what their intimacy had meant to her, say anything to still his fear that their close encounter was an aberration.

Melanie's hair was disheveled, and Sutor wondered if he should say something to her about it before they reached the TradeWinds, in case one of her colleagues was prowling the grounds of the resort. But he liked her hair that way; it reminded him of what they had done, and he wanted to keep this symbol of their love making alive as long as he could.

"I have to give a talk tomorrow," Melanie said when they got on the elevator at the TradeWinds.

"Early?" Sutor asked.

"No, thank goodness—two o'clock. I can sleep late."

The elevator reached the 4th floor and Sutor followed Melanie to her room. "It's a suite," Melanie mentioned as she used a coded card to open the door. "Quite nice—living room, kitchen, and bedroom. The living room is in the back, overlooking the Gulf." A lamp was on in the bedroom when they entered, and a red button on the phone flashed a signal indicating there was a message for her. Melanie turned the television set to the station that broadcasted phone messages. Jesse had called from the friend's house where he was staying to say he was fine, he'd stopped home and the dog was fine, and he loved her. The message made Melanie smile.

"Can I get you something?" Sutor asked, glad to see her good mood.

Melanie switched off the lamp and turned to him. She reached up and put her arms around his neck. "Yes, you can," she whispered in his ear. "You most certainly can."

CHAPTER SIXTEEN

"*I* went to see Alan Kaplan again." Rhonda was trying to talk to her boss, who was so distracted since returning from Florida a few days earlier that he didn't seem to listen to her anymore. "He took me out to lunch," she continued, thinking this would break his concentration.

Sutor didn't answer; he was submerged in thoughts of Melanie Marconi. He had tried to call her a dozen times, at home and at the college but, invariably, he got her voice mail at both places. Only once did he leave a message asking her to call him, which she hadn't done. The one time Jesse answered the phone the kid said his mother was at a friend's house for the night. Sutor had driven into town and, as he expected, Melanie's Camaro was parked in Harold Rosenberg's courtyard. It had been three days since he had opened and read Rosenberg's letter, anticipating its contents: *Please be advised that I, Harold Rosenberg, killed Miriam Lavin. No one else was involved in this deed. I threw the gun in the Schuylkill River.* The letter was signed and dated, but not witnessed.

Sutor knew he was obligated to interview Harold Rosenberg again and he dreaded the thought of it. He didn't want his first meeting with Melanie since returning from Florida to be in Harold Rosenberg's sanctuary. He certainly didn't want to read Melanie's dying best friend his Miranda rights. Nor did he want to enter the home of an AIDS patient again. And most of all, if the love of his life was there with her friend when he visited, he didn't want her to see how frightened he was of being in the same room with a guy whose view of manhood had led him to the point that tons of squiggly bugs were scouring through his body eating away at skin, cells, and organ systems. He knew how devoted Melanie was to Harold Rosenberg, infected or not; and, in an odd affirmation, he had to admit to himself that he envied Harold Rosenberg for his ability to draw more love to his decrepit, skeletal, semi-masculine body than he, Sutor, had ever drawn to his own formidable, healthy, virile, all-male frame. He reasoned that if, after Rosenberg died, there was a possibility of Melanie transferring her devotion to him, that chance would be shattered beyond repair if he did anything to interfere with Rosenberg's peaceful departure from the world.

Sutor forced himself to drive into town again. There were two cars parked in Rosenberg's driveway. Melanie's wasn't one of them, and he was relieved. He hoped to question Rosenberg without her there, in case he came down too harshly for her taste. Sutor parked down the street from the townhouse, then walked through the courtyard and up the stairs. Looking through the sheer curtain on the front door of the Rosenberg home, he could see a group of people in the living room. Harold Rosenberg's mother came to the door in response to his soft knock.

"I'm very sorry to bother you, Mrs. Rosenberg, but I must speak to your son."

"He's too sick to talk to you," the mother advised, looking more pale and fragile than when he had last visited.

"He summoned me," Sutor explained.

Puzzled, Mrs. Rosenberg stepped aside and let Sutor enter the house. Sutor nodded a greeting to the people in the living room—three women and two men—who were gathered around a coffee table going through a stack of photo albums. They were cordial but somber; each said hello; tears were streaming down the cheeks of one of the woman; another woman was comforting her with hugs. If there was anything that made Sutor more uncomfortable than male homosexuals, it was female homosexuals. They were an affront to his sense of masculinity and far more threatening. He couldn't believe that Melanie hung out with these people. It crossed his mind that she might be bisexual, but then he remembered his night with her in Florida, his whole night with her, and the hours of lovemaking after the walk on the beach, and he was certain, without a shadow of a doubt, that she was straight. But then again, as a police detective, if there was anything he had learned in life, it was this: you never know.

Harold Rosenberg's mother led Sutor up the stairs to the bedroom. The door was closed and the room dimly lit. Harold Rosenberg's feeble body lay wrapped in blankets. Much of the equipment Sutor had seen before was gone; only one pole with a bag attached to it remained. There was a square box on the bed, a battery pack of some sort. Harold's face was gray and his body heaved slightly under the covers. A woman wearing a long green dress and a green crocheted yarmulke on her head was sitting on the bed whispering to Harold Rosenberg. To Sutor's surprise, Melanie was sitting in a chair close to Rosenberg's head, holding his hand and rubbing it.

"Did anyone hit the pump?" Mrs. Rosenberg asked.

"Rebecca did," Melanie answered. She looked up at Sutor and gave him a slight smile. Nothing in her greeting hinted that she remembered their St. Petersburg night. Melanie introduced the woman to Sutor, "This is Rabbi Getz."

Sutor, unnerved by this unexpected encounter with Melanie, could hear the rabbi comforting Rosenberg with a poem. *Shall I cry out in anger, O God, Because Your gifts are mine but for a while? Shall I forget the blessing of health the moment there is pain? Shall I be ungrateful for the laughter, the seasons of joy, the days of gladness, when tears cloud my eyes and darken the world and my heart is heavy within me?*

Sutor, after again expressing his regret for coming to the house, stood in the doorway of the room for a few minutes, hesitant to step a toe onto the carpet lest it carry a droplet of this plague he so irrationally feared. He motioned to Melanie, "Can I see you a minute?"

The rabbi murmured on: *Give me the vision, O God, to see that embedded in each of Your gifts is a core of eternity, undiminished and bright, an eternity that survives the dread hours of affliction.*

Melanie let go of Harold Rosenberg's hand and stood up. When Rosenberg opened his eyes, Melanie assured him she'd be right back. Rosenberg turned his head slightly and looked toward the door. He tried to say something to Sutor but it was unintelligible. Melanie leaned across the rabbi and whispered to Rosenberg. *What You give to me, O Lord, You never take away. And bounties granted once, shed their radiance evermore.* She kissed Rosenberg lightly on the lips, an act that repulsed Sutor. "I love you," she murmured.

As Melanie walked toward Sutor, he observed she wasn't wearing makeup and her hair was disheveled. Even haggard, she overwhelmed him with her beauty; and, if he could have, he would have swept her out of this AIDS house and taken her to a clean, healthy, sun-baked place far away, where they could recapture the one day and one night that meant more to him than any other day and night in his 42 years, including the day of his 22nd birthday, the last happy time he'd spent with his mother before she took an overdose of sleeping pills and killed herself, a day that until Florida had been the most significant in his life.

Melanie led Sutor to a small sitting room down the hall from Rosenberg's bedroom. She sat down on a couch and leaned her head against a needlepoint throw pillow. "Morphine pump," she said wearily. "It's almost over."

Sutor sat down next to her. For the first time he noticed tiny lines at the corners of her eyes and a couple of strands of gray in her hair. "Morphine for pain?"

"Morphine to end his suffering."

"It should help his pain," he replied, for lack of anything more erudite and to maintain the pretense that he didn't know what was going on in Rosenberg's bedroom.

"I'm not in agreement," Melanie admitted, "but it was his choice. Everyone's hitting the pump but me. I told him I couldn't do it; I couldn't be a part of it; I couldn't live with it. He understood and said it was all right. I promised him I would help him when the time came, but I couldn't keep the promise."

"Is he dying?" Sutor asked. His mind refused to accept he was a witness to an assisted suicide.

She nodded. "Any minute now."

"I must talk to him," Sutor insisted, alarmed.

"It's too late."

Sutor took Rosenberg's letter from his pocket. "Melanie, I hate to bring this up now. I know how terrible a time this is for you. But I must show this to you." He handed her the note.

Melanie read it and scoffed at the words on the paper. "Ridiculous," she declared, handing the note back to Sutor.

"Why is it ridiculous?"

"He didn't do it."

"How do you know?"

"Because I know."

"How?"

"Don't ask me. I just know. I know Hal and I know what he's capable of. Murder isn't one of the things he could do."

"Why not? He had nothing to lose."

"He had nothing to gain either."

Sutor was about to say "He was trying to keep you from being charged with the crime," but he stopped himself. "Why did he write this?" he asked instead.

Melanie shrugged. "Don't know."

"Did he know Miriam?"

"Of course."

"Did he hate her?"

"Of course not."

"How do you know?"

"Can't you see how silly it is? Hal had a rendezvous with death. He didn't have time for earthly considerations.

His time for love or hate or friendship was over, had been for a long time."

"How do you know that?"

"The poet Robert Frost told me." She recited: *The nearest friends can go, / With anyone to death, comes so far short, / They might as well not try to go at all. / No, from the time when one is sick to death, / One is alone, and he dies more alone.*

"We have to explain this letter," Sutor argued. "What would your Robert Frost say about it?"

"He'd say some things are better left unexplained."

"Murder isn't one of them," he persisted.

"This murder is."

"What makes this murder different from any other?"

"When's the last time you investigated the execution of a little old Jewish lady?"

Her wording disturbed Sutor. "Execution? We've never called it an execution."

"Call it whatever you want, I could care less." She was being nasty and unpleasant, a side of her Sutor hadn't seen before. Was it Rosenberg's imminent death, the murder investigation, or God forbid, him? Could she be distancing herself from their liaison? Why the hell did it matter so much to him? It was one night in a distant town. He'd had a few before in his life, in his younger days, when he'd traveled to Germany for a summer with his father, who had wanted to visit the birthplace he'd always missed. While Henry Sr. reverted to being Henrik Jr., the son of a former SS officer, Sutor had discovered his manhood among the frauleins of Frankfort. It was ironic that what he had learned in the Fatherland should carry him into the arms of this distraught Jewish woman standing before him.

Sutor felt helpless. He wanted desperately to talk to her about Florida, about their relationship, if in fact they had one. Knowing Harold Rosenberg was near death, he also wanted to comfort her, but he didn't know how. His mother had tried to be supportive of him when he was a child, but she was too mired in her own survival needs to give him more than snippets of her emotional energy. He hadn't learned from either of his parents what it meant to bring solace into someone else's life. How could he ease her distress? He struggled to find words that could relieve her suffering, wanting her to hurt less so there would be room for her to love more. Maybe after her friend was gone, she would be so empty there would be nothing left for him. He would console her if she gave him a chance. He'd figure out how to do it, no matter what it took. "How can I help you?" he asked.

"By leaving Hal alone to die in peace."

"He wrote this confession," Sutor argued.

"Use it as you will," Melanie said, putting her hand on his arm and looking up at him. "But, please, don't bother Hal."

Sutor nodded in agreement. "It's too late; I can see that."

"I'll walk you out," Melanie offered.

"Don't bother walking all the way downstairs. I'll let myself out."

"It's fine." She led him down the steps and through the living room, past the mourners-in-waiting, none of whom she acknowledged in any way. "Hangers on," she remarked to Sutor. "It generally happens with dying AIDS patients. Hal has become exceedingly popular in his last months."

They stood facing each other at the front door. "I don't see your car," Sutor observed. "If you need a ride home,

I can come back in town to pick you up."

"Thank you. It's kind of you to offer but I'm going to stay till the end. One of Hal's friends brought me in; he'll take me home too."

Disappointed, Sutor suggested, "See you soon." It was both a statement and a question. He took a card from his coat pocket, wrote his private cell phone number on the back, and handed it to her. "In case you need me," he explained, kissing her on the cheek. "Melanie, anytime, day or night, call me if there's anything I can do for you." He forced himself to add, "or Harold."

"Goodbye," she answered, holding the door open for him.

He left, not knowing if she meant goodbye for tonight or goodbye forever.

CHAPTER SEVENTEEN

"Do you think I'm homophobic?" Sutor asked Rhonda as they drove into Philadelphia to pay a visit to Jerome Eisenberg, Miriam Lavin's grandson.

"No, I don't think you're afraid of being gay." She had her notepad open and was rereading her notes about Jerome Eisenberg.

"I didn't ask you if I'm afraid of being gay."

"Yes, you did. That's what homophobic means. What you probably want to know is whether or not I think you're anti-gay, and, yes, I do. I think you're anti a lot of things."

Sutor became indignant. "What other things don't I like?"

"You don't particularly like sports, you don't like animals, you don't like children, you don't like vacationing, you don't like Jewish people, you don't like coffee, you don't like women."

"What do you mean I don't like women?"

"You never compliment the women in the office, only the men. You'll tell Colin, the Forrest Gump of the force, he did a good job of looking up a license plate on the computer; but when Joanna hands you the 30-page report she stayed late to type, you don't say a word."

Alarmed, Sutor persisted, "And when have I ever said anything disparaging about Jews?"

"I've heard you use the term 'Jew him down.' It's an anti-Semitic comment, and you don't even recognize it as such. I can just imagine what you say about blacks when I'm not around."

"I say black is beautiful," joked Sutor.

"Sure you do," Rhonda mocked.

"I think you're beautiful," Sutor insisted. "But I never told you so because I don't want to get sued for sexual harassment."

"I promise not to take you to court."

"I'm not anti-Semitic," Sutor argued. "I can't be."

"Why not?"

"Because I don't know anything about Jews. I was raised a Lutheran. I went to Christian schools until high school and then I was sent to a military academy."

"Lutheranism is at the heart of anti-Semitism—that's what I learned in the history of religion course I took in college. When your head guy, Martin Luther, tacked up his little notices on a church door, he wrote that Jews were less than animals."

"No one ever told me that," Sutor challenged.

"What did you learn about Jews in school?" Rhonda asked.

"They killed Christ," Sutor replied.

"Say no more," Rhonda lectured. "Can you imagine a more anti-Semitic belief?"

"How can I learn about the Jewish religion?" Sutor inquired. He had been thinking about Melanie day and night, and, even if he couldn't be with her in person, he wanted to understand her, in the unlikely event they might someday be together.

The question struck Rhonda as odd. She turned in her seat to look at Sutor. "Why in the world would you be interested in Judaism?"

Sutor avoided her gaze and looked out his side window into the traffic. "I'm interested in a lot of things."

"Like hell you are."

"I'm looking for a new religion," Sutor teased.

"You don't even have an old religion. I've never known you to go to church."

"I'm very spiritual," Sutor asserted, needling her. "Nobody realizes it."

"What's going on here?"

"Nothing."

"Don't tell me you're dating a Jewish girl," Rhonda exclaimed. "Mister right-wing Fascist conservative."

"I'm not dating a Jewish girl," Sutor responded. "I don't date girls; I prefer women. You're being a sexist, Rhonda. You don't call Jewish men 'boys.'"

"What's her name?" Rhonda urged.

"Whose name? There's no one to speak of. I'm just interested in a new religion, that's all."

"Why Judaism? Why not Baptist, like I am."

"Too much singing," Sutor jested. "I'm anti-singing, too."

Rhonda was silent for a moment, then she had a brainstorm. "It's Melanie Marconi! She's your Jewish girl!"

Sutor almost swerved into the car next to him. "What the hell are you talking about?"

Rhonda slammed her notepad down on the dashboard. "Don't give me that crap. I see your face every time her name is mentioned. I hear you. Or rather, I don't hear you. You clam up whenever she's mentioned as a suspect. Bill, don't insult my intelligence. It hurts me when you do that. If it's true about Melanie Marconi, you need to tell me. You need me to cover your ass."

"I love her," Sutor said simply, staring ahead into the traffic.

"That's it?"

"That's it."

"Does she love you? Are you involved?"

"We're involved." He kept his eyes averted from her.

"You can't do this, Bill! This is crazy! It'll cost you your job. It's probably illegal. It's certainly unethical. She's a suspect in the Lavin murder, a strong suspect."

"I know, I know," Sutor admitted impatiently. "Don't you think I've thought of these things? I can't help it, Rhonda. Didn't you ever love anyone enough to want to look the other way when he did things that hurt you? Didn't you ever have such a passion for someone that you didn't care what the consequences might be?"

Rhonda's body stiffened and she looked out her window. "I'd never let that happen."

"Not once in your life?"

"I said 'no.'" She was annoyed. "Bill, I pride myself on using good judgment. I think carefully before I jump into things."

Sutor said something he regretted immediately. "Then how do you explain Carly?"

Rhonda was stunned. She sensed the blood in her body rushing to her head. She felt faint and it took all her control not to pass out. She couldn't believe he knew. The extraordinary lengths she had undertaken to hide her mistake from the world she now lived in had been for nothing.

"How long have you known?" She was visibly trembling.

"Since I first hired you. Do you think I'd bring someone aboard, make them a part of my team, and not check them out." Sutor reached out his hand to her. "I'm sorry, Rhonda. I shouldn't have said what I did. I'm not in my right mind over this woman. It's no excuse for my intrusion into your life."

"Colin too? You investigated him?" Tears were running down Rhonda's face.

"Everybody who works for me."

"Why didn't you tell me you knew?"

"Why would I? It's not my business if you don't want anyone to know you have a daughter. It's your life. Live it as you want."

"Your tone is judgmental, despite your words."

"I don't mean to judge you."

"You don't think less of me?"

Sutor put his hand on her knee, the first time he'd touched her since they began working together. "Rhonda, I don't think less of you or more of you. Who am I to judge you? I'm a man without a life. Or I was anyway, until I met Melanie Marconi."

"How long have you been seeing her?" She thought it best to move away from the subject of Carly.

"Remember the saying 'what you don't know won't hurt you,'" Sutor warned.

"It'll hurt you, Bill. And if it hurts you, it hurts me."

"Don't get involved, Rhonda."

"I am involved; I know about the affair." She sighed, "Oh, Bill, why? How did it happen?" She imagined their careers going down in flames together. "How can you, of all people, ask that question?"

———————————————————

Sutor and Rhonda entered the 1701 building and took an express elevator to the 25th floor. They entered the reception area of Cardozo Rossen Leonard. Sutor showed his badge to the receptionist as he and Rhonda swept by her. They appeared at Jerome Eisenberg's office unannounced.

Eisenberg was a *putz*, just like Alan Kaplan, who worked five stories below, had said. Rhonda knew it by his hair, combed up from behind in an attempt to hide an expansive bald spot racing toward the back of his head. His nose was more prominently beaked than his mother's and his face a little more pockmarked. Otherwise the scion of the Herzelman family was equally as unattractive as the rest of the clan. His personality fit his appearance. "I have nothing to say," Eisenberg shouted when Sutor and Rhonda walked into his office and introduced themselves. "I'm late for court." He was an associate lawyer, relegated to doing 60-hour-a-week grunt work for a few years until he could move into a practice worth talking about. Rhonda couldn't imagine why anyone would want a job filled with so much paperwork, but she knew that pedantic endeavors appealed to certain personality types, like Sutor.

"This is about your grandmother, Mr. Eisenberg," Rhonda said. "Aren't you interested in having us find the person who murdered her?"

"If you haven't caught him yet, what makes you think you're going to catch him at all? Even I know that most murderers are apprehended within days of a crime." Eisenberg grabbed his overcoat from a hanger on the back of his office door and attempted to slither past Sutor and Rhonda.

"How do you know it's a him?" Sutor inquired, using his large form to block the lawyer's exit.

"Assumption," Eisenberg snapped. "Now if you'll excuse me."

"Assume this, Mr. Eisenberg. If you don't sit down and answer our questions, we will see to it that the next time we come to talk, you won't be a half hour late for court, you'll be days late. Why don't you just invite us in for a chat and save yourself a lot of trouble?"

"I don't have time for this," Eisenberg exclaimed, moving away from the door and beginning to pace the room. "Cut to the chase," Eisenberg demanded, turning his back to his visitors and peering out his window, which overlooked an alley full of dumpsters.

Sutor picked up a photo of Miriam Lavin and the Herzelman clan from a shelf laden with models of antique cars. He pointed to a 1937 Jaguar. "Should have brought Colin," he mentioned to Rhonda.

"He probably has the real thing in his garage, in a million pieces."

The levity annoyed Eisenberg. "What do you want?" he grumbled. "Make it snappy."

"Do you know anyone who drives a burgundy Malibu?" Sutor asked as he looked to see if there was one among the toys.

"Why?" Eisenberg responded.

"A car like that was seen in the garage at the time of your grandmother's murder." Sutor put the photo back and turned to look at Eisenberg.

"I don't know anyone who has a car like that."

"Did you grandmother have any enemies that you know of?"

"For Christ sake, she was an old lady. What the hell kind of enemies can an old lady have?"

"The kind that kill you," Rhonda chimed in. She looked over the books in Eisenberg's office: torts, wills and estates, defense tactics.

"I'm curious, Mr. Eisenberg. Your grandmother sued Alan Kaplan. How come you gave him the estate work? He'll make out pretty well on it financially."

"We went to law school together," Eisenberg replied, moving from the window to his desk. He sat down in a black leather chair and swiveled it so that the back faced Sutor and Rhonda.

Sutor took a seat in front of Eisenberg's desk and began playing with another of the lawyer's toy cars, scooting it up and down along the leather desk pad. Eisenberg swung around and grabbed the car. "I'd appreciate it if you wouldn't touch my things. They're very valuable."

Sutor picked up a glass paperweight. "So what about this friendship with Kaplan?"

"I didn't say we were friends now. I said we were together in law school. "

"Your grandmother was inordinately litigious," Sutor commented. He turned the paperweight upside down. It was made in China. "Could she have angered someone she sued?"

"She lost most of her cases," Rhonda interjected. "The victor doesn't usually get even." She was still perusing the bookshelves when she spotted a wallet size photo of Miriam in a gold frame.

"You represented her in many of her cases, didn't you?" Sutor persisted.

"Too many," Eisenberg exclaimed, exhibiting a hint of hostility.

"Do you know why your grandmother left the bulk of her estate to you?" Rhonda asked

"I got the bulk of her crap, why shouldn't I get the bulk of her money?"

"You didn't get along with your grandmother, did you?" Rhonda suggested.

"I got along with her better than anybody else. From the minute I was born, I was the Messiah to her. First-born male in a Jewish family can do no wrong."

"Sounds nice to me," Sutor remarked, and meant it.

"Don't kid yourself; it's a trap." He asked Rhonda for the photo and, when she handed it to him, he put it face down on the desk. "I became a lawyer for her. Then I got stuck with her legal problems."

Rhonda wouldn't have guessed the *putz* had an ounce of insight in his body. Then she remembered he had been an English major before his family directed him away from anything that might bring him occupational pleasure. It's not too late she wanted to tell him. Half of all lawyers quit to join the circus or take up bird watching.

"Did anyone know about her will before she died?"

"No."

"She never mentioned her estate?"

"Sure she mentioned it. She told each family member something different. My mother was getting the silverware one week, my aunt Susan another. Nobody took my grandmother seriously when it came to her money."

Sutor interjected, "Your grandmother's step-daughter Melanie says your grandmother robbed Morrie Lavin blind and possibly killed him." He hated mentioning Melanie's name publicly for fear his voice would give him away. And he didn't want to hear anything negative about her.

"A flake," Eisenberg advised. "Don't pay any attention to her."

"What makes her a flake?" Rhonda asked. She gave Sutor an 'I'm sorry' look."

"She dresses like she's at Woodstock and hangs out with a faggot. My grandmother fought with Morrie all the time about that bitch bringing her monster dog to their apartment. But she did it anyway. She lives by her own rules. My grandmother despised her."

"What an indictment," Rhonda muttered. "Especially the part about living by her own rules."

"You know what I mean," Eisenberg maintained. He approached Sutor for support. "You've met that kind of woman before, haven't you?"

Can't say I have, Sutor thought. He moved the conversation away from the subject of Melanie. "I'll be candid with you, Mr. Eisenberg. We think someone out for revenge killed your grandmother." His intention was to make Eisenberg uneasy, so he lied, "We're close to finding out who the murderer is. We have a witness."

Eisenberg replied in a peculiar way: "I think it was a purse snatching. Leave it at that."

Sutor wanted clarification. "Don't you want your grandmother's murderer caught?"

"The murderer is not going to get caught. Too much time has passed for that."

"We're in no hurry," Sutor remarked, which, of course, wasn't true, unless the flake was involved.

"Do you know a woman named Allison Long?" Rhonda asked.

"She works here," Eisenberg replied.

"Your grandmother had her phone number in her handbag. Do you know why?"

Eisenberg shrugged. "No idea." He looked at his watch and abruptly got up and walked quickly across the room. "Gotta go," he informed them. "Next time, make an appointment." Before they could answer or stop him, Eisenberg swept out the door, leaving Sutor and Rhonda behind with his toy car collection and not much more to go on.

"Son-of-a bitch," Sutor exclaimed.

"That's for sure," Rhonda countered, her thoughts focused on Miriam.

CHAPTER EIGHTEEN

Rhonda handed Sutor a sheet of paper. "Dr. Marconi's favorite student, Jamal Jones. Try armed robbery and assault and battery; five to ten in Graterford Prison; got out after four years."

Sutor felt a sense of dread. "What's their connection?"

"She got him into the college, wrote letters on his behalf, and helped him get student loans and a grant." Rhonda treaded cautiously. "He owes her," she observed.

His stomach churning, Sutor instructed, "Talk to him," adding "gently," in the expectation that Jamal would recount every word back to his mentor.

Jamal was almost as big a man as Sutor and almost as dark skinned as Wilson Greene. He was dressed in jeans and a printed open-necked shirt with an African motif on it. He was 36 years old and had been out of prison for five years. He had come to the police station willingly after Rhonda called him on the phone.

Rhonda thought she might be on the same wavelength as Jamal because of their similar backgrounds, but he was leery of her as soon as she entered the interrogation room and introduced herself. "You're the good cop, I take it," he challenged. "Man, I have studying to do. Question me and let me out of here."

Rhonda explained that they were investigating the Lavin murder, which Jamal said he knew all about from newspaper accounts and from Dr. Marconi. He insisted he had nothing to hide; he was home studying the night of the killing. Rhonda asked him how he remembered what he was doing so many weeks earlier, and he answered, "I study every night. I have a 4.0 average. I've applied to Penn for the fall. Dr. Marconi thinks I can get in there."

"What's your major going to be?" Rhonda asked. She felt an ache in her chest when he replied, "Psychology."

"You're pretty good friends with Dr. Melanie Marconi," Rhonda commented.

Jamal was a street-smart man and he knew what such a statement meant. "I had two classes with her; one in Western literature and the other in women's literature."

"You're better friends than that," Rhonda suggested.

"What do you mean?"

She felt like she was talking to Bill Sutor again. Did all men when backed against the wall act like they had just been introduced to the English language? She once read an essay in a magazine that maintained that women would have to be mentally ill in order to understand men. Now she knew what the author meant. She opened a diet Coke, put down two plastic cups, and shared the soda with him.

"Is this supposed to make me confess?" Jamal sneered.

Rhonda took a seat across from Jamal and placed her briefcase on the table in front of her. "Jamal, I know where you've been, and I know what led you to prison. I know a dozen men like you, half of them in my own family. And I sure as hell know that a man who's been in prison for the crimes you've committed isn't going to be taken in by a can of Coke. Stop bullshitting me. Melanie Marconi got you into college. What's that about? How long have you known her?"

"She was my high school English teacher years ago, before I fucked up. She read about me in the paper when I was charged, wrote to me while I was in prison, and helped me get out. She worked on my student loan papers and she's working on a recommendation to Penn as we speak. Are we friends? No. Friendship is bi-directional. There's not a thing she needs or wants from me."

"You don't do anything for her?"

"What can I do for her? I took her kid to a 76ers game once. She bought the tickets and paid for dinner."

"Do you like her?"

"Romantically?"

"Yes."

"She's white."

"So?"

"Man, I don't mess with white women. I don't need that kind of trouble." He looked at Rhonda and shook his head in bewilderment. "You guys must be nuts if you think Dr. Marconi and I are having a thing. You guys must be playing with yourselves over this case."

"So if you're not friends and you're not interested in her romantically, what is it for you—ambition?" That was something she could understand.

Jamal became enraged. "Fuck you with these questions about Dr. Marconi. Imagine sitting in prison after committing crimes I was guilty of and getting a letter that says I've always had potential, this bad time will pass and that once I take responsibility for my actions and redeem myself, I'll be able to live a full, free life. When I got out of prison, I wrote a letter of apology to each and every one of my victims. Dr. Marconi was right. Then I was free to move on."

"Are you aware of the fact that Miriam Lavin was Dr. Marconi's stepmother?'

"Of course."

"Do you think Dr. Marconi is capable of committing a murder?"

"Everybody's capable of committing a murder. That's one thing I learned in prison."

"Let me give you a hypothetical situation. If she came to you today and told you she wanted to commit a murder would you help her?"

"I'd advise her against it. Prison wouldn't suit her. They don't serve Kona for breakfast."

"I'll cut to the chase, Jamal. Any idea who killed Mrs. Lavin?"

"Not a clue," Jamal assured her.

"If you knew, would you tell me who it was?"

"It's not my business," Jamal replied.

Rhonda asked a few more questions, but she knew she wasn't going to get much information out of Jamal. "Go study," she concluded. "Do well."

CHAPTER NINETEEN

"He'd move off the planet Earth if she asked him to," Rhonda told Sutor, who knew the feeling. They were driving around looking at apartments. Sutor wanted Rhonda's point of view on where he should live. "I don't think Jamal did it but I'm convinced he knows more than he's saying."

"Aren't we all?" Sutor admitted.

"Are you going to continue being secretive and sarcastic?"

"I don't know what you're talking about," Sutor insisted.

A neighborhood realtor had given him a list of addresses and a handful of keys. All were within walking distance of Henry Sutor's house. Rhonda hated the first three apartments they looked at: not enough closets in one; window-unit air conditioners in another; a decrepit wood fence around the third, a sure sign the landlord wasn't keeping up the place. "Why are you looking at these ratty Narberth triplexes," Rhonda asked. "There are some lovely high rises not far from here."

"I don't like people knowing my business," Sutor answered. "I don't want a lobby or an elevator. I like the idea of walking out of my apartment onto the street and into my car."

"You like the idea of sneaking Melanie Marconi in without anyone seeing her," Rhonda remarked as they pulled up to a brick Colonial converted into apartments.

Sutor looked around the living room of the first-floor unit. The walls were painted a bright yellow and the ceiling was blue with clouds painted on it. It occurred to him that Melanie might like the place. If he took the apartment, the first thing he would do is paint over the clouds.

He liked the apartment, a light and airy space shaded by trees and extensive shrubbery. The kitchen had recently been renovated, it had central air conditioning, and the new bathroom had both a shower and tub. There was a long driveway to the left of the front door leading to private parking spaces behind the house. "Protecting yourself?" Rhonda teased.

"Protecting her," Sutor snapped.

They returned to the real estate office where Sutor filled out an application for the apartment and wrote a check for the security deposit. "I want it completely repainted, in clear white, and the carpet has to be cleaned. Bring in a cleaning company to go through the cabinets and over the woodwork. Sterilize the bathroom. I think the place should be exterminated, too. You never know what the previous tenants were like when it came to cleanliness."

The realtor agreed to Sutor's terms and a date for moving in was chosen. Sutor had two weeks to furnish the place, for which he enlisted Rhonda's help again. "I need a woman's touch. What do I know about dishes and towels?"

"Can't you take stuff from your father's house?" Rhonda asked. "You must have tons of extra things laying around."

"I'm starting over, Rhonda. I don't want a single thing from my father's house. I want everything new."

At IKEA Rhonda picked out a beige couch, a wood laminate coffee table, and two blue and beige chairs for the living room, as well as a trestle butcher-block table, bent-wood chairs, and a shaker-style hutch for the kitchen. "No flowers, no trees," Sutor instructed. "Anything but flowers and trees." Rhonda stretched out a bolt of cloth with a blue, black, and white geometric pattern. "My mother is handy. She'll make your drapes." Sutor bought a bed and mattress, king size, three sets of linens, two pillows, towels, and a comforter. He arranged for a fellow officer with a truck to pick up the bed, chairs, and table and deliver them to his new apartment as soon as the place was painted.

"Expecting company?" Rhonda joked as she helped pile plain white dishes, assorted utensils, trash cans and a couple of plants into Sutor's bulging cart.

Sutor was actually excited, like a seven-year-old who had been given a chance to pick out any bike he wanted. In middle age he was doing something the average guy did in his 20s. In middle age he was in love in a way the average guy had been in high school.

"I hope this works out for you, Bill," Rhonda acknowledged as they drove home from the furniture store, the rear seat of the BMW loaded so high Sutor couldn't see out of the back window. "You've gone to a lot of trouble for that girl."

"It's not for that girl, Rhonda. It's for me. It's time. The girl just makes it special."

Rhonda knew firsthand about special, and she felt truly sorry for her boss and friend.

CHAPTER TWENTY

Sutor hadn't shown anyone the letter from Harold
Rosenberg. He realized that if it appeared Melanie
had committed the murder, he would need the letter to, if
not show her innocence, at least get her off the hook.
He was worried about his delay in revealing the correspondence, it being the most compelling piece of evidence to
date. Sutor understood that Colin knew about the letter
because Colin had informed him of it. But Colin was a
harebrain; he'd never remember discussing the matter—or
so Sutor hoped. He finally decided to tell Rhonda about
the letter.

"I found this under some papers on my desk," Sutor
asserted, handing her the envelope. "I was in Florida when
it came, and I guess someone just overlooked it."

Rhonda looked at Sutor suspiciously, knowing Sutor's
desk was always immaculate. He cleared every last piece of
paper on it before going home at the end of the day, even
if it meant working until midnight. He was obsessive about
order, and he'd never let a letter languish under so much
as one piece of a report.

"What are you going to do with the letter," Rhonda asked, looking across his desk at him, "now that you've found it under this mess."

"Keep it as evidence," Sutor replied. He knew Rhonda wouldn't question his holding back on the letter.

"It solves the case for you," Rhonda suggested. "You'll get the credit, no one else will be charged, and it will be over as far as the law is concerned."

He was curious about how far she would go with him. "You'd be OK with it?"

"If you are, I am," Rhonda confirmed. She had career plans, and she wasn't going to let a little thing like a murder stand in her way.

Sutor took her statement as a sign of loyalty. "I appreciate your confidence in me."

"What are friends for?"

Rhonda instructed Colin to follow Jamal Jones for a week to see where and with whom the man hung out. It was Colin's kind of assignment: he got to ride around in a car all day and half the night. The best part of the duty was sitting inside the college lobby while Jamal took his classes. Colin could look over the mini-skirted, tight-sweatered, gum-chewing Italian girls, whose acres of dark hair he longed to dive his fingers into. This is how I got in such a mess in the first place, he remembered: the back seat of his favorite car, the rebuilt Mustang, a lack of foresight, and the next thing he knew a potentially half Irish bambino, an enraged maternal grandfather-to-be, and a guilt-provoking family priest shoved him down the aisle of St. Monica's, a place he had been trying to escape since first grade. He had begged his *innamorata* to get an abortion, but she, her whole family, and his whole family were outraged. In little ways his wife still let him know she'd never forgive him for the suggestion.

"Why do you think working-class women oppose abortion?" Rhonda asked him after he had told her his tale of entrapment over one of their marathon lunches. "Pregnancy is the only way out of their parents' house. The daughters are slaves in the family home and, if they work outside the home, the jobs are menial. Getting knocked up and married is their ticket out. The only challenge of their lives is to find a nincompoop willing to impregnate them. Unfortunately they get stuck with the nincompoop for the rest of their lives."

She saw me coming, Colin thought, as he surveyed the freshmen class, spotting a young woman who looked the way his wife had the night she lured him into the rear of the Mustang. "Fool that I am, I'd do it again."

The novelty of girl-looking wore off as the week wore on. Jamal Jones led the dullest life Colin had ever encountered, next to Sister Mildred's. Jamal left his North Philadelphia brownstone, walk-up apartment each weekday at 7 AM and traveled south on the Broad Street Subway until he reached Spring Garden Street. He went to his classes, had a bite to eat in the college cafeteria afterward, and by 3:30 he was on his way home, where he stayed until the next morning sent him back to school again on the subway. In the cafeteria, Jamal nodded acknowledgments to a number of people but always ate alone, his books open and a thick highlighter pen in hand.

"The guy's a monk," Colin reported back to Rhonda, who was now running interference for Sutor when it came to anything connected with Melanie Marconi. "He's got no life."

Rhonda instructed Colin to keep at it.

When Colin complained to Sutor that he was bored and wanted to quit the assignment, Sutor said coldly, "Do what Rhonda tells you."

As ordered, Colin followed Jamal into the subway after Jamal's last class on Friday. Instead of heading north as he had the previous four days, Jamal got on a train heading south, into the center of the city. After getting off near City Hall, in the heart of the city's legal and financial district, he made his way up Market Street and into the 1701 office complex. Colin watched Jamal walk to the bank of elevators programmed to floors 15 to 25. When Jamal got on one of the elevators, Colin followed, squeezing himself toward the back, behind three attractive women who were chatting about their Friday night plans. Distracted by the women, Colin almost missed Jamal's exit at the 24th floor. Before he could follow Jamal, the elevator doors closed and he was forced to ride to the 25th floor, wait for another elevator, and head back down. The down elevator was crowded and he had to stand at the front. He pushed 24 and, when the doors opened, he saw Jamal standing in the reception area of Cardozo Rossen Leonard talking to a lanky, dark-haired woman dressed in a slinky red dress and black spikes, who he knew instantly, even from the back, was Allison Long. Afraid she would turn and see him, Colin quickly spun around and faced his fellow travelers. "Thank God it's Friday," he remarked cheerfully.

After waiting in the lobby for about 10 minutes, Colin saw Jamal emerge from the same elevator he had ascended in, a manila envelope in his hand. Colin followed Jamal as he walked back to Broad Street, where he hopped on the line heading north, and home. Colin returned to 1701, stood to the side of the bank of elevators, and waited. Just after five o'clock, Allison Long emerged along with scores of other people racing to their Friday night rendezvous'. He was dying to see who Allison was hooking up with, and followed her to a parking lot a block away. Her car was parked on the first floor, in a reserved area. Alone, she got into her Mercedes and drove away.

When Colin called Rhonda to report what he had seen, she instructed him to get back to following Jamal.

———————————

Rhonda summoned Sutor into a private interrogation room to be sure no one else heard their conversation. Carrying two shopping bags, she sat down at a gray metal table and put both bags under her chair.

She had seen a change in Sutor over the past two weeks. He seemed both softer and more animated at the same time. He had given Rhonda a present, it's wrapping paper covered with stars. Turned out it was a Barbie doll for Carly—a black Barbie doll, in a red dress and high heels. Rhonda had pledged not to raise her daughter to model after the vampish character, but she appreciated the gesture and told Sutor so.

"You don't have to worry, Rhonda," Sutor volunteered. "It's between you, me, and your little girl." He assured her no one else knew about Carly. "It's time you brought her out of the closet, though" Sutor suggested, amused at himself for using a homosexual reference. Rhonda said she'd think about it.

Rhonda pulled out one of the shopping bags from under the table. "My mother finished these drapes last night. I have to pick up rods. I'll be over to help you put them up." Handing Sutor the second bag, she smiled and said, "This is a special housewarming gift from me to you."

Sutor reached into the bag and pulled out a box with Victoria's Secret embossed across the top. He gave her a quizzical look.

Rhonda gestured toward the box. "Open it."

Sutor picked up the lid of the box, folded back the tissue paper in it, and lifted out a purple silk bathrobe trimmed in pink piping.

"I figure she's a medium," Rhonda explained.

Sutor was moved beyond words. "What can I say?"

"Be happy, Bill," Rhonda replied.

Jamal left his house at 7 PM on Sunday night, traveling again on the Broad Street Subway. He was dressed in nicer clothes than when he had picked up the package from Allison Long. Instead of jeans he was wearing a pair of dark-colored pants and, to Colin's surprise, Jamal had a tie and jacket on under his overcoat. He was still on the train when it passed the City Hall stop, and he remained seated another ten minutes until he was in South Philadelphia, not far from the sports stadiums. Colin hoped he'd get lucky and have to follow Jamal right into a Flyers hockey game, but no such luck. Jamal got off the train at Snyder Avenue and emerged in the heart of the city's Italian community.

Jamal walked down a dark, quiet street and stopped in front of a Mom and Pop restaurant with fake Tiffany lamps visible in the window. He looked around for a minute and then waved to a woman who stepped out of a car parked across the street. Colin got a clear view of the woman wearing a long, black coat with a fur-trimmed hood covering her head. As she crossed the street and passed under a street lamp, the hood fell back and a mass of red curls tumbled out. It was Melanie Marconi. She gave Jamal a kiss on the cheek as he handed her the manila envelope, and together they disappeared into the restaurant.

Chapter Twenty-One

*B*ill Sutor sat alone in his new apartment. He leaned back on his new couch, a cup of raspberry tea resting on his new coffee table, and wished that Melanie was there with him, the Saks parking lot murder be damned. It hadn't been easy leaving his father's house. The old man's reaction to his son's departure was that he couldn't care less what Sutor did, he didn't need him and never had, the sooner Sutor left the house the better. Sutor had asked, "Is this how you want it to be?" before his father had turned his back on him. Henry Sr.'s actions hadn't made it any easier for Sutor to drive away from the house where his mother had raised him. He even found it hard to leave behind the next-door neighbors, whose passion for each other he finally understood. He hoped he was driving toward a life with Melanie Marconi, and, if not a life, at least enough days and nights to make the effort of moving worthwhile.

Sutor had called Melanie's house repeatedly on his first Saturday in his new place. He left messages saying he'd moved to a new apartment and would be in most of the day getting organized. She hadn't called back. On Sunday morning he drove by her house, but the purple Camaro wasn't in the driveway. He stayed home most of the rest of the day, hoping she would call. By midnight, when she hadn't, he convinced himself the affair was over. He tried to remember the poem Melanie and Rhonda had discussed at their first meeting—*I am that I am, your late and lonely master, / Who knows now what magic is.* When he arrived at work on Monday morning he told Rhonda he'd just spent the worst weekend of his life.

Rhonda told Sutor to cheer up; they were making some progress on the case. "Colin did a good job of following Jamal Jones. Melanie Marconi met Jamal at an Italian restaurant in South Philly last night; the owners are Antoinette and Carlo Marconi, an aunt and uncle of Melanie's late husband, Richard."

Sutor felt annoyed that Melanie had taken the time to dine out with Jamal but hadn't returned his calls. "How does that help the case?" he asked.

"Colin interviewed Mr. and Mrs. Marconi, the aunt and uncle. He found out some interesting things."

Rhonda repeated to Sutor what Colin had told her: That he had intended to enter the restaurant as a cop asking questions about the mixed-race couple who had just left, but when he saw the name "Marconi" on the mercantile license posted over the bar, he hopped on a bar stool and ordered a beer. The restaurant was nearly empty so it had been easy to strike up a conversation with the owners.

Old army photos of Carlo Marconi were plastered around the place, and Colin showed a keen interest in them, examing each as if it were the Hope diamond. When asked his occupation, Colin honestly identified himself as a police officer, figuring these people must have at least one relative on the Philadelphia force and they'd be receptive to chatting with a colleague of a family member. He had been close. The aunt, who had introduced herself as Antoinette, mentioned, "My next door neighbor, Mrs. Angeloni, her son Tony, 18 years on the street, he'll retire soon with a pension."

After Colin remarked that he was hoping to get a bite to eat, they gave him one of the best tables in the house, in the back section of the restaurant, where a mural of St. Peter's in Rome was painted across the wall. Colin ordered *Vitello alla Milanese* and, before he had finished his *antipasti* appetizer, he had endeared himself to the Marconis' with his boyish, bumpkin manner and his revelation that he had an Italian wife and four bambinos at home.

"We're from Milan, in the north," Antoinette Marconi told him. The Marconis' were well into their 70s, a handsome couple; his hair was pure white and hers still solidly black; they were both built as if they had eaten pasta at all three meals of the day for 30 years.

"My wife's family is from the south," Colin said. In truth, he hadn't the faintest idea where his in-laws had originated, even though they had mentioned their village a thousand times.

Colin invited Antoinette to join him. She brought over a bottle of homemade wine, sat down, and poured two drinks, handing one to Colin. "Salute," she announced, holding up her glass. Colin returned the toast.

Colin proceeded to show Antoinette pictures of his wife and children, and ask her family questions: Did she have children? Nieces or nephews? Did they work in the restaurant business? Was she a grandmother?

"Wait," Antoinette declared, going behind the bar and bringing out a worn photo album. She showed him her family, page by page. He sat patiently through dozens of pictures of her son and daughter, their combined six children, and her three great-grandchildren. He listened patiently to tales about family christenings, confirmations, weddings, and funerals. When Antoinette pointed to a wedding picture of her sister, her eyes had filled. "Dead 20 years. It's like yesterday. I say a prayer for her every day." She crossed herself and continued, "Here, look. My sister's son, Ricardo, may he rest in peace. He's with his mother in heaven. He married a professor, my nephew. Had a boy. You just missed her; Melanie; nice girl." The aunt gave Colin a look of resignation. "Jewish. What can you do?" She whispered in his ear, even though there wasn't another soul around, "She sometimes comes with a friend. A Negro." She lifted her eyebrows. "Not her boyfriend, don't get the wrong idea."

"I'm sorry I didn't get to meet your niece," Colin remarked.

"Niece by marriage," Antoinette corrected him. "Not my real niece. Not family, if you know what I mean." Colin knew exactly what she meant—after more than ten years of marriage to Carmela, he was still "the Irish son-in-law," the outsider.

"How often does she visit? Do you see your nephew's boy?"

"She comes every two weeks but only brings the boy, Jesse, once in awhile. She's raising him Jewish. My nephew, he didn't care, God should forgive him." She crossed herself again. The aunt insisted she liked Melanie, even though her niece by marriage was "one of those people" and too soft on her son. "Always worrying about that boy," the aunt observed. "Already she's saving for college. She tells me she needs $25,000 a year for four years, and then some more for school after that. Would you believe she has more than half of it—$70,000?" She shrugged. "I have two children. I didn't push them to college. That's how you lose them. I warned her: Make your children better than you are and they're not around to take care of you when you're old. You know what my nephew's wife says? She says that's no reason to keep them down on the farm. We don't even have a farm so what's she talking about?"

His mouth full of veal, Colin wondered, "Where the heck does a school teacher get her hands on that kind of money?"

"Don't ask," Antoinette said, reaching to the next table to get a leftover basket of rolls for Colin. "She works overtime, teaching extra courses. She's so busy that the banks are closed by the time she gets out of work. She brings her extra money to me, and I go to the bank and get her those certificates she likes. I put them in the boy's name. Carlo thinks it's stupid to put money away and not be able to get it back for four or five years. He told her to put her savings in a box and keep it in the closet or under her bed. It will be there when a rainy day comes."

Colin took a long sip of his wine. "$70,000 already? That's a lot of overtime," he asserted.

"Too much," Antoinette replied sadly. "It's not healthy. I tell her, 'Look what happened to Ricardo.'"

Colin finished his dinner as quickly as possible. He was anxious to call Rhonda to tell her about the money. When he finished eating, he pulled a wad of cash out of his pocket to pay for his meal but Antoinette Marconi would have none of it. "No, no," she insisted, "it's our pleasure to feed a policeman."

Colin wanted to tell the aunt that he would be reimbursed for this expense, but he didn't want to raise the Marconis' suspicion about his visit. "That's very kind of you," he acquiesced, accepting the gift of an Italian dinner. "The meal was wonderful." He kissed Antoinette on the cheek and shook Carlo's hand, promising to bring his wife and her entire family there.

Carlo Marconi walked Colin to the front door and waved him off. *"Faccia attenzione,"* he said.

"I'll try," Colin answered.

Colin was on his cell phone to Rhonda before he reached his car, parked a few feet away. Rhonda was impressed with what he had found out and told him so. "Good work. You did great," she declared, offering him his second gift of the night.

Chapter Twenty-Two

"Checking up on me, I hear." It was Melanie. Sutor was tongue-tied for a minute. He had picked up the phone on his desk thinking it was the call he was expected from Rhonda.

Sutor stammered, "I wouldn't call it that." He fiddled with a Boston fern and sprayed water on it from a Windex bottle.

"What would you call it?" Melanie asked. "Aunt Antoinette got worried. She was upset that she talked about the money I give her, which of course you know about now. When she told me a nice policeman had dinner at her restaurant I figured it was someone you sent. My aunt is an old lady, and your pal tricked her."

"I'll explain it to you," Sutor said.

"It speaks for itself."

He held his breath for a moment. "Can I see you?"

"I don't know. I'm pretty pissed right now."

Sutor felt desperate but tried not to show it in his voice. The desperation was mixed with anger at how she was treating him. He wanted to ask her about the money she gave her aunt but decided not to. "Let me take you out for a cup of coffee and we'll talk."

"I'll consider it; I'll call you back."

"When?" He couldn't keep his anxiety in check. He figured if he was going to make a fool of himself, he might as well go the distance. "We can have dinner together later. I'll take you out. You can use a break."

"I eat with Jesse."

"After dinner then," Sutor suggested.

"I'll call you later."

"I'll be home tonight, after 7:00."

"I'll try to get away. Maybe we'll meet for coffee and you can explain what's going on."

Although he was dying to hold her in his arms again, coffee was better than nothing. She had a hell of a nerve asking him to explain himself. She was the one up to no good, moving money here and there. He'd get her to explain what was going on before he uttered a word. He hung up the phone, his day ruined, unless she found her way to him at some time.

She walked through the door of Café Society 20 minutes late. Sutor was glad for the time to think of something to say that wouldn't ruin his chances with her. He had solicited Rhonda's advice, and she had warned him he was in over his head, that he should end the relationship until the Lavin murder case was solved and pick it up again—if it turned out Melanie wasn't guilty. For all of Rhonda's background in human behavior, an understanding of love wasn't one of her strong suits. Even Sutor, boob that he was about relationships, knew that if he abandoned Melanie now, when he thought she was guilty, she'd never forgive him if she were found to be innocent. Conversely, if he stayed with her believing she was guilty, maybe she'd love him later if he proved she was not responsible for Miriam Lavin's death. It wasn't looking good in either case.

Sutor had gone over in his mind what he knew for sure of Melanie's involvement in the Lavin murder. There was a good chance she had been in the parking lot the night of the murder, driving the burgundy car. The car was seen on City Line Avenue, a mile from Saks, a woman and a man in it. The handbag sailed out of the burgundy car. One of Harold Rosenberg's caregivers parked a burgundy car in Harold's garage every Friday night. Even Harold Rosenberg, who loved and trusted Melanie, thought she had killed Miriam Lavin. But where did Jamal fit in? Was he the man in the car with her, the one who threw the purse Wilson Greene's way? Greene would have noticed a white woman with a black man, wouldn't he? Probably not. That left the mystery of Allison Long. Her phone number was in Miriam Lavin's handbag. And Jamal Jones knew Allison well enough to visit her at work. Maybe they were all in it together: Melanie, Jamal, Allison, and Harold. Clearly, he was losing his mind over the case—and the woman.

Before leaving the station to meet with Melanie, Sutor had given Colin the assignment of a lifetime: Watch Allison Long. "Find out who she knows, who she parties with, who she sleeps with. Where does her money come from? How does she spend it? And find out where that little Mercedes came from?"

Sutor rehearsed in his mind what he would say to Melanie when he saw her. He decided not to mention the money right now.

He stood up when she came in the door. She smiled and waved and, when she reached the little French bistro table where Sutor waited, she kissed him arduously on the lips.

"I've missed you," she declared, taking off her black coat. Sutor took her coat from her and placed it on a nearby chair. He held her chair for her as she got comfortable. There were snow flurries in her hair, and her cheeks were red from the cold. Fluffing her hair with her hand, she admitted, "I wasn't going to come but I couldn't help it." She was wearing green, a matching sweater and long skirt. A string of thin pearls fell onto the sweater and three strands of pearls dangled from her earlobes, almost reaching her shoulders. She looked at him and, unsmiling, asked, "What are we doing, Sweetie?"

Sutor couldn't remember what he had planned to say. "You look beautiful," is all he could manage.

"What are we having?" she asked, looking up at the choices listed on a blackboard pinned to the back wall of the café. Melanie ordered hazelnut decaf from the waiter who approached them, mentioning, "I'm having trouble sleeping." Sutor picked apple spice tea.

Sutor took a small box out of his jacket pocket. It was delicately wrapped in purple tissue paper and tied with a pink ribbon. He handed it across the table.

Melanie's eyes widened and she smiled broadly. "For me?" She took the box and unwrapped it. "I love presents." She blew him a kiss. "I especially love presents from lovers."

The tissue covered a delicate white Limoges box with the inscription *The Best Is Yet to Be* on the top.

"Robert Browning, I think," Sutor noted. He had checked that out with Rhonda.

"I adore it," Melanie said enthusiastically, holding the box in her hand.

"It reminds me of you," Sutor responded.

"Are we crazy?" Melanie asked.

"What do you mean?"

"Why are we here?" Melanie put the gift back in the tissue and tied the box again.

"You know why I'm here," Sutor maintained.

"Tell me."

"What do you want me to say? Isn't it obvious?"

"Sex," Melanie suggested. She averted her eyes from his by toying with a packet of sugar.

"Do you want me to lie and say that's not part of it? I think about making love to you all the time. Why wouldn't I?" He reached over and took her hand. "Melanie, I'm here because I love you. I was in love with you before Florida, before we ever made love. That's why I went down there, to be with you. I couldn't stand the idea of you being away from me. I jeopardized my job to be with you. I'm jeopardizing my job right now."

Her eyes filled with tears. "It's no good, you know."

"You're wrong," he insisted.

"You think I'm a murderer," she argued. "That's why you're having me followed. If you want to know where I go, just ask me, I'll tell you."

"Melanie, I don't know if you're a murderer or not. And I'm not sure I care. I want you to know that if you did kill Miriam Lavin, I'll stand by you. I'll try to understand why you did it. I won't abandon you." He had a feeling he was saying too much and he stopped talking.

She noted, mockingly, "How romantic of you. It's clear that you think I did it."

"It's not about romance," Sutor challenged. "It's about love."

"Are you expecting a confession? Maybe in bed one night, when I'm vulnerable."

He was surprised she was so suspicious of him. "Don't you trust anyone?" he demanded.

"Men drive women into madness."

"I don't think I ever have, and it's not something I aspire to."

"You haven't had the opportunity yet."

He didn't know what to say to her. He felt checkmated. How could he agree or disagree when he knew so little about women and their internal lives? Maybe that's what drove them so crazy. "You sound like Rhonda, one of my detectives," he remarked, leaning forward and touching her cheek. "Melanie, I don't know about this madness stuff. Lately I've been a little off my rocker too. Men drive women crazy, women drive men crazy; it's the same thing. All I care about is you. I don't know what to do about the Lavin case. I hate thinking about it or working on it; I've just about let Rhonda handle it all. I don't know what to do about you. I don't know if I'm coming or going anymore."

"I'm afraid to get involved with you," Melanie confessed.

"You're already involved with me, in case you didn't notice."

"Don't mix up physical attraction with involvement. I don't think it can go further than that. We can see each other from time to time, make love, and go our separate ways; that's the most we can hope for."

"Why are you placing limits on our future?"

"I have my reasons."

"I'm entitled to know."

"Richard," she admitted sadly. "I can't reconcile myself to what life was with Richard and losing Richard."

"I can't fight a dead husband," Sutor responded.

She continued, "There's Jesse, too. I can't get involved with anyone until he leaves for college."

"Why not? He's 15, living his own life."

"Fifteen-year-olds *think* they're living their own lives. This is the time kids need their parents most. A person can't be a good parent and also be involved in a serious relationship outside of marriage."

"That's ridiculous," Sutor argued.

"The kids always suffer; they're always neglected."

"I was supporting myself totally by 15," Sutor recalled.

"That's because you're not Jewish, and that's the other thing. Gentiles see child rearing differently than Jews. They see everything differently. I married an Italian because I loved him, but it wasn't an easy life. Our values were different; our interests were different; we didn't want the same things for Jesse; we had different styles of arguing and making up. His family never accepted the marriage, or me. I swore I'd never get involved again with a man from a different culture. I know you're not Jewish, Bill, and it's a problem for me."

He didn't understand what she was saying. "I don't see why. You can be as Jewish as you want and I can be whatever it is I want."

"So what are you?"

"I can't see that it's important," Sutor replied, afraid to tell her the truth.

"What are you?" she repeated. "What's your religion?"

"I was raised Lutheran," Sutor answered, "but I'm non-practicing."

"You're of German heritage?"

"German and French." The French part was minimal but he threw it in for balance.

"Two anti-Semitic cultures. Do you consider yourself a Christian?"

"I don't know. I don't think much about religion. I don't care much about religion."

"I do, you know. I care a lot about Jews and being Jewish."

The waiter brought their coffee and tea. They drank for a while in silence. Sutor didn't know what else he could say in defense of his background. He decided that he'd have to be with her at least 20 years before telling her about his visit to Germany with Henrik. Melanie finished her coffee and looked at her watch. "I'm teaching tomorrow. I have to run."

Trying to hide his disappointment, Sutor asked, "When will I see you?"

"I don't know," Melanie said. "I think it best that you don't call me for a while. Let's give this thing a rest. When I'm ready to get involved in a way that would make you happy, I'll call you."

Melanie rose and put on her coat. She walked over to Sutor, leaned down, and kissed him lightly on the lips. Then she turned, left the café, and vanished into the night.

CHAPTER TWENTY-THREE

"I forgot how good-looking you are," Allison Long said in greeting, when Colin walked into the office she shared with two other paralegals at Cardozo Rossen Leonard. She looked different from when Colin had first met her, more sophisticated in her black wool suit, with a huge gold pin on her lapel. Her dark hair was pulled straight back into a ponytail ringed by a jeweled clip.

"Same here," Colin responded, trying to contain his surprise. He still thought her the prettiest woman he'd ever seen, the kind he dreamed he might have ended up with if it hadn't been for high school. He asked if there was some place they could talk privately.

"My place or yours?" Allison flirted.

They moved to a conference room and sat next to each other at a teak table that could seat an entire NRA convention. Allison pulled her chair up close to Colin's, crossed her legs, allowing her skirt to slide up her thigh, and leaned on the table with her elbow. "What's this about?" she purred.

Before Colin could reply, she took off her suit jacket. He could see through her pink sweater and noticed she wasn't wearing a bra. "You met with a black guy last Friday—Jamal Jones," he managed to comment, trying to concentrate on police business.

"Don't know him."

"You met with him in the reception area. You gave him an envelope."

"He must have been from a messenger service. I send out packets of legal documents all day."

"How many did you send out last Friday?"

"Three or four."

"This guy wasn't a courier."

She shrugged. "What can I tell you?" Leaning forward suggestively, she suggested, "Why don't you forget all this silliness about meetings and envelopes? Don't you have better things to do with your time?"

"Like what?"

"Like getting together with me."

"It's one of my life's goals, only there's one problem: I'm a married man," Colin responded.

"Meaning?"

"Meaning if I get caught by my wife and her family, I'm a dead man."

"There are ways," Allison persisted, taking his hand and sliding it up her leg.

"How come a drop-dead gorgeous woman like you isn't attached?"

"Who says I'm not? I see someone once in awhile."

"I'm married. How do you figure we can get together in secret?"

"No sweat. My parents have a place on the Chesapeake. We could go there. It's great in the winter. Deserted. We're on a marina. It's quiet and romantic."

"Give me some notice so I can set up my alibi."

"I'll do that," Allison retorted, abruptly rising from her chair. "I have to get back to work. You're adorable, but not worth losing a job over."

"You never met with Jamal Jones?" Colin asked again, as Allison bounded out of the conference room. "Is that what you're telling me?"

Allison disappeared without answering.

Rhonda couldn't get used to Colin's lack of education. Once, over lunch, she had asked him what the premise of the movie "Pulp Fiction" was, and he had answered, "What does premise mean?" She had clarified herself by saying "underlying motive."

Sutor had laughed at the exchange. "If he doesn't know what premise means, how the hell would he know what underlying motive means?"

Rhonda had turned to Sutor, "Then how do you communicate with him?"

"Just say, 'Colin, what was the movie about?'"

This Colin had understood. "Absolutely nothing," he asserted proudly.

With answers like this, Rhonda was sure Colin would be promoted before she was.

Today, for the first time since she had begun working with him, Rhonda was impressed with Colin. He was a car man, and this was the area of expertise in which he did his best work. "Guess who bought little Allison her little blue Mercedes?" Colin handed Rhonda a copy of an agreement of sale from a dealer.

"Jamal Jones," Rhonda guessed. She was joking but Colin didn't pick up on it.

"No. Try again."

"Bill Sutor." Rhonda had become more spirited and personable since Sutor had freed her from her secret life with Carly. She had been able to show her boss a photo of the girl and talk a little about the things the child did.

"Are you going to tell me or not?" Rhonda snapped in exasperation. "What the hell is this, Jeopardy?"

"None other than the married Jerome Eisenberg. Want to know where they meet?"

"Is this going to go on much longer?"

"The Sheraton, in Valley Forge, near Miriam Lavin's apartment, not far from my own mansion and the place I've taken many a lady to."

"How long? How often?"

"A year. Once or twice a week."

"Expensive hobby," Rhonda observed.

"Her family owns a place in St. Michaels, Maryland. I went to every luxury car agency in the area until I found the dealer in Easton who sold the car."

"What made you poke around the Eastern Shore?"

"Allison mentioned boating on the Chesapeake. A fatal error. I tracked down her family, found them listed in St. Michaels. Then I took a chance and looked up every boat registration in Maryland, Delaware, and New Jersey. I found a Nimble Nomad, a strange little boat, outboard motor, trailable, runs about 8 knots...."

"Colin! Shut up about the boat!"

"Hey, the boat's the key. It's registered in Allison's father's name, Edward Long. I found the owner of the marina it's docked at. Talked to him. He identified photos of Allison and Jerome. They hung out down there last summer." He gave her an exaggerated grin. "Are you impressed, my dear?"

She had to admit she was. "Great work. I underestimated you." She offered him the highest compliment he could aspire to: "Bill will be proud."

"That babe Allison invited me to go cruising with her. She'd dump Eisenberg for me in a second."

"You're full of it," Rhonda declared, impressed with him nevertheless.

Sutor and Rhonda waited for a night when Colin assured them Jerome Eisenberg was at the Sheraton with Allison Long before driving out to the countryside to meet Jerome's wife. Rhonda was overwhelmed by the beauty and stature of many of the homes they passed as they drove through the suburban villages with names like Coventry and Chester Springs.

"Who lives out here?" Rhonda wondered, trying to imagine herself the owner of one of the fieldstone manor houses they passed as they drove far west of the city.

"Too secluded for my taste," Sutor noted. "I'd die of boredom."

"Jerome Eisenberg isn't dying of boredom," Rhonda joked. "I wonder why he goes to a hotel in Valley Forge instead of Allison's place?"

"Society Hill is a long way from here," Sutor suggested. "This way he's almost home. It gives him more time to rock and roll. Afterward Allison can drive herself home in that little Mercedes he bought her. Not a bad exchange."

Doris Eisenberg graciously invited them into her newly built stucco and wood English Tudor after verifying their identities through a camera attached to the front doorframe. Her kitchen was as large as Fromma Freedman's but, unlike Fromma's, this one was filled with the smell of meatballs and spaghetti sauce. Two children sat at the center island playing with the remains of their meal. The boy looked about 10 and the girl only slightly younger. Mrs. Eisenberg introduced them. "Michael, Laura, say hello to our guests." The children complied with their mother's request after which she gave them permission to go to the downstairs playroom to enjoy their new Xbox. Cheery and talkative, Doris Eisenberg told Sutor and Rhonda all about the house, how she and Jerry came to buy it, what improvements they had made, and how wonderfully her kitchen worked since they had put on the new addition.

Sutor explained the reason for their visit, indicating they wished to speak to her and her husband about the Lavin murder and hoped they both could give him a few minutes.

"I'm awfully sorry," Mrs. Eisenberg informed them, "Jerry had to work late tonight. He has a big case coming up in court next week and had to take depositions." She was a plain but pleasant-looking woman whose lack of vanity allowed her to display a few white strands in her dark brown hair. She wore wire-rimmed glasses and only a dab of pink lipstick for makeup. Dressed as she was, in a black and white print skirt and white silk blouse and wearing one-inch black leather pumps on her feet, she looked more like a third-grade teacher than the creator of a million dollar software program.

Mrs. Eisenberg called Jerome's office and cell phone but got no answer on either. "He must be tied up. Can you wait?" she asked, inviting her visitors to sit down at the kitchen table. "You've come a long way and it's freezing out. I'm sorry Jerry isn't here to help you. He hates driving home late when it's this cold out." She poured two cups of tea for her guests while Sutor leafed through a gardening book from the stack on the table.

"I'm on the committee of the Philadelphia Flower Show," Mrs. Eisenberg explained.

"The show is next month," Sutor noted. "That's how I know spring is almost here. Right before the *forsythia suspensa* appear in my mother's garden."

Sutor and Mrs. Eisenberg talked awhile about the unfolding of nature. He liked the guileless woman and wondered what she saw in her lawyer husband, her cheating lawyer husband at that.

"Does your husband share your interest in gardening?" Rhonda asked, trying to get a fix on the marriage.

"Oh, yes. Jerry loves to garden out back when the weather permits and when he's home, which isn't a lot given his job and hours. Last year he planted a *cornus kousa* and a ton of bearded irises. They're his favorite. The year before he went on an azalea and hosta kick," she laughingly continued. "I don't know what he'll be up to this spring."

Rhonda avoided Sutor's eyes after that comment, least she give Jerome Eisenberg's secret away to Mrs. Eisenberg. "It's getting late, Bill," she suggested, looking at her watch.

"Maybe you can help us, Mrs. Eisenberg, so we won't have to bother your husband at his office tomorrow. Tell us about Miriam Lavin. What was she like?"

"Hated gardening. Not even much use for real flowers either. She had those phony silk arrangements on her tables. She treated me very well considering that I'm not Jewish. She believed in marriage and family and, though she had opposed my marriage to Jerry, she came around once it was finalized, particularly after I got pregnant with Michael. I worked hard to please her. She had asked me to get married by a rabbi and I did; she insisted we raise the kids Jewish and I agreed. I even converted to Judaism from Catholicism, and that took some doing on my part. I make a nice home for Jerry. She was very grateful."

"So you personally got along well with her?"

Mrs. Eisenberg chuckled. "I made it a point to get along with her. If she liked you, she treated you wonderfully. She was very good to me." She fingered the Waterford sugar bowl and creamer she had placed on the table. "She gave these to me." She pointed to a cupboard full of china and art objects that had once belonged to Melanie Marconi's mother. "Most of those are from her. She was very generous."

"What happened if she didn't like you?" Rhonda asked.

"Cut you dead," declared Mrs. Eisenberg. "She could pass you on the street and pretend she didn't know you."

"Did you ever know her to do that?"

"Only by rumor. It was kind of a family joke—'Don't cross grandma.'"

"Do you know of anyone who disliked her enough to kill her?" Sutor inquired.

"She could be extremely difficult, but people who knew her got used to it. She was a control freak. Everything had to be her way."

"What if it wasn't?" Rhonda asked. "Didn't anyone go up against her?"

"People got mad all the time, but she was an old lady and everyone humored her."

"Did your husband humor her?" Rhonda persisted.

"They got along perfectly. She relied on Jerry. He was her lawyer, handled most of her affairs and all her legal and financial work."

Rhonda took a long shot. "I wish Mr. Eisenberg was home because I understand he's an astute attorney. I wonder if he has any idea who killed his grandmother?"

"He thinks it was a carjacker or purse snatcher," Mrs. Eisenberg answered. "He says it's a hopeless situation, no one will ever be charged with the crime. He's trying to put it in the past. He doesn't want anyone to talk to him about the murder; it upsets him too much."

Rhonda said, "Sounds like they were very close. It must be hard for him."

Mrs. Eisenberg looked at the clock. It was past 8. "He doesn't realize how upset he really is. He's been throwing himself into his work to avoid thinking about what happened. He's been very quiet lately; sits in his den brooding. It's so sad. I wish I knew how to help him."

Rhonda made a casual observation, hoping to lure Doris Eisenberg into a trap. "Your house is lovely, Mrs. Eisenberg, but I don't think I could live way out here. I'd be too scared. I'd have to have a gun." She stood and looked out the kitchen window, into the darkness. "Aren't you frightened? Do you keep a gun around for protection when your husband's not home?"

"It's safe as could be out here," Mrs. Eisenberg assured Rhonda. "I have an alarm system that I keep on at night when Jerry's not here. Jerry had a gun but, after the children were born, I made him take it to the office."

"Good move," Rhonda commented. "It's better that it's in the office."

"He doesn't have it anymore. It was stolen. The cleaning people, I guess."

Sutor and Rhonda small talked with Mrs. Eisenberg a while longer as they finished their tea. Then Mrs. Eisenberg walked them to the door. "Say goodbye to the children for us," Rhonda said. Sutor added, "Your husband is a lucky man." And he meant it.

"The no good bastard," Rhonda declared as they pulled away from the Eisenberg house. It was so cold out that the heating system of the BMW just about managed to warm them. "She's a really nice lady," Rhonda continued, huddled in her quilted down coat. "He should drop dead."

Sutor was trying to put the pieces together. "So what do we have here? The married Mr. Eisenberg gets a girlfriend and the family matriarch finds out about it. Miriam Lavin liked her granddaughter-in-law and tells her grandson to get rid of his girlfriend. How's it sound so far?"

"I doubt that Miriam Lavin liked Doris but I think she would have sided with her when push came to shove over Jerome's roaming eye. The girl had gone the distance for the Herzelman family; she's the mother of the next generation; she kept her part of the bargain. Miriam wouldn't have tolerated Jerome cheating on his wife and, God forbid, leaving her for some twit."

"How did granny find out about Allison Long?" Sutor probed. "Where did she get Allison's phone number?"

"Maybe she went to Jerome's office and Allison was there," Rhonda speculated.

Sutor didn't agree. "They were too smart for that. I suspect they never crossed paths at work except for things professional. Furthermore, I think Mrs. Eisenberg hasn't a clue. I wonder why he doesn't just run off with Allison Long?"

Rhonda understood completely. "And ruin his career?"

"The wife is loaded," Sutor suggested. "He doesn't want to give up his lifestyle."

"And the kids," Rhonda added. "Too much trouble. Too much family trouble."

"Jerome likes his dual life and has no intention of losing it."

"Good theory," Rhonda commented.

"See any problems with it?"

"Just one," Rhonda chuckled. "Some proof."

CHAPTER TWENTY-FOUR

The phone rang in Bill Sutor's house just after midnight, waking him from a sound sleep. He heard only, "I need you," and he was out of bed and on his way to taking the quickest shower in the history of running water. It took him 15 minutes to shave, dowse himself with cologne, dress in pants and sport shirt, grab his overcoat from the hall closet, and get out the door. In another ten minutes he pulled into Melanie Marconi's driveway.

She opened the front door when the spotlights came on. He saw the German shepherd at her side as soon as he came onto the porch. He hesitated, thought "to hell with it, I'd rather die trying," and pulled open the storm door. Melanie reached out to him as he came through the doorway. He held her so tightly the dog growled. Wrapping her arms around him, she buried her head in his neck.

"Hal's dead," she cried, tears running down her face.

He had known that from the moment he picked up the phone. "Yes," he confirmed, stroking her hair, which was more disheveled than the last time he'd seen her.

"It was bad."

Sutor nodded. "I'm sorry," he murmured, not quite truthfully. From what he'd seen of the guy, his sickness, and his relationship with Melanie, Sutor figured it was time. Now maybe she could think about him a little, which she obviously had.

He led her into the living room, to the velvet couch. "Come here," he urged as he sat down. She willingly complied, and he laid her across his lap, cradling her in his left arm like she was a child. The room was dark and a bit chilly. He wished the fireplace were going so he could see her better. The dog had followed them into the living room but, after staring at Sutor for a few seconds, left and took a place in the hallway. "Jesse?" Sutor questioned. "At a friend's," Melanie whispered,

He held her close and stroked her hair; neither of them spoke for a long time.

Though he acutely desired her Sutor restrained himself. He sensed that she needed a friend tonight not a lover. "I'll stay with you," he offered.

She led him upstairs to her bedroom, a massive space decorated in white lace. They lay on the bed fully clothed. She began to sob and he gathered her in his arms and held her. After awhile they fell asleep. To Sutor's surprise she reached for him in the middle of the night. After they made love, Melanie fell asleep with her head against his chest. Sutor didn't move the rest of the night for fear of disturbing her. He lay awake, cradling her, looking at the moon through the floor-to-ceiling window directly across from the bed.

Sutor went downstairs at dawn, just as light seeped through the lace curtains in Melanie's bedroom. The dog greeted him at the bottom of the steps. He forced himself to pat the dog on the head hoping she would take a liking to him, even if it were doubtful he ever would to her. That was enough for Gertrude, who followed him into the kitchen and sat by his side while he surveyed the cabinets for what he needed.

He noticed a 3 x 5 card stuck to the front of the refrigerator by a magnet. On it was written a quote, from a novel she had read, he assumed: *It was like a stone, something in me. The way a hook needles a fish, it hurt when I tried to move away from it. And then it turned and I was worse. Love sunk like that in me once—like a hook—so I couldn't think of anyone else. It was a long, long time ago, too long. And I was alone, dwelling.* At the bottom of the card she had added Richard. There was a recipe for something called *sufganiyot* next to it, with a note attached that read, "bring down menorah."

There were photographs in frames everywhere. Jesse as a baby. Melanie holding Jesse as a baby. Richard bathing Jesse as a baby. Jesse and the dog, both as babies. Melanie in a wedding gown, dancing with an older man—Morrie, he supposed. Melanie, Richard, and Jesse as a family. Melanie and Harold Rosenberg in front of the Eiffel Tower. Sutor tried to imagine living among the odd pottery, strange sounding foods, sentimental pictures, dog hair, and abject grief of Melanie Marconi's life. He couldn't envision it. Rhonda had said he was anti a lot of things. She was right. He liked a simple life, with no encumbrances. When he ate out, he went to one of two places serving the meal he most enjoyed: a sirloin steak and baked potato. There was a store in the suburbs that sold him his suits, shirts, ties, underwear, and shoes, items he always paid for with a personal check, on the spot. He'd used the same barber for 20 years, and the same doctor, dentist, and accountant.

The only thing he changed every three years was the date of his car, but not its make or color.

A batch of CDs was strewn on the kitchen table: Bob Seeger, Van Morrison, Nina Simone, Joe Cocker, Chris Isaak, Emmylou Harris, Paul Simon. Most of the names were foreign to him. Lord, give me strength, he thought. How am I going to love this woman properly? What changes in myself do I have to make? How do I make them?

She had called herself a madwoman, Lilith, the first wife of Adam. How in Adam's name had an Italian man from South Philadelphia come to marry her? And how did this madwoman come to love this Italian man? And please, God, would this beautiful, strange first wife of Adam ever come to love him?

Sutor made a cup of coffee for her and tea for himself. He looked through the kitchen closet and cabinets until he found a tray. There was a bouquet of pink mini carnations in the center of the kitchen table; he broke a stem off, placed it in a glass of water, and put it on the tray. The table was littered with bills, magazines, and catalogs. Detective that he was, he skimmed the debris. An American Express statement, *Sports Illustrated*—for Jesse, he assumed—*Time Magazine, Country Homes*, three different VISA bills, a Bloomingdales' catalog. Her checkbook was on the table, and he had glanced at the balance column. There was no figure there; she had never once reconciled her account. Her address book lay open to a page that held the business card of a funeral director. He had taken a minute to look through the book, automatically turning to the *L's*. Morrie and Miriam Lavin were in there. Next to Morrie's name was a date, 10/10, a birthday maybe, or date of death. A line was drawn across Miriam's name with a sketch of a happy face next to it. Underneath this listing were four more addresses and phone numbers, none of them beginning with *L*. Letters, easily deciphered, coded the information. *BE* was obviously Bernice Eisenberg and *SG* represented Susan Ganardo, Miriam's daughters. *JE* had to be Jerome Eisenberg, the lawyer grandson. There was another citation, *AL*. Sutor couldn't think straight this morning. *AL*. He had wanted to call Rhonda to ask about *AL* but had been afraid to break the madwoman's spell. Then he realized that *AL* meant Allison Long.

The dog Gertrude came up to him, drawing him away from his spying. Sutor thanked the dog for pulling him back to his task. "Good girl," he said. The dog walked to the kitchen door, whined, and looked at him. He remembered that on his first visit to the house the dog had been locked in the yard. He felt safe in opening the back door and letting the animal out. It occurred to him that this was probably what poor, dead Richard had done every morning of his married life. "Sorry, pal," Sutor said aloud to the photo of his predecessor.

He carried the tray up to the bedroom. It was a Wednesday morning, and he wondered if she had classes to teach. She stirred when he came in the room. "Gertrude," she mumbled from beneath the comforter. She was curled on her side with her back toward the door. "I have to let Gertrude out."

"I let her out already," Sutor responded, feeling like a husband, which never in his life before this had he aspired to be. He went around to her side of the bed, put the tray on the night table, and sat down on the lacy comforter. She rolled over on her back and pushed herself up with her hand. "Thank you," she said softly as the blankets dropped away from her, exposing her breasts.

"For what?" He tucked two pillows behind her so she would be comfortable, then he pulled the comforter up around her.

"For being with me."

He held her cup of coffee as she had sipped from it. She told him that it had taken Harold Rosenberg four days to die. His TPN had been taken away, leaving him without food. The morphine drip hadn't worked because he had built up a tolerance for pain medication, so the hydration had been turned off. A drug called Versed, used for surgical sedation, had been tried but failed. Hal grew weaker and grayer every day, until he begged her to shoot him in the name of friendship, out of love, finally from a place of mercy. She refused. He insisted she didn't love him; she told him he was confusing love with courage. When the end came, she wasn't with him because she had gone downstairs for a while and had fallen asleep on the living room couch. After the private duty nurse woke her to report there were no longer any vital signs, Melanie and the nurse went back upstairs together. The nurse had already straightened out the bed and fixed the body into an acceptable position. Harold Rosenberg's eyes were partially open and he didn't looked like himself, nor did he look at peace. "He looked painfully, miserably, horribly human no more."

The cup and saucer in Sutor's hands shook slightly. As much as he tried to understand it, Sutor couldn't fathom a friendship that demanded so much. He realized that Melanie was capable of doing extraordinary things, and the scope of those things was something he didn't want to think about. "Do you want me to stay with you today?" He figured after more than 20 years on the job, he was entitled to take a personal day, even though it might cost him his pension if the reason for his absence were known. "Are you going into the college?"

"No," she replied, "I have to make funeral arrangements for Hal today. I'm going to pick up his mother at noon. I took off the whole week knowing this was coming. The funeral will most likely be tomorrow and then shivah will start. Hal was religious so there's a lot to do."

Sutor insisted, "Call me if you need me."

"I already did, didn't I?" she responded, smiling.

He forced himself to tell her what he was feeling so he wouldn't be tortured with the secret of it all day. "Melanie, you should know this before I go: I love you. I've loved you from the moment I walked into your office at the college."

"It's the sex," Melanie retorted.

"We weren't having sex in your office that first day."

"Weren't we?" she teased.

She touched his cheek and admitted, "If I were ever to love again, I would pick a man like you."

It was the best he could hope for and he had accepted the fractional compliment. "I'm a patient man," he advised—an understatement considering his lifelong wait to fall in love. He took the empty cup from her and stood up to set it on the tray.

She moved toward the other side of the bed and turned down the comforter where he had been sitting. "Can you go in a little late?"

He hesitated until he saw her rounded body under the covers. "As late as you want," he declared.

CHAPTER TWENTY-FIVE

Sutor took an inconspicuous place in the next to the last pew of Goldsteins' Chapel, the same funeral home that had ushered Miriam Lavin to her final resting place. He was relieved to see Melanie Marconi in the front row looking rested and composed, and he flattered himself that her demeanor had everything to do with the comfort he had provided two nights earlier. She was dressed in a floor-length black velvet skirt and black sweater, and her scarlet hair was pinned up with a black, feathered clip. Jesse was by her side, wearing a suit and tie and looking like a miniature version of his late father. Harold Rosenberg's mother, weeping into a tissue, was sitting on the other side of Melanie.

The chapel was brimming with people, more than half of them couples of the same gender. A handsome young man with long blond hair gathered into a ponytail sat down next to Sutor. He leaned forward and put out his hand in introduction. "I'm Sage, an old lover of Hal's." Sutor took a deep breath and reached out to the man. "Bill here," he said. "A friend of a friend."

Bill took a prayer book out of the slot in front of him, opened it, and pretended to read the Hebrew prayers. Sage tried to strike up a conversation. "I met Hal when...."

A woman with white hair, seated across the room, waved to a man entering the chapel through the door behind Sutor. Sutor waved in the woman's direction. "Excuse me," he announced to his new pal, "I just spotted my wife." Rising to let Sutor out of the pew, Sage commented, "Nice meeting you." Sutor didn't answer. He moved quickly up the aisle and stood in the back of the chapel for the rest of the service.

Sutor recognized the officiating rabbi as the woman he had seen in Harold Rosenberg's bedroom, but he couldn't recall her name. It had been one of those experiences he wanted to forget. The rabbi began the service with a verse written by a woman named Mimi; it had half the audience in tears. *The soul has its own schedule. While we check the clock, talk on the phone, plan vacations or rush to work, the soul consults its inner ledger, asking: "Have I done what I have come to do? Have I settled accounts?" While the cat licks her back, the water boils, the nurse makes a joke and checks your pulse, the soul tallies each victory with its pain and asks: "Have I made my mark? Have I set things right?" While the car engine sputters and the coffee steams, the soul—full of longing—stands in the doorway and asks, "Can they live without me? Have I suffered enough?" Last Friday you answered, "Yes."*

The rabbi spoke of Rosenberg's spirit as he tackled the disease that had robbed him of his youth. After leading the congregation in a number of Hebrew prayers, she invited audience participation, turning the Jewish ceremony into a Quaker meeting. A series of Harold Rosenberg's friends took to the pulpit to describe their own relationship with

Rosenberg. One dark-haired young man admitted to having had a long affair with Harold, during which time the couple had traveled to Greece and Spain. A bald-headed former lover wearing a camouflage jacket remembered Augusts in Provincetown and winter weeks in Key West. A pockmarked woman wearing a housedress, one of the hangers-on Melanie had identified to Sutor, credited Rosenberg with helping her discover her true nature—lesbianism—leaving Sutor wondering how Rosenberg had accomplished that.

Melanie spoke last. She was escorted up to the pulpit by Jesse, who held her hand until she was situated comfortably behind the lectern. Sutor found the gesture endearing, and he vowed to remember it if he ever got close enough to the kid to compliment him. Unlike the previous speakers, Melanie didn't say much about her relationship with Rosenberg. Instead, she used the occasion to thank people in the audience, those she thought had made Rosenberg's life fulfilling. She was especially kind in her words to Rosenberg's mother, who had personally cared for her son throughout his illness. She credited Rosenberg's doctor, the rabbi who helped him accept his inevitable death, and the many people from AIDS charities who delivered food and medicine, kept bedside vigils, and even cleaned Rosenberg's house when it needed it. Melanie talked about Rosenberg's career, his realized dreams, his intelligence and sense of humor. She mentioned his good taste and manners, the two things she loved best about him. What she'd miss most, she said, was his professionally wrapped birthday presents, the bows glittering and real flowers attached.

Sutor was impressed that she said nothing self-serving, uttering not a word to describe her days and nights of caring for Rosenberg, or her suffering now that he was gone. She finished up with a piece from *Romeo and Juliet*. As she did so, tears filled her eyes and her voice quivered. *And when he shall die, / take him and cut him out in little stars, / And he will make the face of heaven so fine / That all the world will be in love with night / And pay no worship to the garish sun.*

The rabbi rose from a chair behind the lectern and put her arms around Melanie. Jesse came up the steps and took his mother by the arm to help her down to her seat. Melanie looked up as she came down the steps and glanced toward the back of the room where Sutor was standing, but it was hard to tell if she saw him through her tears.

The rabbi ended the service with the 23rd Psalm. Jesse and seven other pallbearers then carried Hal's coffin to the hearse outside the chapel's side door. The mourners were directed down the aisle, row by row. Most of them were going to the cemetery, and they hurried to their cars so that they could follow the hearse. The rabbi remained behind, sitting pensively in the first row of the pews.

Sutor approached her gingerly. "Do you have a minute?" he asked, startling her. He showed her his badge. The rabbi greeted him, saying she remembered him from their previous meeting. Sutor apologized for forgetting her name. "Getz," she reminded him. "Rabbi Getz." Sutor asked if he could drive her to the cemetery so that they could talk, but the rabbi informed him that she wasn't going to the cemetery, adding, "Someone else is doing the service there."

"We can talk now," she suggested, rising from the bench and leading Sutor to a sitting area behind the chapel. As they seated themselves on a red velvet loveseat, Sutor observed her long, brown tweed skirt and beige blouse buttoned to the top. Like most men who had no understanding of lesbianism, Sutor thought that if the rabbi would only feminize her wardrobe, change her hairstyle, and put on a little lipstick, she could find a boyfriend and put aside her perverted lifestyle. "I understand you were Harold Rosenberg's spiritual advisor," Sutor began. "You helped him."

"Yes," the rabbi concurred, "I helped him reconnect with Judaism. He was a Bar Mitzvah when he was 13 but he lost track of his roots after that."

Sutor, who was trying to lose track of his own roots, acknowledged, "I can understand how that can happen." Continuing the conversation, he suggested, "You and Mr. Rosenberg must have gotten very close."

"We did, thank God. I hope I helped him to die in peace."

"I'd like to ask you about some of the things he might have talked about." Sutor was trying his best to be tactful. He'd never had a conversation with a rabbi before and he didn't know the rules of etiquette in such a situation. The relationship between the rabbi and her flock seemed to be less deferential than he remembered it being between Reverend Mirkin, the Lutheran pastor of his childhood, and the church congregants.

"I can't reveal what Hal and I talked about," the rabbi noted. "I consider our talks confidential."

"Now that he's gone, I don't think it's a breach of confidentiality to talk about some of the things he might have revealed to you."

"The relationship exists whether Hal is alive or dead."

"I respect that," Sutor responded, "and I respect you for feeling that way. But I hate to think that Harold's name is about to be besmirched for something he didn't do."

"What do you mean? Why would Hal's name be besmirched?"

"Was he capable of murder?" Sutor asked.

"The man wouldn't kill a moth when it flew into the house. He rescued stray cats."

Sutor took Rosenberg's letter from his pocket. "He confessed to the murder of Miriam Marconi's stepmother," he related, handing the letter to Rabbi Getz. "How do you explain this?"

Rabbi Getz took the letter from Sutor. She shook her head as she read it. "This is ridiculous," she exclaimed. "There's an explanation but I'd rather not talk about it."

"You have to talk about it," Sutor insisted. "We're talking about murder."

"Hal wouldn't want me to."

"You have to talk about it," Sutor repeated,

"He wouldn't want anybody to get into difficulty."

"Anybody or somebody specific?"

"Somebody specific."

"Who?" urged Sutor.

The rabbi gave the letter back to Sutor. "I'd rather not say."

"Look, Rabbi Getz, I don't know a lot about Judaism, but I assume it's a religion that does not condone killing."

"On the contrary, killing is often justified. There is a lot of smiting in the Old Testament."

"Well, murder then. I don't imagine murder is condoned."

"It isn't."

"So help me catch a murderer."

"How can I possibly do that?"

"Who was Harold protecting? You know and I know that this murder wasn't the final act of a dying man. I hardly think Miriam Lavin was on Harold's mind when he was hooking up those tubes. Someone else was on his mind, though, and I want to know who it was."

"I can give you a name," the rabbi observed, "but I don't know if this is the guilty party."

"I'll figure that out," Sutor responded. "Just tell me why Harold Rosenberg wrote that confession."

The rabbi looked away. "I'm not sure I should be doing this. I don't know if this is what Hal would want."

Sutor appealed to her sense of friendship and the ambivalence he detected. "Do you, as Hal's friend, want the case to be closed with Hal's name on the file as a murderer? I assume he lived a decent, law-abiding life. It doesn't seem that he deserves this."

"He was protecting his friend Melanie," the rabbi admitted, "He didn't want her to be charged with the murder."

"Why would she be charged with the murder?"

Tears formed in the rabbi's eyes. "I hope Hal doesn't hate me for this," she murmured, looking down at the floor. "Melanie Marconi was in the Saks garage the night of the killing."

"How do you know that?" Sutor felt his heart rate increase at hearing this. He began to perspire so heavily that he could feel his shirt getting wet under his jacket.

"Hal told me. Two days after the murder, he was in bed and I was reading the Sunday *Inquirer* to him. He liked to keep up with the news but he had trouble with his vision, so I read the paper to him. I stayed with Hal for two hours every Sunday morning. After he listened to the newspaper story about the murder in the garage, Hal said, 'I hope they don't find out about Melanie.' 'Find out what about Melanie?' I asked, and he replied, 'She was there. In the garage.' I asked him why in the world Melanie would be in the Saks Fifth Avenue garage on a Friday night, which was her night to stay with him. It wasn't like her to miss her night or even be late. The schedule was set. But Hal told me that Melanie had gotten to his house until after 10:00 that night; generally she came about eight o'clock."

"Did he think she committed the murder?"

"He didn't say."

"Did you get the feeling he thought she had?"

"I got the feeling he was worried that she might have."

"Would he cover for her if he thought she did it?"

"Wouldn't you?" the rabbi exclaimed, startling him.

"What makes you say that?" Sutor asked, wondering if the rabbi had telepathic powers.

"She's a pretty woman. If she were gay, I'd cover for her myself."

He wondered if Melanie would be flattered by such a compliment. "Would Harold cover for her if he thought she did it?" he repeated.

"Undoubtedly," the rabbi declared. "Why wouldn't he? What did he have to lose?"

"Would he have approved if she had?" quickly adding, "If it turns out she did it."

"That wouldn't have mattered to him. Whether he approved or disapproved of an action, he believed that people have to do whatever it is they have to do. He and Melanie were alike in that respect. They both would have sworn by anything the other did."

"You're saying that even if he was against it, if Melanie killed Miriam Lavin, Harold would have protected her."

It occurred to him that he had more in common with Rosenberg than he'd ever imagined.

"Yes," the rabbi insisted. "He loved her. Isn't that what love is all about?"

Indeed.

The rabbi asked Sutor if he was driving down Broad Street toward the city. She had parked her car at Harold Rosenberg's house and come to the funeral in a limo with the immediate family. Sutor wasn't heading that way but decided to use the opportunity to explore something that was on his mind. It took him most of the 20-minute trip to get up the courage to say his piece. Just as they reach Hal Rosenberg' street, Sutor said, "Rabbi Getz, I was raised as a Lutheran but I'd like to learn more about Judaism." He quickly added, "Not for conversion but just out of interest. Some of my friends are Jewish, and I think I should know more about their religion."

Rabbi Getz suggested a number of books, noting it depended on how strict a faith his friends adhered to. She said there were many parts to the religion, the philosophy, the history, the holiday rituals. What was he most interested in?

"I don't know," Sutor admitted. "I just want to know enough to get by, I guess."

The rabbi was amused. "Enough to get by what?"

Sutor drove up the driveway to Rosenberg's house. The rabbi got out of his car and thanked him for the lift. "You don't just get by in Judaism," she advised Sutor before closing the car door, "just as you don't just get by in life. You jump in with both feet, commit to it, embrace it. Then it will become a part of you forever."

Sutor thought of Melanie. "I have one foot in," he told the rabbi, knowing it wouldn't take much before the other followed.

Chapter Twenty-Six

Colin brought them the proof they needed, but there were still some missing pieces. "I personally went to every car rental agency on the Eastern shore," Colin declared, triumphantly throwing a receipt from a Hertz agency onto Rhonda's desk where she was going over her Jamal Jones file with Sutor. "A discount on Daddy's senior citizen's card, the cheap bastards. A burgundy Malibu, rented the morning of the Lavin murder in Cambridge, Maryland, returned the following day. Mileage to Philadelphia and back and not much more."

"It doesn't make sense," Sutor argued. "Fromma Freedman identified a redhead, probably Melanie Marconi, as the woman in the parking lot driving the burgundy car."

"It's weird alright," Colin agreed. "Maybe Melanie Marconi and Allison Long are friends who planned and carried out the murder together. I wonder which one drove the Malibu?"

Rhonda looked at Colin in disbelief. "Stick to tracing cars," she suggested. "Stay away from homicide theory."

Sutor turned to Rhonda. "Fromma Freedman definitely said she saw Melanie in the parking lot driving the burgundy Malibu?"

Rhonda nodded. "That's what she told me. I even taped the interview."

Rhonda went through her desk drawer and pulled out a miniature tape and a recorder. The three of them were listening to the playback when, after hearing Fromma's discussion of the car in the parking lot, Sutor exploded, "Run that again!"

Rhonda, startled, replayed the tape. At first she didn't realize what had transpired between herself and Fromma Freedman.

Mrs. Freedman, what did you see? I'm not leaving here until you tell me the truth.

A car.

What kind of car?

What do I know from cars? A car. I saw a car.

What was the car doing?

It was sitting there. And then it drove off.

Sitting where?

Near my parking space. Near the handicapped section of the lot. You know, I am within my full rights to park in handicap—my husband and his stroke. It gives me the right even though I don't have a license plate.

What color was the car?

I don't know. The parking lot doesn't have many lights.

Concentrate for a minute. Can you remember anything about the car? Try to remember the color.

An unusual color. Maybe purply.

Purply? You mean wine colored?

Purply. Sort of purply. dark purply, I'm not sure.

Like a burgundy maybe?
Could be. I don't know. Yeh, I guess so. Yeh, that's it.

Sutor slammed his hand down on Rhonda's desk. "You put words in her mouth! God damn it! She said the car was purply; she didn't say burgundy!"

Rhonda finally grasped the significance of her mistake. "Oh, my God. Mrs. Freedman saw a dark purple car that night. Melanie Marconi drives a purple car."

Colin chimed in. "She even told us what kind of purple car it was."

Rhonda looked puzzled.

"Play the husband's part again," Colin directed.

Sutor fast-forwarded to Sam Freedman's part in the discussion.

Any idea about the year?"
New.
How do you know that?
It looked like the car my husband was going to buy for my son, against my advice, I might add. He never thinks enough is enough when it comes to the kids.
Do you know what kind of car it was?
No.
But it looked familiar?
It looked like my son's car-to-be, which, for all I know, he already owns.
Would you please ask your husband what kind of car he and your son were looking at?

Rhonda avoided Sutor's gaze as she listened to Sam Freedman on the tape.

The year, make, and model of the car you were planning to buy your son.
Which son? I bought all three of them cars.

Which son, Mrs. Freedman?

The last one.

Does he have a name?

Stephen.

He's looking at a Corvette. It's loaded—GPS system, satellite radio, the works.

"A purple Corvette?" Rhonda interjected. "Melanie doesn't have a purple Corvette."

Colin spoke authoritatively. "It's easy to mix up a Corvette and a Camaro. Similar body type and design. The woman saw a purple sports car in the parking lot, of that we can be sure. And a woman was driving it."

Sutor played the rest of the tape.

Did you get a look at the driver of the car you saw the night of the Lavin murder?"

A woman was driving. I didn't see her clearly. I only saw her for a second, driving away from where my car was parked. I didn't think much of it then, and I don't think much of it now.

Did you hear anything? A shot, maybe?

No. I had just come into the parking lot and was walking toward my car.

Did you notice a license plate number?

Of course not. I would have told you if I had, wouldn't I?

How many people were in the car? Anyone besides the woman?

Just the woman.

Think carefully, Mrs. Freedman. Did you notice anything distinctive about the woman? Her face? Her clothes? Did you recognize her?

I didn't notice anything.

She drove past you, didn't she? You must have seen something. What else can I tell you?

Was she white or black?

White. Definitely white.

Are you sure?

Sure I'm sure.

What make you so positive?

How many black women do you know who have red hair?

"What does it mean?" Colin asked.

Sutor saw it clearly and laid it out for Colin and Rhonda. "Mrs. Freedman did see Melanie. There were two cars in the parking lot that night. Melanie Marconi was in her purple Camaro, and Allison, either with or without Jerome Eisenberg, was in the burgundy Malibu. Mrs. Freedman didn't see the Malibu. It had come and gone by the time Mrs. Freedman got to the parking lot."

Rhonda was so upset she was trembling. "I'm sorry, Bill."

Sutor didn't answer but continued unraveling the chain of events. "It makes sense now. Melanie Marconi witnessed the murder. She was in the parking lot, driving the purple Camaro. She was following Miriam Lavin or Jerome Eisenberg."

Rhonda finished the scenario. "She saw the murder and now she's blackmailing Jerome Eisenberg. He's passing money through Allison to Jamal. Jamal is giving the money to Melanie and she's slipping it to her aunt, who's putting it in the bank."

"So who did the killing?" Colin asked.

"The loving grandson," Sutor said, in relief, "and his girlfriend. They rented the Malibu in Cambridge, drove up to Saks, and shot Miriam. They took her handbag and threw it out to Wilson Greene, minding his own business on City Line."

Rhonda added, "They didn't know at the time that Melanie Marconi, alone in her Camaro, had seen them. Wilson Greene stated there were two people in the burgundy car. They were Eisenberg and Allison."

"We knew the murder was personal from the looks of Miriam's injuries," Colin observed. "This personal we never guessed," he acknowledged, shaking his head. "The grandson. Who would have thought it?"

Rhonda was still upset that she had set the investigation off its course for so long. "Bill, I was careless. I screwed up."

"Yes, you did," Sutor agreed coldly. "Now make up for it and go trace the money. Where's Eisenberg getting it? Certainly not from his wife. Go see Kaplan. He's the executor of Miriam's estate. Eisenberg chose him even though he and Miriam were on the outs. He knows something. This time no socializing, Rhonda. Find out what we need to know."

Colin sensed the tension between Sutor and Rhonda. In an effort to break the spell, he joked, "Does this mean I won't get to sail the Chesapeake with Allison?"

"In about 40 years," Sutor answered. "When she gets out of jail."

Chapter Twenty-Seven

"Where's Jerome Eisenberg getting the money he's giving to Melanie Marconi?" Rhonda confronted Alan Kaplan in his office. She arrived unannounced and, despite her attitude, he was pleased to see her.

"Rhonda! How are you?" He rose from his desk and came around to greet her. "I've tried to call you." He gestured toward a chair. "Sit down. We'll talk." The man didn't have a worry in the world.

Rhonda sat down and Kaplan returned to his desk chair. "I enjoyed having lunch with you. Can we graduate to dinner now?"

"I'm here on business only, Alan. We need some information, off the record and confidential. I know there's the tricky matter of attorney-client privilege, but this concerns you as much as your client. We want to know about Jerome Eisenberg's money." Despite herself she was glad she had worn her Perry Ellis navy wool suit, which made her look younger, and slim.

"What money are you talking about?" Kaplan leaned back in his chair.

"You know exactly what money I'm talking about. We think you're in cahoots with Eisenberg in siphoning funds from the estate to Melanie Marconi. We want to know why. Are you writing checks to Eisenberg out of the estate account?"

"As executor of the estate, I've abided by the letter of the law. I'm not about to jeopardize my license and career for Jerry Eisenberg or anyone else by doing something illegal."

Rhonda began to strong-arm Kaplan. "You're going to jeopardize a lot more than your license," she warned him. "You're going to jeopardize your freedom. My boss wants to charge you with being an accessory after the fact to murder. I offered to talk to you first."

Kaplan shot forward in his chair. "What! It's ludicrous! I had nothing to do with Miriam Lavin's murder."

"You're taking money from her estate account."

"Only my executor's fee. Not a dime more."

"You're giving Jerome Eisenberg money from the estate account."

"No, I'm not."

Rhonda rose to go. "We're not getting anywhere here. I just wanted to let you know what's going on."

"Wait!" Kaplan pressed a button on his phone and instructed his secretary to bring him the Lavin file. "Please, Rhonda, sit down. Relax a minute."

"I'm out of relaxing time," Rhonda countered. "We're down to the wire on this, Alan. You're either in or out." She couldn't stop thinking about her mistake and desperately wanted to hand Sutor something that would make up for it.

They waited in silence until Kaplan' secretary dropped a thick manila folder on his desk. Kaplan skimmed the pages until he got to the document he was looking for. "I'm Jerry's attorney, Rhonda. I'm held to privilege here."

"We'll keep it off the record," Rhonda offered again. "My word on this is good. We need the story. We'll pull it together our way."

Kaplan handed the document to Rhonda. "Jerry gave this to me after his grandmother's death. Said he had found it among her papers. It's a promissory note for a $100,000, payable to Melanie Marconi. It's dated a week before Miriam's murder."

"Miriam Lavin promised to pay Melanie that kind of money? It doesn't make any sense," Rhonda declared.

"I think the note is a forgery. Eisenberg gave it to me when he hired me to handle the estate. The estate is substantial so it meant a nice piece of change for me. There was one condition attached to the agreement: I'd pay the money in cash to Melanie in installments, as we cash in Miriam's assets. The money is paid through Allison Long. Melanie Marconi has something on Jerry. What it is, I don't know; and I don't want to know. Six months ago Melanie sent a nasty note to Miriam Lavin informing her that Jerry was having an affair with Allison Long. Miriam hit the roof, called Allison and threatened to ruin her, told Jerry she'd cut him out of her will and not leave him a cent if he didn't end the affair. That's all I know. Honest. All I do is get the money, legally, I might point out again, and pass it on to Jerry. That piece of paper makes taking the money out of estate funds completely legal."

"How did Melanie find out about the affair?"

"She was following both Miriam and Jerry, and sometimes Miriam's daughters, trying to annoy and intimidate the Herzelman family by video recording them as they went about their business. She used a digital camera or her cell phone. Sometimes she'd just sit outside Jerry's house in the country. Twice she appeared in the courtroom when he had a trial to handle. She walked into his health club a couple of times and filmed him on the Stairmaster. She has this harebrained idea that her son is owed $100,000. She was determined to get the money out of Miriam and the family, even to the point of harassing them at work and home to do it. Both Miriam and Jerry wanted Melanie arrested, but it's not illegal to sit in a courtroom or follow someone into a movie theater or restaurant. Melanie never spoke to them, she never threatened them, so there was nothing they could do about her harassment."

"Did it do any good?" Rhonda asked. "Was Miriam paying Melanie before she died?"

"Miriam wasn't paying, but I think Jerry was. Once Melanie let Miriam know about Jerry's affair, Jerry swore to his grandmother he'd give up Allison. Of course, didn't. Melanie knew he hadn't because of her habit of trailing him. She let Jerry know she was set to go to his wife next. Jerry freaked out about that. If Miriam and Doris pounced on him together, Jerry wouldn't have been worth as much as a chopped liver sandwich. Doris would divorce him and take the kids and the money. Miriam would have changed her will. Poor Jerry would have been left with that crummy job of his and, you better believe, pretty Allison would have been gone too. He was giving Melanie money to keep her mouth closed. He was giving her money before Miriam died, and he kept it up afterward."

"Why didn't he give Allison up? Wouldn't it have been simpler?"

"Have you seen Allison Long?" Kaplan asked. "Her legs reach to places Jerry has only dreamed of going in his teenage fantasies. A man like him gets a woman like her once a Purim."

Rhonda, feeling a tad of jealousy over Kaplan's description of Allison, observed, "A woman like that doesn't come cheaply to a man like Jerome."

"Like I've said before, you get what you pay for," Kaplan retorted.

"Where was he getting the money before Miriam died and you guys began dipping into the estate account?"

Kaplan flinched. "That hurts, Rhonda." Then he laughed out loud. "The guy was struggling. With what Allison costs him, he didn't have a lot of extra change. He paid Melanie a little here and a little there. With Miriam dead he can pay her off and be rid of her."

Rhonda was relieved to have gotten the information Sutor sent her for. "I'd like a copy of this note."

Kaplan buzzed for his secretary again and, when she appeared, he handed her the document. While they waited for the copy, Alan Kaplan relaxed enough to ask Rhonda out again. "Dinner tonight? You owe it to me after threatening me with life in prison."

"I don't think so," Rhonda replied. "This case takes all my time. I haven't got a minute to spare."

"The case will be over some day. How about then?"

"Alan, you should know that I have a little girl. I'm a single parent." She couldn't believe she had blurted that out.

"I'll pay for your babysitter, or you can bring your daughter along."

"You don't mind?" Sutor had been right: there was something freeing about owning up to Carly.

"What's to mind? I like kids. I have two of my own, remember? Do you have a picture of your daughter with you?"

Rhonda opened her purse and took out a photo of Carly sitting on Santa Claus's lap. She handed it across the desk. "Last Christmas," she explained.

"Cute kid," Kaplan remarked. "I'll bring my five-year-old along when we go out."

Rhonda rose to go. "I'll think about it, but not until this case is over. I won't take any more of your time today. I'll pick up the note from your secretary on my way out."

Kaplan walked Rhonda to the door. "I know what's going on in your mind, Rhonda, but nothing about you is a problem to me. I think you're a terrific woman. I like being with you. That's all. If you want, we'll just be friends."

"I'd like that," Rhonda replied. "For now, that's good." She kissed him on the cheek and walked out of the office. She wondered if she could ever be worth as much to Alan Kaplan or any man as Allison Long was to Jerome Eisenberg and Melanie Marconi was to Bill Sutor.

CHAPTER TWENTY-EIGHT

Sutor surprised Melanie by appearing at her office just after her last class of the day. Jamal Jones was there when he arrived, sitting in a chair next to Melanie's desk.

In a tone that made it clear he had come about serious business, Sutor said to Jamal, "Please excuse us."

Not intimidated, Jamal turned to Melanie, "Want me to leave?"

"It's OK. I'll see you later," Melanie replied, looking up from her work.

Jamal stood and breezed past Sutor without speaking to him.

Melanie was working at her laptop. "Hemingway's Women. A new lecture." She continued to type, her eyes on the computer screen. "Moment of truth," she declared, "the choice we make determines the rest of our days. This is what Hemingway found out when he left his second wife for a woman he had met at a Key West bar."

"I've already chosen how I want to spend the rest of my days," Sutor announced, standing in the doorway. "This is something different."

She swiveled in her chair to face him. "Have you come to arrest me for murder?" She pulled a page out of her printer and began editing it.

"No."

She looked up, surprised. "What then? Why are you so somber today?"

Sutor came into the office, closed the door behind him, and sat down at a chair next to her desk. He closed the lid on her laptop so she couldn't avoid him. "You were in the Saks parking lot the night of Miriam Lavin's murder."

"Was I?" She looked directly into his eyes.

"I know you were there. You were following either Miriam or Jerome and you stumbled upon the murder."

"Someone identified me?"

"Your car, yes."

"And me driving?" She thought Sutor was bluffing and wasn't the least concerned.

"Why did Jamal meet with Allison Long?"

"Ask Jamal."

"I don't have to ask Jamal. I know what happened."

"Pray tell," Melanie said.

"Here's what I think. You were following either Miriam Lavin or Jerome Eisenberg or Allison Long. You saw Jerome or Allison shoot Miriam. You probably have it on videotape, maybe on your cell phone. You're getting money from Allison Long, who's getting it from Jerome Eisenberg. We've checked up on Allison Long. We know she rented a burgundy Malibu in Maryland the week of the killing. The killer or killers drove a burgundy Malibu." He pulled his chair closer to Melanie to face her directly with his accusations. "Melanie, you saw the murder and you're blackmailing Jerome Eisenberg. You've given Aunt Antoinette $70,000 over to invest in Jesse's name."

"Interesting theory," Melanie suggested.

"Blackmail is not a theory, it's a serious crime," Sutor reminded her. "So is obstructing justice."

"Obstructing justice? Isn't that what you guys do? Miriam Lavin robbed and killed my father. What kind of justice did he get?"

"This isn't about Miriam Lavin and your father. It's about you and Jerome."

Her answer convinced him his theory was correct: "It's not blackmail, it's about rightness. The Herzelman family has to make right what their mother made wrong. It's about redemption."

"Redemption?"

"In Jewish law that when you do something wrong you can't just be sorry; you have to redeem yourself. Miriam robbed my son. She's not alive to redeem herself so her family must do it for her."

"Are you telling me that Jerome Eisenberg voluntarily decided to redeem his grandmother's thievery?"

"He was convinced it was the right thing to do. It was in his family's best interest. He stole a hundred thousand dollars from my son's trust fund. I intend to get it back. Every cent. Fair really is foul, isn't it?"

Sutor became furious. He was tired of her hiding behind poetry and literature, her invisible allies when she wanted to justify herself. She was so busy intellectualizing about life, she missed the reality of it. "Goddamn it, Melanie, this isn't funny. You're in over your head. Jerome and Allison murdered Miriam and you were a witness to it. You've been withholding information. You can be charged as an accessory to murder for being there and watching it. If they're charged, they might even say they saw you do it. Melanie, let me handle this. If Jerome and Allison murdered Miriam, and they know you saw them, they might kill you too."

"They can try."

Sutor grabbed her by the arms. "What the hell do you mean 'they can try'? This is not a game." He pulled her up from her chair and shook her hard. "This is dangerous stuff. You don't know what you're doing?"

"I have insurance," Melanie challenged, breaking loose from him.

"Insurance? What insurance? What the hell are you talking about?"

"I mean, I'm insured, in case they plan to kill me."

"Are you crazy?" Sutor yelled. "Do you think that video or whatever else you have on Eisenberg is going to save you? You're naive and you're foolish. You live in this dream world: the college, that house of yours on the Main Line, these books." He waved his hand at her bookshelves. "Emily Dickinson won't protect you, Melanie, and neither will Hemingway. You're out of your league."

When he saw he wasn't getting through to her, Sutor changed his tack. "Melanie, don't you care that Jerome and Allison are going to get away with committing murder?"

Melanie leaned over her desk, grabbed a picture frame and forced it upon Sutor. The photo in the frame was of a handsome elderly man, arm and arm with Melanie. "I don't view Miriam's death as murder; I see it as justice. What about my father?" She began to cry. "She killed my father. She got killed. Case closed."

Sutor put the picture down. He took hold of Melanie's hands and held them tightly together. "Melanie, I beg of you, let me handle this. You must tell me everything you know. We won't charge you with anything if you help us, I promise. You're a witness to a murder. I know you saw it all. For your own sake, please let me handle this."

Melanie pulled her hands out from his. "I can't help you," she persisted angrily. "If you understood me at all, you'd know that. For you, this is about work. For me, it's about family. This isn't about murder for me."

It took all his control not to continue trying to shake some sense into her. Instead, he pleaded, "Think about Jesse. You must think about Jesse."

"He's all I ever think about," Melanie acknowledged, "other than you."

In his present worried state, Sutor ignored her last comment, trying every way he could think of to convince her to tell him what she knew, to no avail. "This is going to end badly," he warned her. "It's going to end badly for you."

"It already ended badly for me," Melanie maintained. "My father is dead and Miriam stole his money."

"Believe me," Sutor insisted, "that's nothing compared to what Eisenberg could do to you, given what he did to his grandmother."

"It's my life," Melanie argued, "I'll take my chances with it."

"It's not just your life you're gambling with. It's Jesse's too." Sutor didn't mention that it was also his.

"Don't worry about me, Bill. Go home. I have work to do." She sat down and turned again to her computer.

Sutor saw that there was no reasoning with her. "You're putting me in a difficult position," he lectured. "I know what you did. I can't protect you legally. Everything will come out. "

"Do what you have to do," Melanie advised. "I'll be OK with that." She began typing on her laptop, in effect dismissing him.

Sutor wanted to ask her to come home with him, but it was clear she wasn't interested. Her unpredictability drove him half crazy. He never knew whether she'd be hot or cold when it came to his advances.

"I'm really busy here," Melanie announced, clearly running cold.

"Let's get together soon," Sutor suggested, despite his better judgment.

Melanie returned to her work without responding.

Sutor left her office feeling panicked. The street in front of the college was deserted, and the security guard wasn't on duty at the front desk. Sutor sat in his car for a half hour, sorting through his options, none of them appealing. He talked out loud to himself while driving home. "'Do what you have to do,' she said. But what the hell is it that I have to do?"

Chapter Twenty-Nine

Allison met Jamal Jones in Harold Rosenberg's courtyard and handed him a manila envelope. It had been snowing for the past hour, coming down heavily enough to blanket Center City in white. "This makes it an even hundred," Allison said, tightening her scarf around her neck. There were no lights on in Rosenberg's house and a *For Sale* sign was staked into a snow bank just outside the driveway.

Jamal took his hands out of his pocket and handed Allison a small video tape. "I won't be seeing you again," he declared, turning to go.

A voice came out of the darkness. "No, you won't." Jerome Eisenberg appeared suddenly, a gun in his hand.

Jamal threw up his hands when he saw the gun and yelled, "Hey, man," just as Eisenberg shot him through the heart. Jamal fell backward into a snowy bush. The envelope flew into the air, landing in the shrubbery beside the house.

"Shit. Go get that envelope," Eisenberg commanded Allison.

"I don't see it," Allison insisted, sifting through the bushes. "There's no light in this place. I can't see anything."

Eisenberg began crawling around in the bushes.

"Are you nuts?" Allison exclaimed, glancing back at Jamal's body. She saw a light go on in the bedroom window of the townhouse next door. "I'm getting out of here." She hurried across the courtyard and down the driveway to a rental car parked by the curb, another Malibu, this one black. She got in the driver's side and started the car.

"I'm coming!" Eisenberg called after her, abandoning his search. He stood, dusted himself off, ran down the driveway, and jumped into the passenger's side of the car. "Go!" he ordered. "Get the hell out of here!"

Melanie called Sutor at his apartment and blurted out, "I'm at my office. Jamal was supposed to be here two hours ago. He's never late. Something is wrong."

Sutor was watching television in the living room. He was in the middle of eating a pizza, his third such dinner of the week. He hadn't seen Melanie since their argument a few days earlier, and he was despairing of ever hearing from her again after their confrontation. "Where was he coming from?"

"A meeting with Allison Long at Hal Rosenberg's place."

Sutor jumped up, knocking the pizza box over. "Stay in the office! Do you hear me? Don't leave the building! I'm on my way." He warned her again. "You hear me, Melanie? Stay in the office!" He added frantically, "And lock the office door."

"I have to find him! I sent him there!" Melanie insisted before hanging up.

Sutor called the homicide department of the Philadelphia police department and got hold of a detective he'd worked with before. "Two down so far," the detective said in response to Sutor's inquiry about shootings that night. "One in North Philly, the other in town."

"Where in town?" Sutor asked.

"Delancey Place, near the Square."

"You get a name?"

"Let me check." The detective put Sutor on hold for five minutes while he called one of his men at the crime scene. He came back to Sutor with "A black guy named Jones." He added with a chuckle, "It's Friday night. A lot of black guys named Jones get killed on Friday night."

Sutor yelled into the phone. "That's our case. Send everybody you have on the street in town to the Temple Campus on 17th Street. There's a woman working in the Main Building. She's gonna be killed tonight. We're looking for a middle-aged white guy and a young woman. Hold on to them. They're prime suspects in our murder case." He slammed down the phone, grabbed his holster and coat from a rack by the front door, and raced out of the apartment, leaving the door partly open behind him in his haste.

The BMW held its own in the storm, hitting 60, then 70, not once skidding in the snow, but Sutor was too scared to appreciate it. He called Rhonda. She was still in the office trying to come up with a lead that would make up for the error she was torturing herself over.

"Go into Philadelphia." Sutor ordered her. "Get to Harold Rosenberg's house. Don't take the Saturn. It won't make it. Find Colin. He's still at work. He can drive that tank of his in anything. Just get there. Jamal Jones got killed. I'm heading for the college. Rhonda, I'm counting on you! The Philadelphia police are there already. Take charge of this." Before hanging up, he snapped, "You know what you have to do!"

After talking to Sutor, Melanie called Jamal on his cell phone for the tenth time, text messaged him for the third, and waited for a call back. When it didn't come she grabbed her coat and handbag and headed for the college parking lot. She had driven the Honda to the office after hearing that a snowstorm was predicted. The car could make it to Hal's place if she hurried. She stopped outside the front door of the Main Building to button her coat and pull up her hood. It was close to 10 o'clock and, except for a Hispanic couple negotiating for drugs on the corner of 17th Street and a security guard watching the storm from the front desk of the lobby, the street was deserted.

The faculty parking lot was a block from the college and Melanie walked quickly, looking behind her every so often in case a druggie saw her as easy prey. She was worried about Jamal but tried to calm herself by rationalizing that perhaps the Broad Street Subway wasn't running on time because of the bad weather. But he was hours late. It didn't make sense. She knew deep down something awful had happened to him. Bill was right, she had miscalculated. It was to be the last payment, an even hundred thousand, exactly what was stolen from her son's trust fund. She never imagined something would go wrong this close to the end. She'd go to Hal's and then up Broad Street to Jamal's and back to the college. She had gotten him involved in this, and she'd keep looking until she found him.

Melanie crossed a small street that divided two classroom buildings. It was snowing heavily, and she didn't notice a car with its lights out parked on the sidewalk outside one of the buildings. As she passed in front of it, her head down and cold hands stuffed into her coat pockets, the car pulled slowly away from the curb and turned right to follow her. Melanie reached the parking lot, a vast flat surface protected by a chain-link fence. She walked around the black-and-white striped wooden barriers blocking the entrance to the lot. The Honda was the only car in the place, parked just past the five handicapped spaces designated beyond the entrance. Melanie unlocked the Honda's driver's side door, pulled it open, and began to rub snow off the door window with her bare hand. Her back was to the lot entrance so she didn't see a black Malibu pull up and block the only way in or out.

Bill Sutor's "German sweetheart" hit 90 on the Schuylkill. He weaved in and out of the meager traffic, oblivious to the danger he was putting his beloved car in. The BMW swerved in front of a city salt truck and sped up the Spring Garden Street ramp. He was livid with himself. He hadn't taken control of the Lavin murder case the way he should have. Because of Melanie, he had handed many of the details over to Rhonda and Colin. Deep down he had been convinced Melanie had killed Miriam Lavin. He'd thought it from the day he first saw her in the funeral home. Harold Rosenberg even believed it. That had settled it for him. The car, the hair, the parking lot, Harold. It was a logical conclusion, and he prided himself on being a logical man. But he hadn't considered the other side, the person she was. She was a woman who talked about books for a living. She had been a devoted wife. She was a mother who loved her child and accepted responsibility for him.

She had assisted a student get back on track after a prison term. She had helped a friend die. Melanie was right. It was the sex. It had blindsided him. He saw her breasts, her skin, her legs wrapped around him. This is who he thought she was, other than a murderer. It was enough to make him a believer in the madwoman conspiracy. He felt like crying. His lack of faith in her, and his passion, had led him to neglect the case, and now he feared he was going to pay for it with her life, and in turn his dreams for the future.

Melanie turned when she heard footsteps behind her. She faced Jerome Eisenberg, who held a 9mm automatic in his hand.

"I thought we were even," she challenged. "We had an agreement. You gave me the money; Jamal gave you the tape of you and Allison killing your grandmother. It's finished. We never have to see each other again."

"I don't trust you," Eisenberg said menacingly.

Sutor turned down 17th Street and pulled in front of the Main Building. Two Philadelphia police cars were already parked there. A third pulled up behind the BMW. Sutor had just rolled down his window to say something when he heard the shot. It came from down the street. Not realizing he could get to the parking lot faster if he drove, he jumped out of his car and began running. He pulled his revolver from his holster. "No," he shouted. "Please, God, no!" He slipped and fell in the snow and struggled to his feet. Trembling from fear, he ran and slid his way down 17th Street, frantically looking for signs of Melanie. He reached the chain-link fence and tried to see her through it, but he was moving too fast to notice anything but a shadowy figure. He heard the motor of a car and saw the Malibu pull out into the street in front of the lot entrance.

A Philadelphia patrol car, it's siren flashing, sped down 17th Street. The driver, his homicide detective pal, slowed when he saw Sutor. Sutor pointed his gun in the direction of the fleeing Malibu and yelled, "He just shot a woman." The patrol car tore after the Malibu.

Sutor turned into the lot and spotted Melanie's Honda. A body lay next to its open front door. "Melanie!" he cried out. "Oh, my God. Melanie! Melanie!"

She was standing there, staring down at Jerome Eisenberg's dead body, her hair covered with snow, her Saturday night special, the Raven, in her hand. "I didn't trust him either," she explained, without a trace of remorse. "He was Miriam Lavin's grandson."

CHAPTER THIRTY

*R*honda, Colin, and a half dozen Philadelphia cops were scouring the Rosenberg courtyard looking for shell casings. The medical examiner was there, going about his business of examining the body.

"He never had a chance," Rhonda remarked to one of the cops. She wasn't referring to the killing but rather Jamal's existence.

The snow was falling densely, and the medical examiner's people were in a hurry to get out of the storm. Rhonda and Colin searched the bushes with flashlights while Jamal Jones' body was lifted onto a gurney and covered with a tarp.

"What's this?" Colin asked as he reached out for an envelope hanging from two entwined branches. He shined a light on its front side, which was blank.

"Let me see that!" Rhonda grabbed the envelope from Colin's hand, folded it in half and quickly put in her coat pocket. "We'll look at this later. Let's finish up and get the hell out of here."

Melanie bent down, pulled back the tarp, and looked at Jamal's face. Sutor held tightly onto her arm, lest she fall. She rose and buried her face in Sutor's chest, crying. He helped her to his car, parked in the middle of the street, blocking traffic, and settled her into the passenger's seat. He turned on the engine and set the heat up high. He told her, "I'll be right back."

Rhonda was waiting for him on the landing outside the front door to Rosenberg's house. "I have something for you," she said, her back to the courtyard. "It's in my right pocket."

Sutor put his arms around Rhonda and slipped the envelope from her pocket. He looked inside before putting the envelope in the inside pocket of his coat.

"Colin knows about the envelope but I'll figure something out," Rhonda whispered. "Count on me this time."

Sutor kissed her on the cheek. "I always do," he replied before leaving her behind on the landing.

Sutor stopped to talk to Colin, who was helping a cute ambulance driver load Jamal's body into her vehicle. "They stopped the Malibu a block from the college. Allison was driving. They got the tape," Colin told him.

Sutor hit Colin on the back affectionately. "You did a terrific job. We couldn't have solved this without you." The compliment warmed Colin through his coat. He was dying to brag to Rhonda, but he knew she thought she was Sutor's right-hand woman, and he didn't want to hurt her feelings. "I'm going to see that you get a commendation for this," Sutor announced.

Sutor returned to his car. Melanie was inside leaning against the passenger's side door, her eyes closed. Sutor took the envelope out of his pocket and held it out to her.

"This belongs to Jesse. It's from his grandfather."

Melanie sat up and looked at the envelope for a moment. "Are you sure?"

"It's Jesse's. Give it to him." He dropped the envelope in her lap.

Melanie reached out to Sutor, took his face in her hands, and kissed him on the lips. "Stay with me, Bill."

"I'll drive you to madness," Sutor warned her.

"You already have," she admitted, looking lovingly at him.

Sutor put the BMW in gear and headed down Delancey, through the center of Philadelphia, onto the Schuylkill Expressway, and west, across City Line. He was driving Melanie to a safe place, away from Harold Rosenberg, away from Jamal, away from Miriam and her clan, and finally, hopefully, away even from Richard. He was driving right through the blizzard, away from Melanie's past, and his own.

Order Form for Invisible Loyalties
ISBN 978-0-615-17801-1

Internet Orders: www.pinkrosespublishing.com
Fax: 610-537-3077
Postal Orders: Pink Roses Publishing,
PO Box 307
Merion Station, PA 19066-1019

Also available through Amazon, Borders, Barnes and Noble,
and area bookstores.

Please send the following book (books) at 14.95 each plus shipping:

Name: _____

Address: _____

_____

City: _____ State: _____ Zip Code _____
Telephone: _____
E-mail Address: _____

Sales Tax; Please add 7.75% for products shipped from California.

Shipping by Air: US: $4 for first book; $2.00 for each additional book;
International: $9 for 1st book; $5 for each additional book.

Subtotal of copies@ $14.95 = _____
CA Residents add 7.7% = _____
Shipping for 1st book = _____
Shipping for each additional book = _____
Total = _____

Payment: ❏ Check   ❏ VISA   ❏ Mastercard
❏ American Express   ❏ PayPal

Card Number: _____
Name on Card: _____ (Please print)
Exp. Date: _____

BOOK SIGNINGS, AUTHOR WORKSHOPS, SPEAKING ENGAGEMENTS AND READERS' GROUPS

Malinda Jo Muzi is available to speak to groups about non-fiction or fiction writing, or specifically her novel, Invisible Loyalties. She is also available for book signings and charity events.

If you are involved in a reading group, feel free to contact Mrs. Muzi about chatting with group members and answering their questions when it meets. For further information:

Phone: 610-667-2072
Fax: 610-537-3077
E-mail: mmuzi@pinkrosespublishing.com

Request Form: Fax to 610-537-3077

_____ is interested in Malinda Jo Muzi speaking to our group, on-line or telephone chatting, signing books, or conducting an author's workshop. Desired date:_____.

Please provide details: _____

_____

_____

Name of Group:_____

Contact Person:_____

Phone No:_____

Fax:_____

E-mail:_____